The Seed of Immortality

Mahjong at Changshou Shan

A Fantasy of Ancient China

by Wayne Goodman

wayne goodman books

waynegoodmanbooks@gmail.com
Instagram: @waynegoodmanbooks

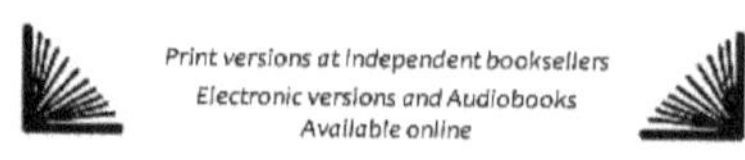

洗麻将牌

The characters and stories contained in this book are based on Chinese mythology as well as actual places and events. This might be difficult to believe, I realize. That is why I have included this proviso. There might also be a few anachronisms along the way, but it is all in the spirit of telling a good story.

Also interwoven throughout the tale are some comical references to the three major philosophical schools prevalent in China: Confucianism, Buddhism and Taoism. I believe these competing systems helped to develop the country's amazing and enduring culture. It all inspired me to create this work. A classical drawing entitled "The Vinegar Tasters" also supplied some of the story's flavor.

The paintings come from Dall-E, the Artificial Intelligence program from Open AI (with some modifications by the author, including an artificial chop). According to current law, these images cannot be copyrighted.

At the very end I have included a glossary to help define some of the unusual terms I used. Because I did not want this story to sound like a lesson in Chinese Culture, I mentioned many of these terms without supplying definitions.

Mahjong itself has evolved over thousands of years. The version I present is more like the modern game than what was played at the time of this tale.

承認

There are a few people I must take the time to thank, for this book would not have been possible without them.

First, my mother. If she had not tried to teach my partner Richard how to play Mahjong, I might never have had the inspiration for this book. At first, he couldn't remember what to say when he won, and because we had been playing a popular dice game with other family members the prior evening, he shouted, "Yahtzee®!"

Second, the people and culture of China. Without them, I would not have had the wonderful traditions and lore upon which to base this tale.

Also, my friends who took the time to read the manuscript and provide helpful critique: The Benicia Outlaws Writing Group and Andrew Chen.

Most importantly, my partner, Richard May. His assistance, support, and amazing suggestions along the way helped propel me over the mountains and rivers, as well as though the forests and deserts. "Yahtzee®!"

Units of Measure used in this book

Cun – The length of one's thumb
Chi – The length of one's foot
Li – 1,800 chi, or a little over half a kilometer

Mu – Area covering approximately 500 square yards, or one-tenth of an acre

Fen – A Chinese weight equal to half a gram

Table of Contents

1. White Dragon

"White Dragon!"

I look up, thinking I would see the formidable beast flying in the cloudless sky. How silly. If, indeed, the White Dragon hovered above, it would have already singed me with powerful flames or slashed me with its sharp claws.

There are many Dragons in our culture:

Red Dragon: Symbolizes benevolence and presides over the animal kingdom,

Green Dragon: Represents sincerity and presides over the plant kingdom,

Yellow Dragon: Signifies royalty and the emperor,

Blue Dragon: Indicates purity of action and controls the weather,

But it is the White Dragon that symbolizes filial piety and presides over the spirit world. We cannot see the White Dragon, for it is inherently invisible, but I run in fear, hoping to find shelter before the soaring beast catches me. Great gusts blow, and I hear the crack of lightning.

Crack! A slung tile struck others on the table, waking me from the terrifying daydream.

"White Dragon, I say!" called Fa Sha, a former military man, on my left in the North position.

Despite cool breezes of a planting season day, my sweat-drenched tunic hinted at the fear I felt playing Mahjong with these distinguished gentlemen. At thirty-and-five years of age, I appeared to be the youngest, and least worthy, person here.

This secluded mountain site loomed over the jade green valley below. Late afternoon sunlight stippled through the pines and cypress trees. Birds chirped. Water from the nearby stream flowed over mossless rocks, cackling and burbling.

Fa Sha stared at me with his one remaining eye. "Do you need this or no?" he queried as he tapped the discard with a long fingernail. "You fell asleep again, Qing Chun. Do you want to play this game, or do you need to nap?"

I fumbled the next available tile from the wall in front of the player on my right in the South position, Xin Bu Hao, a wealthy banker. The pretty Spring tile greeted me, and I placed it face up. This entitled me to an extra, and I reached across to the stack in front of Lao Peng You, a person of unknown status wearing expensive silk brocade, who sat East this hand. I drew a North Wind, which I did not need but feared that Fa Sha, in the North position, might be collecting for bonus coins.

At this point, my hand consisted of worthless tiles, not an honorable one with Winds or Dragons. Only one pathetic run of little numbers. Almost worthless.

Much the way I felt about myself. Years of struggling and scraping in the Dong Ping cinnabar mine since childhood had devastated my nervous system. When the acupuncture, herbs, and moxibustion did not cure me, the doctor suggested a trip to this mountaintop retreat for my condition as the final hope.

I had little money saved, but a week of Mahjong at Changshou Shan sounded beneficial. Regrettably, this picturesque setting seemed more like a gambling den for prosperous swindlers to take advantage of the old and infirm. If I did not win, I would have to pay dearly, and I had very few coins left.

Having no reason to keep this tile, I placed it on the table and announced, "North."

Xin Bu Hao laughed aloud, like a stout, contented rich man, then yelled, "Mahjong!" He turned up his tiles, showing three sets, a run, and the pair of North Winds. Not a high-paying hand, but a Mahjong, nonetheless.

"Idiot!" Fa Sha lambasted me. "You threw his winning tile!"

How was I to know the man in the South position needed a North? More sweat soaked my already stained garment.

The enigmatic smile of Lao Peng You across the table surprised me. He sat East and would pay or collect double.

Everyone stared with open mouths as the player opposite me revealed his tiles. He already displayed a collection of valuable flowers, but when two sets of Dragons and a set of East–the Prevailing Wind this round–turned up, I knew it would be a limit hand. The other two men calculated their values and settled with polite grumbles. I knew my remaining coins would not total the amount I owed. My nerve-wrecked body trembled.

"You have only the Spring tile, Qing Chun, and you cannot afford to pay me what is proper. However, Spring is my favorite, and I shall settle with you later in private." Lao Peng You winked at me, and one corner of his mouth raised. "You must now leave the table as you have no more money." He pointed at my chair and shouted, "Next!"

I stood and walked away, my head flagging. The embarrassment of losing all my savings at the table only added to my pain. I worried what type of payment this charlatan might exact. Although, given my intolerably wretched state of health, what further fresh fears could trouble me?

Other men at Changshou Shan made surreptitious remarks about Lao Peng You, labeling him an undead man. Perhaps a thousand years old and possibly a Mandurugo, an immortal blood-sucking creature. I knew him as a fit-looking well-dressed, man of about forty years. His wide-brimmed hat identified him as being from Xiyu, one of the Western regions.

Whatever his nature, I found myself indebted and must treat him as honorable.

Before returning to my room, I stopped at the kitchen for a bowl of rice and fish soup. I hoped the cook prepared it well, as I could no longer smell nor taste food. Losing these senses tested my broken spirit, the ultimate insults of this cursed disorder.

In my room, I lit the lantern so I could continue the teachings of Confucius. I opened *The Classic of Filial Piety*. It began:

"The body, hair, and skin, all have been received from the parents, and so one doesn't dare damage them–that is the beginning of piety. Establishing oneself, practicing –"

Sharp knocking interrupted my reading. I set down the bamboo strips and went to the door. Lao Peng You stood before me brandishing his puzzling smile.

The room only had a bed and a table, nothing more, a supposed medicinal retreat. Lao Peng You entered and stood near me. He closed the door behind him.

"Good evening, Qing Chun." He glanced down at the floor where I had set the bamboo strips. "Confucius? An interesting fellow, but hopelessly flawed in judgment," he said as if he had known the great man personally. "I hope you enjoyed your meal."

I could not provide an assessment of the rice and fish soup. "Good evening, Lao Peng You. How may I serve you?"

He laughed. Perhaps he had a merry disposition, or I amused him. I preferred to think him easy to entertain. The rice wine on his breath pierced through my inability to smell.

"Very funny. You are not my servant. I am here merely to collect my debt from the game." He looked at me with a hungry eye.

My face displayed many scars from years of work in the cinnabar mine, and I judged myself unsightly. "What is it you require, my lord?"

Again, he laughed. "You amuse me, my friend. I am neither lord nor master, simply a debt holder." His head moved down and up, examining me as if evaluating an animal for purchase. "You have something I want, something I need. I am here to collect."

I had nothing. Compared to his fine threads, my tattered clothes held no value. My work-damaged body could hardly complete a half hour's labor. The ruined internal organs rendered me but a worthless corpse from Hunan Province. What could I have possibly possessed that this rich man would want?

"My lord, I have nothing, but you are welcome to anything if it settles my debt to you."

His crooked smile returned. "Anything?"

"Please name your desire. If I can give freely, I shall give."

Lao Peng You narrowed his eyes and assessed me once more. "Qing Chun, I want your seed."

My what???

Had I any shred of my former strength, I might have considered performing an act of physical harm against this degenerate individual. Unfortunately, my wretched illness left me deficient in muscle. Furthermore, I felt compelled to repay the debt.

I had never been with a woman, although I desired it greatly. However, my misshapen form did not attract lovers, and I could not afford a woman to lean on the door and sell me her smile. As far as men, I had no wish to be with another, although I knew there were those with such tastes. Perhaps this Lao Peng You had such passion.

"Do I understand correctly that you wish to make love to me?" I could not believe I asked this of another man.

He tittered a gentle laugh. "Not so much love making as love taking. I want your seed."

This confused me, and he must have read that in my face.

"You may choose which manner you prefer." He pointed toward his mouth, then his bottom. The accompanying grin did not reassure me the way he might have intended.

The man to whom I owe a debt wanted me to put my organ inside his body for the purpose of obtaining my seed. It did not make sense, but I needed to honor the obligation.

"Is there no other way?"

"What else have you to offer me?" Lao Peng You shook his head. "Nothing. This is the only way to settle your debt with me."

I had no wish to touch another man as I would a woman and pointed at his mouth with a quivering finger.

"Good," he said, indicating the bare bed. "Please, be comfortable."

As I attempted to sit, the pains started again, and I grimaced. He reached to untie my pants. I grabbed his hands.

"Relax," he cooed with a smirk. "You will receive great pleasure."

I had not pleasured myself in a while because the prolonged nerve ailment had been so formidable. Once I lay down, he undid my pants and touched my thigh. My body shivered without intent, but I convulsed with purpose. It might have been my nervous condition; it might have been my shame.

He slid a finger along the shaft of my little brother, and it began to swell. Even though I had no desire for this gentleman, the sensation of his skin on mine produced a very unexpected reaction.

Before I could object, he had me in his mouth. My eyes flapped shut. I tried to think of anything to take my mind off this abuse. Mahjong, hot tea, rice wine, working in the mine.

An idea burst into my head: *Why is my seed so important to him?* I needed to understand the significance of this act.

"Stop!" I shouted.

Lao Peng You pulled his head away from me. "You cannot refuse. The debt must be repaid."

I swallowed before continuing. "I wish to know why you value my seed so highly. When we have finished, I want your word as a gentleman you will tell me."

His eyes shifted from side to side, and he squinted for a moment. "I promise to explain everything. Please let me continue. It is urgent that I resume."

I nodded. A gentleman's word still held credence with me.

When he returned to my body, I winced thinking about my circumstances. His expertise overcame my resistance, and within moments, he gulped my reluctant seed. Pain reverberated in my chest with each rapid breath.

When I looked again, Lao Peng You stood licking his lips as if he had just eaten a sweet Moon Cake.

I stared at him while my composure returned. His expression changed from an ecstatic beam to a satisfied grin. I hoped this carnal act fulfilled my gambling debt to him.

My unwelcome visitor then captured my gaze with his eyes. I felt a wave of warmth as his spirit entered my own through the two portals. For a few uncomfortable moments, I sensed his soul within me.

"Qing Chun," he began, "You are an honorable man. Years of working, scraping at mercury ore with your fingers, has reduced you to a miserable state." He looked down his nose at me as one would with inedible fruit rinds. When he turned away, I saw the embroidered design on the back of his robe, a large blue dragon hovering over a small, cultivated plot of land.

"A long time ago"–he continued, turning to face me–"I was like you. An old man, a peasant farmer, with nothing to live for." His eyes examined the plowed fields of my patchwork face. "One day, while I tended my crops, I heard a deafening roar above me. When I looked up, I saw the Blue Dragon, Shen Lung, bringer of the rains. My crops needed moisture badly and I prostrated myself upon the field in deference to the beast for hope of being rewarded with life-giving water from the heavens. Without warning, the Blue Dragon swooped down and grabbed me from the ground with his powerful claws."

As he told his tale, Lao Peng You stared off into a dark past. He spoke but not always in my direction.

"The beast penetrated me from behind, and it hurt like no pain I had ever endured. He grunted, he groaned, he slathered me with his vile saliva." My visitor moaned. "When the dragon finished his business, he whispered into my ear, 'I have given you a gift.' 'A gift?' I asked, 'A gift that cannot be returned or exchanged?'"

The man faced me front on and I could no longer see the intricate design of his gown. "'One could say that,' the dragon purred. 'A gift you cannot return or exchange. Yes. I received my gift of longevity when I first bit into the Celestial Queen's Immortal Peach. I have now given you the Seed of Immortality. From today forward, you will be known as Lao Peng You. To make best use of this gift, ingest the seed of mortal men. This act will return your youth to you, and you will live a long, prosperous, happy life. You can give this gift to others but be very judicious because it will change a man forever, and that may have unforeseen consequences you cannot predict.'"

Lao Peng You stared at me. "I asked the dragon if he would visit me again, and he answered that he would from time to time but not in the immediate future." He paused to observe my face, but I focused on his story without expression. "Since that time, I have sought the seed of many men. The Blue Dragon spoke truth, and I have been returned to this state," he indicated his present condition, "and I have lived countless years."

I looked at him with a half-closed eye. "Thank you for sharing your tale with me. It is late now. I am tired, and I wish to sleep."

"No!" he shouted. "You do not understand. I did not tell this story as entertainment. I confided in you because I want to offer this gift to *you*. When you turned up the Spring tile at the table today, I realized you are a compatible soul, and I believe we can live together for many years, enjoying the richness of our lives in happy communion."

My expression changed to surprise at this revelation. I did not know what to think. More questions. "Does that mean you will be wanting my seed on a regular basis?"

His face eased into a smile. "If you choose not to accept my gift, I can live a long life by taking your seed regularly, but you will soon die because of your ill health." The smile dropped. "Should you choose to join me in immortality, your seed will no longer nourish me. We shall have to search together for our new life force."

A daunting dilemma confronted me: Die soon of my medical condition or bite the fruit of immortality and learn to take pleasure in another man's affection.

"Within a few hours you will regain your lost facilities. Everything will function again as it used to."

Tasting and enjoying food would be a welcome addition to life. But the cost, so great.

Another question formed in my head. "If I choose to join your lifestyle, how would you initiate me?"

His smirk suggested I would not like the response, "I would have to do to you what the dragon did to me."

My anal muscles clamped shut. No man had ever touched me there.

"And I would have to take other men's seed to maintain my youth?" I inquired.

"Yes. Either fashion." He pointed to his mouth and then his backside. "Think it over, Qing Chun. Sleep with this tonight and I shall return in the morning for your answer." Something in my countenance must have compelled him to say, "Heed me, my friend, if you choose not to join me, due to your pitiful infirmity, tomorrow will most likely be the last day you will ever see. Good night." He opened the door and strode away.

Yes, I have much to consider. Perhaps I shall sleep, but I would have not set a wager upon that.

During the night, Shen Lung, the heavenly Blue Dragon, appears to me. My first instinct is to protect my backside so that he would not take advantage of me the way he did with Lao Peng You. In my dream I stand in the Dong Ping cinnabar pit, and I turn so that my back is against a nearby wall.

The dragon chortles. "Fear not, Qing Chun, for I am not here to burst your chrysanthemum."

I wish to relax, but dragons are not always the best truth-tellers.

"But I am here to give you a gift." His eyes shimmer and bedazzle.

My body goes rigid. "I do not want the gift you gave Lao Peng You. He is a dishonorable man because of it."

A smirk creases the scales on Shen Lung's face. "Lao Peng You is not without honor. He merely obeys my commands. For it is I who requested him to invite you into our immortal society." The dragon holds a peach in one claw. He puts it up to his mouth and nibbles on it.

My curiosity stirs. "Is that a peach from the garden of the Celestial Queen?"

"Yes," he replies, "I have just come from Kunlun Shan. The tree only bears fruit every three thousand years, and Queen Mother of the West gave me a ripe beauty to share with you."

"With me? I am but a humble servant, not a heavenly spirit like yourself, oh, great lord of the sky." I bow in obeisance.

He smiles. "In your mind you are but a humble miner from Hunan. To us, you are another Immortal awaiting the invitation to join our group."

I? An Immortal? Legend tells there are only eight Immortals at any given time.

"To answer the question fluttering in your head, Zhang Guo rode off once again on his donkey and has not been heard from for years. We fear he has been lost." He moves the bitten peach to my mouth. Even though my olfactory sense no longer functions while awake, the fruit smells fragrant and musky in the dream.

"What if I refuse to join your order? Will you slay me here?" My body trembles, possibly from the nervous disorder or mere trepidation.

Shen Lung's bejeweled eyes sparkle nearer to my own. "You fear death?" His breath smells pungent but not unpleasant, more like fermented duck eggs. "Your health is quite precarious at the moment, and you will otherwise perish tomorrow. I have no reason to harm you now."

Perhaps he demands filial piety. Again, I have something that another wants but do not understand what it is.

"Yes, I expect your piety, Qing Chun. In return you will have a healthy, adventurous, long life." He backs away, his long, forked tongue flicking the air. "The something you have that I require is purity. Lao Peng You serves us well, but at times his actions are questionable. Your service to me will be to guide him toward a better existence."

Even after he explains it, I still do not understand what I can give him. However, the choice seems clear: Because my body approaches its final hours, I shall die tomorrow if I do not eat from the peach and achieve immortality. My life has been good, and I have conducted myself well in all things. To end it now would be honorable.

The idea of living forever also appeals to me. But would I eventually become like Lao Peng You? Without the fear of death, men do not always act with scruples. Perhaps Shen Lung chooses me because he knows I possess strong will-power and could resist such temptations.

The Immortals offer me this choice for a very important reason unclear to me. They may never reveal their rationale, and I may never fully grasp my function. A blinding ray of light projects from the peach into my eyes, my heart thumps, and I feel an intense obligation to take on the binding commission of protecting others from Lao Peng You's greed and gluttony.

"You will be known as Hao Lan," he whispers.

The Blue Dragon places the peach closer to my mouth, and I crane my neck to take a bite...

Knocking on the door startled me to awaken.

"Qing Chun. Wake up!" The voice seemed familiar. Yes. Lao Peng You. So early.

I tried to move but could not. The nervous condition had conquered me at last. Pain, pain, horrible thunder pain bolted through my withered body. I struggled to yell out, but no sound came.

The door opened and his shadow inched over me. He observed my broken shell wracked in anguish.

"When you did not appear at breakfast, I thought to look for you here." Lao Peng You shut the door, knelt beside me and touched my shoulder, perhaps in an attempt to comfort. "You are not well. Shall I call for the medic?"

I did not want anyone else to see me in this pathetic state. "Er… Uh… Ahh…" I could not manage to utter any words. Useless. Totally useless.

"Did you consider my offer? Do you wish the gift?" I could sense him examining me. "I do not believe you have much time left, my friend."

My friend? This man was not my friend. I considered him self-centered and overconfident. I did not want his friendship. I did not want his gift. I did not want his lifestyle. *Let me die, let me die. Just go away and let me die.*

Lao Peng You turned my weakened frame so that my backside faced the ceiling. Without consent, he lowered my pants again. As much as I wanted to resist, I lay like a helpless lump because my body would not respond to thoughts or commands.

He whispered into my nearly deaf ear, "I give you this gift as an act of compassion, not from physical desire."

Feeling his rigid member inside me would have produced great discomfort at any other time, but at that moment, with so much hurt, so much ache, I could not differentiate this pain from all the others.

Wishing my mind to blank and my life to end, the image of Shen Lung, the Blue Dragon, swooped into my head. His great claw held the partially eaten Peach of Immortality out to me.

As ethereal wisps of death enveloped my body, I reconsidered the offer. Perhaps a long, healthy life might not be so bad.

I strained to get my mouth around the tempting fruit, but he pulled it away from me, *cun* by *cun*. The great dragon tested my resolve in this way perhaps a dozen times, and I stretched as much as I could, until–

at last–part of the peach rested between my teeth. I bit its flesh as hard as I could.

A great flash of light erupted and blinded me. I spat out the pulpy bit. It tasted sour and bitter, not sweet at all. Until that moment, I felt heavy with exhaustion. My body all in a sudden felt lighter, as if a weight lifted and disappeared.

When I looked up again, Lao Peng You stood over me with closed eyes and a grand smile. He exhaled in the manner of an exhausted horse.

My clothes, gone. The pain, gone. My grief, gone as well.

Hunger. I felt a powerful craving to ease the pangs. Without understanding why I did this, I reached under Lao Peng You's tunic and grabbed for his little bird. I had an intense urge to put it in my mouth, a pursuit I had never desired before.

He batted me away. "Yes, you are hungry, newly reborn one, but you cannot have *my* seed. We must find you another." He turned to the door and pulled it open. "Wait here. I shall return quickly."

He left me alone in the little room on the big mountain, wondering why the birds and the trees and the water on the mossless stones spoke directly to me, singing my spirit, calling my new name. *Hao Lan.*

A short while later, the door opened, and Xin Bu Hao entered, slamming it shut as if he had seen a dragon shadow. Fat, bald, old, and smelling of overripe fish, he began undoing his trousers. My hands flew to his hips flanking that protuberant belly. Acting upon some instinct I had no control over, my mouth engulfed his rather small member. It doubled in size and got a bit firmer as well. I found it difficult to breathe, given the almost unbearable tang of his body odor. The bristly, white porcupine hair poked me in the eye and nose, but obtaining his seed had become the most important thing in the universe to me.

As if suckling my mother's breast, I pleasured the man and received my reward. The taste of his fluid did not differ much from the stench of his body. While I had no desire to swallow this sticky goo, instinct instructed me I had no choice and must do so, without delay.

The gentleman did up his pants, bowed with respect, opened the door, and ran off.

My body convulsed with spasms, and I grunted from the slight discomfort. The inflow and outflow of air no longer caused my lungs to ache. I observed how my hands showed no evidence of scars from working in the mine. Making fists and rotating my wrists no longer sent shocks of pain up my arms.

Lao Peng You entered, holding a finely-embroidered jacket, pants and matching shoes. He handed them down to me and closed the door.

"Here. Put these on. You can purchase your own later. For now, I will lend this suit to you."

As I stood and fumbled into the finery, I realized it did not cause physical aches. When I took in air, I could smell the freshness of the silk and the delightful aroma of bean cakes.

He handed me a small, warm package. "I brought these for you. You are probably very hungry."

Indeed. Very hungry. Tearing off the paper first, I gnawed at the soft pastry as if I had not eaten in a week.

For the first time in many years, I could taste the delicious, savory treat. *What has happened to me?*

"You have many questions," Lao Peng You declared. "I shall answer them all in time. First, you must finish the cakes so that you can hear what I have to say."

He stood watching me devour the meal. Then he produced a small flagon, opened the stopper, and handed it to me. The pungent taste of rice wine filled my parched throat, welcome rain upon the scorched desert.

I looked back at my guest. He half-smiled and regarded me again with what I perceived as renewed interest.

"Did the dragon inform you of your Immortal name?" he asked.

When I went to speak, words caught in my throat. "No," I whispered, shaking my head while looking down at my fancy new shoes. "Wait..." I looked up. "Yes, he did say something. What was it...?"

Even though the dream ended but a few hours before, I had difficulty recalling the conversation. In my head, I replayed the ethereal events: the mine pit, the Dragon, the Peach, the offer. "He said, 'You will be known as Hao Lan.'" I gazed upon Lao Peng You's admiring face.

"Hao Lan it is," he smiled. "Your previous life has ended, and for the rest of eternity you will be known as Hao Lan."

The rest of eternity. Eternal. Immortal. For *ever.*

"You might be wondering why I chose you," he rattled on. I just looked back at him as I ate. "The previous night, Shen Lung appeared to me in a dream. He said, 'During the game, a rumpled young man will draw the

Spring Flower tile and you will take all his coins. He is to receive immortality. You are to provide the gift.'" He smiled at me again.

Was it luck that I drew the Spring Flower tile or was it preordained, as Shen Lung foretold? Either way, I have joined an elite group of formidable people and must learn to discipline myself in accordance with their special rules. I had been taught that the true test of power would be the ability to refrain from using it.

"When you are ready," Lao Peng You continued, "you must return to the Mahjong table."

It seemed a lifetime ago that I sat across from this disreputable man, drawing the special Flower tile, losing all my money, and owing a sizable debt. "But the other players will know that I have no money. I have been discredited."

He produced a polished bronze disk and held it up. In its reflective surface I saw a man I barely recognized. My unblemished face as a boy but with additional years, like a young adult. No one would recognize me as Qing Chun, including me. He put the mirror back in his pocket. Then he brought forth a small bag and put it in my hand. It sounded metallic and felt heavy.

"You will start with this seed money, but when you have earned enough to pay me back, we shall be even."

This seemed like a very bad idea. My Mahjong abilities lacked proficiency, certainly not equal to those here at Changshou Shan, and especially not even close to this expert.

"How can I be certain of winning? You are a master player, and I am lower than an apprentice."

Lao Peng You laughed. "I have many years of experience, it is true. I can read my opponents and know their intentions." He looked into my eyes. "However, there is something much more important than skill and knowledge. Do you know what that is, Hao Lan?"

At first, I did not realize he addressed me by my still unfamiliar new name. Before I could calculate an answer, he blurted one out for me.

"A confederate!"

Thus, he revealed his double-dealing. I liked him less and less.

"Xin Bu Hao feeds me the honor tiles and makes low-value Mahjong. No one suspects, and I split the winnings with him."

While I had never considered myself a man with a violent disposition, his disclosure caused me to contemplate striking the scoundrel. However, it seemed best to contain my thoughts and let the rest of the universe deal with him. It felt like the first test of my new abilities.

"And now you will sit with me at the table. We shall remove the coins from the pockets of the unfortunate others." He opened the door and glanced back at me. "Come, we are expected."

I observed Lao Peng You as he left my room, his gait soft, his shoulders gliding. For the first time as Hao Lan, I exited the small chamber and followed my new mentor, hoping that the quality of my second life would surpass that of the first one.

2. The Wall

News of Xin Bu Hao's death surprised no one. His health seemed questionable at best. I prayed with sincerest wishes that my impulsive act did not contribute to his demise.

I moved into his vacated cubicle as Hao Lan, a newcomer. No one questioned the disappearance of Qing Chun either. He had been disgraced at the table, losing all his money to Lao Peng You, and owed a rather significant sum.

We played many rounds of Mahjong together. As agreed, I fed him the high-scoring honor tiles and would occasionally have a low-scoring Mahjong hand to draw attention away from his winnings.

I used the building of our walls–the stacked rows from which we drew–to provide my partner with good tiles. After the traditional shuffling or "washing," each player built a double height line of eighteen in front of him. I would catch a glimpse of the tiles and arrange a few good ones in the stacks. At the start of the game, we took two sets of two tiles at a time until we had twelve, plus one more each, to start our hand. Lao Peng You taught me that even the apparent randomness of the dice could be controlled to one's advantage.

Following the initial draw, players traded tiles in sets of three with each of the others in a sequence known as *Tai Feng*. At this point, the deception could best be carried out. When swapping with my confederate, I passed him the Winds and Dragons. No one ever knew.

By the end of the playing sessions, we had amassed a substantial fortune, with the other players donating a generous portion of their treasuries to our coffers. I believed we accomplished this without the opponents' knowledge of our scheme.

Lao Peng You divided his winnings with me as he had promised. However, his idea of *sharing* did not match the fashion I learned from my elders. To me, it involved splitting as equally as possible, or at least according to the proportion of work performed. Lao Peng You's version involved him keeping all the gold coins but giving me the silver and copper ones. This allocation amounted to a three-quarter, one-quarter split, yet it still afforded me sufficient funds to repay him the seed money and purchase his splendid robes outright.

One evening, we sat in his suite eating our meal, and it gave me the chance to ask more questions. "How long can we maintain this devious trickery without people becoming suspicious?"

He exhibited his inscrutable smile. "They all know I am an expert at Mahjong. That is why they come here. Pride. Bravado. They want to beat the Master at his game and claim superiority. Ha!"

I looked at him with a skeptical eye. "You mean no one has ever discovered your system?"

A loud cackle burst from his mouth. "Ha, ha. No. They all suspect me of chicanery or magic, but as you know, I am no sorcerer." He picked up a riblet and suckled the juicy meat from it. "Most of them are near death, and do not leave the mountain alive anyway. None of them ever suspects me of having an accomplice!" Lao

Peng You pointed the bare bone fragment at me before tossing it into a nearby vessel.

"I can only imagine you have employed this idea for years... with many different associates." I picked up a redbean cake and placed it in the bowl before me. With my fingers, I broke off small pieces and nibbled while he continued.

"Yes, it took me many years to develop a fool-proof system like this. And I have gone through many, many fools indeed. Ha, ha, ha." He scooped some saffron rice into his bowl. "However, as you will soon learn, people quickly forget. You can take advantage of the same tactics–time after time–as long as you leave a sufficient interval between uses." With sticks, he shoveled rice into his mouth as if someone might jump out and remove the food from his hands. "I can tell you are not used to such sumptuous dining." His eyes rested on the bean cake. "As the days go along, I do hope you acquire a taste for more sophisticated dishes."

He grabbed an oyster shell and slurped the ivory-colored meat into his mouth. I had never tried ocean food because of its expense. Lao Peng You absorbed it like air.

"Here. Try this." He handed me another half shell. The oyster quivered.

"Is it alive?" I had no desire to eat other living beings.

His sly grin raised my anxiety a bit further. "Yes. They are inedible after death." He looked into my eyes. "Eat it, Hao Lan. One gulp. *Go!*"

With some apprehension, I opened wide and placed the cold, chalky exoskeleton to my lower lip. When I tipped my head back, the loose flesh fell and wriggled in my throat. The slimy glob felt particularly disagreeable, and I winced in disgust. However, I realized I must get used to ingesting unfamiliar substances if I am to live the life of an Immortal and swallowed it with a quick spasm of my throat. Fortunately, this creature displayed little taste, unlike my experience with the seed of a man.

Lao Peng You reached across the table and patted my shoulder. "There. I knew you could do it. Believe me, this is most enjoyable compared to some of the things you will have to put in your mouth from now on. Ha, ha, ha!" he bellowed.

In serving my heavenly masters, I accepted that regret would not be a realistic option. I had an ascribed duty to perform and must accept all accompanying inconveniences.

"By the way," he went on while choosing another oyster. "I suggest you purchase yourself a title as quickly as you can. Having a noble-sounding epithet commands a respect you cannot engender as a commoner." His fingers lifted a medium-sized shell, and he inhaled it quick as lightning. "I, myself, am a Marquis. The title, a bargain. It has opened numerous doors for me that had been previously barred." Again, he looked into my eyes. What did he seek? "The news has come to me that a Barony is available nearby. Shall I acquire it for you?"

Baron? I had no desire to be a titled person. Not born into royalty or a landed family. It would prove a false label, a sham pretense. Not the way I wanted to pursue my god-ordained, solemn responsibility.

Lao Peng You nodded to himself. "We shall play again tomorrow, and I shall take my fees from your share."

He paid no attention to my discomfort with his plan. However, he has lived this lifestyle for a very long time, and perhaps I should allow him to guide me at first, uncomfortable as it might feel. "Yes, that sounds like a good idea, Lao Peng You," I acquiesced.

The Marquis laughed again. "My friend, you no longer need to address me by my full name. We shall be close, and in private you may refer to me as *huoban*. It is only fitting."

Huoban. No one had ever allowed me to use that term. From the sound of things, Lao Peng You appeared to have grand plans for our association. I wondered if he knew of my assignment from Shen Lung.

"In public, you may also call me Marquis Pichan. Soon you will be Baron Dongting."

Baron Dongting, sounding much like my former Dong Ping cinnabar mine, a place of hard labor. Perhaps over the years I shall grow into this title. As it appeared, I shall have much more time in my life purse than I ever imagined.

"By the way, I know you are having difficulties adjusting to your newfound immortality. Please allow yourself the liberty to acquire a familiarity with it. There are many advantages to be enjoyed, but a few drawbacks, as you are soon to discover."

A very cryptic remark indeed. This fellow, my *huoban*–as he calls himself–has much to learn as a teacher and mentor.

"Finish your wine," he ordered, "and take a stroll in the evening air. It will help you to think and acclimate."

Yes, that sounded like a good idea after all. "*Kan pei*," I toasted, downed the dregs of the cup, and stood to leave.

"While you amble throughout the area, I shall make the necessary arrangements for your new title, Baron Dongting."

It will take some getting used to that name, let alone Hao Lan. So many new labels. So confusing. I hoped the evening air would help to clear my thinking.

As I strode along the roundabout stone paths, I heard delicate footsteps behind me every so often. At one point I stopped and looked to see who trailed me. To my surprise, a young woman–a young girl more likely–stood peering down at my feet as we paused in a small patch of moonlight next to the burbling stream. Her face hid below layers of powders and creams, but the surface appeared lovely and magnificent. The wide black belt encircling her waist accentuated the slight frame of her torso.

Qing Chun–weak, ugly, scarred, poor–could never have had this opportunity, but Hao Lan–Baron Dongting, young, handsome, virile, rich–could have his fill of dainty women. A test of my will, for sure, but at that moment, the desire for companionship to ease my anxieties overpowered my reasoning faculties.

With a tilt of my head, I motioned for her to follow. We strolled through the bamboo stand in silence to my new quarters, a generous room with a comfortable bed. Once inside, I closed the door, and a wave of excitement washed over me as I anticipated the great pleasure to come.

The youth faced away from me and undid her garment. It fell to the floor in a way only silk flutters in butterfly ripples downward. In contrast with the alabaster face, the rest of her firm skin glowed as if it had been polished ivory. When she turned to face me, I could see her petite breasts with lychee nipples. She represented everything I could have ever wanted in a woman. I reached out to touch her, and she grabbed my hand by the wrist and guided it to her chest, a homesick spoonbill returning to its nest.

"Twenty silver," she whispered.

I reached in my pocket to retrieve the hefty coin purse. From it I extracted a handful of coins–most likely more than twenty–and placed them in her other hand. She counted and, with a small smile, dropped them on her robe.

Because I had never been with a woman before, I had no idea how to love her in the polite and proper fashion. She looked up at me and grasped my predicament. With confident choreography, she conducted my hands over her breasts and up her neck to the gossamer face. My heart palpitated within my chest as it had never before. A naked female and I proposed to experience the heaven of intercourse.

Every nerve tingled. I looked into the dilated pupils, her young, luminescent eyes peering back in presumed anticipation. I only needed to release my member from its hiding place to embark upon this erotic ballet.

Oh, no! I reached down to undo the flap and realized my manhood had not yet responded. This transient companion seemed to understand as she moved a hand down to assist me. Even with her expert fingers my member did not respond. What was happening? What was *not* happening?

She gave me a few more squeezes in an attempt to ignite my passion. Nothing! I wanted this intimacy more than anything, but my body would not respond.

A volcano of fury erupted inside me. My face felt like fiery lava.

"*Longyang*," she cried as she pulled her hand away.

"Get out! Get out!" I shouted.

In one rapid motion, she grabbed her robe along with the coins I had given her and ran from the room without dressing.

When I had reassembled my clothing to appear tolerably presentable, I marched over to Lao Peng You's suite and knocked with aggravated force.

"Enter," came the voice from within.

I opened the door and stood staring at the man who forever changed my life, a strong question on my face.

"Ah," he quipped. "I see you have discovered one of the few disadvantages of immortality. Come in," he waved his hand. "I shall explain."

An explanation, indeed. I slammed the door behind me and sat at his table.

He took a full breath then began. "As you have just found out, we cannot have sexual relations with females. It is not permitted."

"*Permitted*?" I interjected. "Who needs permission to enjoy oneself?" I attempted to suppress my anger but feared a lack of success.

"Yes," Lao Peng You replied. "We cannot reproduce. It is not allowed."

"Not allowed? But why?"

He paused before responding. "There are rules we must obey as Immortals. I have never questioned the reason for this, but I would imagine if we were allowed to reproduce without self-control, our world would become overpopulated, and we would all starve in time."

With a cooler head I am sure this would have made more sense. "I have never *been* with a woman, and, if what you say is true, I shall never *be* with a woman."

Lao Peng You hung his head slightly. "Yes, that is true."

"Then what is the point of a long life if one cannot enjoy its pleasures completely?" I asked before pausing for my mind to regulate itself first.

"This is only one of a very few sacrifices in exchange for our long lives." His expression suggested an attempt at comfort, but comfort did not arrive.

"Then I wish to go back to my old life."

He stared through me. "You cannot go back. Besides, if you did return to your former life, you would now be dead. Is that what you want?"

Perhaps. Death seemed more honorable than the life my newly found *huoban* proposed. Lao Peng You turned away from me and I could once again see the Blue Dragon design on the back of his magnificent robe. Shen Lung gazed out at me, vivid eyes twinkling. A clear message: *Get back to work and stop complaining so much.*

While this felt like sitting on a carpet of needles, I recognized I must have water in my brain not to remember how the road to heaven unearths many hardships. A straight man must, at times, follow a crooked path.

"No, *huoban*, you are right," I demurred. "I shall learn in time to enjoy the fruits of immortality, sour and bitter though they may be."

He faced me, smiled, and nodded. "Today you may see clouds, but, soon enough, the moonlight shines through." He indicated the door with a hand. "Good night. Sleep well. Tomorrow, we play again. Once you have earned the money to reimburse me for your title, you will no longer be indebted, and your profits will be yours. Welcome to the sweet life, Baron Dongting."

I left his suite wondering what other pleasures I would have to forfeit in exchange for eternity.

No dragon visits me during the night, but my mind and heart travel back to the small village of Wu Chu where I had lived before making the journey to Changshou Shan. As I walk along the main street, people I had known my whole life ignore me, as if I didn't even exist.

Though my parents have been dead for years, I go to our family house, even if others may live there. When I look through the window, I see mother and father sitting at the table, a pot of delicious-smelling fish stew between them. Both have tears in their eyes.

I walk to the front and shout their names. Father opens the door with mother behind him. Neither of them seems to recognize me.

"I see you have tears in your eyes, and the fish stew smells wonderful." That sounds like a silly thing to say, but in a dream, I have no control over my speech.

My parents grab each other in a tight hug.

Father speaks. "We cannot allow you to join us for a meal. Our son has died, and we are in mourning." The door shuts in my face.

I am their only child. They refer to me. I am dead to them as they are to me. I go back to the window and see them sit at the table once more. Neither takes any stew.

A strange dream, indeed.

As I walk away, I feel the ground rumble. Loud thunder peals. I gaze upward to see if the dragon appears after all. Nothing but the occasional bird and cloud in the otherwise clear sky.

When I look back toward the family house, a great wall had risen up from the ground, separating me from my parents. This barrier–unlike any I have ever seen–consists of solid gold with intricate silver inlaid marquetry patterns, inset jewels and gemstones sparkling in the sunlight. The riches of the world right in front of me. I cannot take my eyes off this alluring partition. I stretch my arm out to touch it...

Loud chirping of morning birds brought me to consciousness. Changshou Shan. Mahjong. Marquis Pichan awaits.

After a quick wash and a bowl of cold rice, I approached the ceremonial table of gamblers. My *huoban* played in a game with three men I did not recognize.

Lao Peng You looked up at me, "You, sir. Did you wish to join us?"

Did he not remember me? Had my appearance changed that much? Or is this another of his clever ploys?

"I seem to remember you from yesterday," he continued. "Who are you?"

Without thinking about it, my old name almost fell from between my teeth. I coughed to cover up the misstep. "Hao Lan," I replied.

"Yes, now I remember. Please, be patient. A seat will open for you very soon." As long as *he* played, I would not even have time for a cup of tea.

I moved to stand behind him as a lucid watcher to observe what tiles he held. His hand consisted of honor tiles. All he needed for Mahjong was–

"White Dragon!" called the man across the table as he flung down his discard.

"Mahjong!" declared Lao Peng You as he picked up the tile and showed his previously concealed ones. Another limit hand. He would collect most of the money stacked on the table.

The man who threw the dragon tile exploded in speech too discourteous to repeat. He had but a few coins left, nowhere near enough to make adequate payment to my *huoban*.

"Li Duan, you do not have sufficient coins to compensate me." Lao Peng You displayed his trite smile accompanied by squinting eyes. "I shall settle with you later in private. You must now leave the table as you have no more money. Next!"

He turned to me with a vacant countenance, as if we had never met. "What is your name again, sir? Sit down before someone else takes that seat." Lao Peng You motioned to the recently-deserted chair.

"Hao Lan," I mumbled as I sat. My displeased stare bounced off his polished exterior.

Throughout the remainder of the day, we played hand after hand, round after round. Because I let my anger regarding his behavior engulf me, I could not concentrate in my customary way, and our winnings did not match previous endeavors. However, the funds we garnered still amounted to a treasure great enough for a family of nobles to live in its accustomed comfort for at least ten years.

At our private dinner that evening, Lao Peng You divided the coins as before, gold for him, silver and copper for me.

"The price of your Barony is forty-and-nine gold. Please make payment now." Together, we counted out pieces to his satisfaction. "There. Your indebtedness to me has ended, Baron Dongting." He smiled, and I realized it as the first time he offered that gesture toward me all day.

Your indebtedness to me has ended, he said. I owed nothing to anyone. I possessed money of my own. Enough to feed myself, clothe myself, enjoy myself. Well, enjoy myself in most ways.

No comforts would I need to forgo. Lao Peng You and I held more wealth than the whole town of Wu Chu put together, even if you add in the contents of Dong Ping mine and the accumulated fortune of its owner.

I never wished for riches and could have been happy living my whole life as a simple, poor man. My father taught me to put a few coins away every day according to Confucian thrift, and that allowed me the luxury to visit Changshou Shan for the purported medicinal cure. To my great disappointment, the small pittance did not last very long, as my *huoban* purloined it from me with his nefarious ruse.

What, at first seemed like a disaster, Lao Peng You appeared to be able to transform stone into gold. Without his subsequent assistance, I would be a corpse, rotting in the bright sunlight. My unfortunate luck would have me a *Jiangshi*, hopping toward my little village many, many *li* away, unable to rest until I returned to the outset of my journey.

Every advantage has a disadvantage. I exchanged my old life for immortality but not without shortcomings. Oh well, as has been said, "Better to be a diamond with a flaw than a pebble without."

"*Huoban*, I observed you did not play to your best today," Lao Peng You declared. "Something bothers you, I would imagine." His eyes appeared to analyze and diagnose me. "Perhaps we should undertake a small journey together."

Until coming to Changshou Shan, I had never left Wu Chu. As I had heard, "A good journeyer has no fixed plans and is not focused on arriving." This newfound adventure of mine had no specific terminus, and I should probably just follow the meandering path at my feet. An Immortal had the time to pursue unknown destinations, and it might be possible that I would gather some wisdom along the way.

"Yes, a small journey together sounds quite enjoyable," I said, standing and moving to the door.

"Good. Get some sleep and we shall set out after breakfast. Good night, *huoban*." His smile felt more sincere.

Before leaving I turned to ask, "Where shall we be traveling?"

Lao Peng You laughed at my reasonable question. "You are so curious, Baron Dongting. Would you not like it to be a surprise?"

Yet another surprise? I did not really need to know where we journeyed, just that we headed somewhere. And with my *huoban*. "Yes, a surprise sounds quite enjoyable. You have reasoned well, Marquis Pichan." I smiled at myself for using his noble title.

"Until morning," he uttered.

"Until morning," I repeated and returned to my room for the night.

In my dream, I stand next to the jewel-encrusted wall in Wu Chu again. My desire to touch it increases with every second. Gold, silver, diamonds, pearls, emeralds, rubies, opals, jade. A cornucopia of eternal wealth. Exceedingly enticing.

When I reach out, the wall moves away from me! The whole structure retreats as if gliding on glass. As much as my arm length. I take a step forward and stretch out again. As before, the entire wall backs away! It must weigh many, many fen. *How can such a hefty object do that? Oh well, I remind myself, it is but a dream.*

I attempt to put reason to the events. The obvious interpretation might be that I can never have what I want, or that wealth will always elude me. But this being a dream, most likely induced by Immortals, I have suspicions. What I perceive as obvious may not be the truth.

This complicated relationship with the universe has drawn me into its maelstrom. My inadequate education did not include such lofty ideals as discussions regarding the importance and nature of nighttime dalliances.

Perhaps I am the Immortal, and this is someone else's dream. Who can distinguish between the dreamer and the dreamt?

There is so much I need to learn...

The sound of clanking plates returned me to reality.

"Hao Lan. Wake up. It is almost time to leave." Lao Peng You entered my cubicle without asking permission. He held two bowls of cold rice. "Here, eat quickly." He handed one to me. "I have hired an oxcart for us. We leave when the sun clears the treetops."

An oxcart? I have never had such luxury before. Most of my life I walked from place to place, my feet accepting the associated pain as part of the journey's cost. To ride in a rich man's vehicle will surely feel like the epitome of my life.

"Normally, I ride on a palanquin"–Lao Peng You ruffled a hand flourish–"but I could not find four carriers willing to take us all the way to our destination and back. We must suffice with this most common method." He tipped his bowl so that the few remaining grains of rice fell into his open maw. "Eat up! We shall be late!"

His grandeur knew few, if any, bounds.

We sat in a plain wooden box on wheels pulled by a pair of oxen. Lao Peng You held the reins, as I had never driven before. The road down the mountain wound left, right, left, right, left until we reached the mossy valley below.

Before leaving the area completely, we paused at a stream to allow the team to drink. I laughed aloud as I looked about, observing such new wonders. My giddiness seemed to amuse the Marquis. I imagined it had been such a long time since he had been a poor farmer that he could not remember a simple man's experiences. My idea of luxury probably struck him as merely commonplace.

Our ride lasted several days. I continued to find amazement in the surrounding countryside. Tall, slender hills and lithe willows lined the pathway. Elegant buzzards drifted overhead. Every once in a while, one dived to catch a luckless pika popping up from underground.

We stayed at stopovers along the way to sleep at night and replenish our supplies. When we entered the village of Jiayu, Lao Peng You guided our cart up to what looked like a brick tower connected to a long stone fence.

"Here we are," he announced, as if I knew exactly where *here* might be.

"Yes," I responded. My eyes darted about. "Here we are."

He smiled and laughed. "I know you have no concept of where we are or what *this* is." He waved his arm to indicate the structure behind him.

"You are correct, *huoban*," I said.

"*Huoban*," he mused. "I like the way that word sounds when *you* speak it."

He hopped off the cart and walked to the tower's base. I followed him without being asked.

"This," he said, pointing to the large stack of bricks, "is a defensive wall conceived by our Emperor Qin to keep the *Xiongnu* people out of his territory. It separates the civilized China from the uncivilized hordes to the north." He gazed left and right, surveying the earthwork barrier.

"It is magnificent," I gawped.

"It is rubbish!" he squelched. "Large and impressive it might be, and someday people flying to the moon will be able to identify it from high above, but it has many flaws. Eventually, impassioned invaders will overcome its ramparts to pillage our land." His gaze dropped to the dirt.

This man seemed to know both the days that have passed and those to come. Quite an onerous burden to bear. As it has been written, "If you wish to know the future you must first study the past."

When I looked up again, I noticed a single brick that lay in the middle of a ledge, all by itself, looking quite out of place.

"There is a legend," Lao Peng You began, "of a young engineer given the responsibility to design and build this particular tower." His eyes pointed to the building but seemed focused elsewhere. "After careful calculations, he reported to the supervisor it required exactly 99,999 tiles to complete. The cynical overseer told him it sounded like a ridiculous, made-up number. In an effort to placate his superior, the engineer increased his request by one to equal 100,000 bricks."

I tried to count the number of stones but gave up after a dozen or so.

"The supervisor warned that if so much as one tile went unused, all the workmen would forfeit their salaries in compensation for the engineer's wastefulness."

His story sounded dreadfully contrived, and I wondered if Lao Peng You might have been one of these characters.

"Upon completion, 99,999 turned out to be the exact number of tiles needed, as originally calculated by the engineer. When the overseer learned of the extra brick, he beamed in anticipation of administering his premeditated punishment."

What a dreadful man! Thrift may be laudatory, but such a tiny error could have been overlooked.

"The brash engineer explained how the Monkey King had appeared and directed him to place the single tile on the ledge, where it now sits, as a pivotal counterbalance. It is *Ding Cheng Zhuan.* Should it be removed, the entire wall would fall."

He fell silent, his hands clasped at the waist.

Curiosity drove me to inquire about the story's culmination. "How did the greedy supervisor respond?"

Lao Peng You scrutinized me before speaking. "I... *he* was not happy."

My suspicion confirmed.

"Now that we have dispensed with nostalgia"–his lighter energy seemed rekindled–"on to our personal business."

I had no concept of the agenda for this trip. My *huoban* conducted our itinerary with or without my blessing.

"We shall follow the wall toward the East until we find the first site of new construction. There, we shall engage the workers." He strode back to our wagon. I followed close after for fear of being left behind in this unfamiliar territory.

After we climbed aboard, Lao Peng You took the reins and directed the oxen to head East along the road next to the great wall.

"*Huoban*, Marquis Pichan," I addressed him. "May I ask a personal question?"

His mouth curved into a gentle arc. "There are no personal questions between us now, merely matters of curiosity. What is it you wish to know, my friend?"

Something had been bothering me since the second day we played Mahjong together. "Do you remember your original name? The one your mother and father gave to you?"

A soft, wistful smile enveloped his face. "That was such a long time ago, but, yes, I do remember my birth name." He paused and looked up, as if in prayer. "Da Xin they named me but then left this deprived babe at an orphanage full of monks and nuns. My unhappy childhood haunted me for a long, long while, but I have outgrown it over the years."

Soon thereafter, our oxcart arrived at a work camp. Many sweaty men labored in the heat of the afternoon. Some carried mud to the brick makers, others carried the completed tiles to the emergent wall.

Lao Peng You pointed at them. "These fellows are serving the will of our great Emperor Qin. When the exalted one ascended his self-made throne, he banished all books save those in his personal favor. Any who refused to burn the offending treatises got sent here to serve their master's need for cheap construction workers."

How awful! One cannot open a book without learning something. Could a man banish knowledge? Ideas and philosophies outlive the scholars who developed them. This felt like a silly endeavor by our glorious Emperor.

"Some of these men require or desire personal attention." He turned to me. "That is why I brought you here. You will be hungry soon, and this group will most likely be more to your… taste, shall we say."

So, that is it. Our need for replenishment seed to maintain our immortality. My aching heart had not yet concluded this most challenging transition, and I had no idea how long it would take for me to become accustomed to my new immortal life. Time flows away like water in the river, and at some point, my self-possession will float up to the surface.

42

3. The Three Great Scholars

Late that afternoon we arrived in Fulu, a town near the construction site. As it lay along a major trade route, Lao Peng You had no difficulty arranging suitable rooms for us at one of the plentiful lodgings. Unfortunately for me, his expensive taste for luxury just about emptied my purse. We could have found less costly, less fancy, less spacious rooms, but he wanted me to become acquainted with the fineries of living as a titled gentleman. The Marquis Pichan with his *huoban*, the Baron Dongting, roomed at Da Huang Gong, Fulu's most expensive public inn, in its two most supreme suites. One would have been sufficient for me, but Lao Peng You informed me he wanted to demonstrate his air of our superiority to the locals.

Each suite included three grand rooms: one for sleeping, one for bathing, and one for lounging. Poetic wall hangings and small statues adorned the space. I had thought my quarters at Shangshou Shan luxurious and extravagant with its two small rooms.

In the evening, we returned to the construction site. My *huoban* approached prisoners sentenced to labor on the Emperor's isolating wall and made some enquiries to find gentlemen who would be willing to supply us with our immortal needs.

"Baron Dongting," he announced, "here are three suitable, available, and agreeable participants." His hand indicated the men to his right standing with downcast eyes. I found none of them particularly unattractive, old, or bald, but I determined none of them to my *taste* either.

A woman–a woman of almost any size, shape, or splendor–would have been preferable. As my long-life condemnation dictates, the primary source for sexual expression will consist of extracting the seed of fellow men. So far, my two experiences have included once in the bottom and once through my lips. In the mouth produced a bad taste, but in the rear ended in great pain.

"Well, Baron, we are waiting." Lao Peng You stared at me, arms crossed.

One of the workers looked up and smiled, much like a woman might have in the same situation, awaiting a lover to make a choice among possible wives-to-be. I pointed at him, and my *huoban* grabbed the man's wrist, pulling–then pushing–the unremarkable fellow in my direction.

"Enjoy your evening, gentlemen." The others strolled off together, back to the Marquis's room, I presumed. "I shall see you in the morning, Baron."

"Baron," my chosen companion uttered in a reverent tone, bowing his head, which made me shiver. In my previous life, I would have been the one demonstrating humility. I had not yet grown comfortable with this new social station.

I motioned with my hand and started walking back to Da Huang Gong. Like a silk shadow, the man followed me, step for step. In my suite, with the door closed, my temporary mate began to disrobe.

"Wait!" I needed to know what expectations this stranger might have. "What did the Marquis Pichan tell you about our business?"

The visitor lowered his eyes. "Baron, the Marquis informed us that the two of you sought the company of men, preferably those who eat the bitten peach."

I have certainly had my bite of the peach, bitter and sour. "I see. And are you such a fellow?"

His head shook from side to side. "No, your lordship. I have a wife and daughter."

"Then what brings you to my suite this evening?"

"Nothing but the desire to earn money, your lordship." I wished he would stop calling me that. "My family needs food."

"And how much did the Marquis Pichan promise you for your complicity?"

"One hundred silver, Baron. But I am willing to take less... if that would please you."

As it turned out, I could no longer enjoy what would please me. A quick tally of my coins showed about twice the promised amount. "I shall give you one hundred fifty silver, and you can leave now." I understood how it felt to be taken advantage of physically.

He produced a wide smile. "If that pleases your lordship." Again, with the unnecessary title.

As I counted out the payment on the table, his eyes grew in size. I held out my hands with the coins for him to receive. When our hands touched during the exchange, my member stiffened to its fullest, and a sudden impulse consumed me. *I must have his seed! I must have it* now!

Without discussion, I pulled his trousers down and lifted my tunic up. The coins disbursed in all directions.

After removing my own pants, I knelt and lubricated his manhood with saliva. He achieved engorgement as well. Lying on my back atop a woolen rug, he burst my hungry chrysanthemum. I experienced the expected pain, but not as fervent as I had feared. His thrusting hips suggested pleasure for others could, indeed, be found in the back yard.

After about fifteen repetitions, his face grimaced, and he cried out, "Ah, ahh, *ahhhhh!*" I could feel the warm deposition, but the uncomfortable sensation of his penetration irritated me.

"Out!" I shouted, meaning for him to remove himself from my body. However, he must have thought I meant for him to leave the room. After grabbing his trousers–and as many coins as he could–he ran off.

I realized I had unfinished business of my own and stroked little brother to completion. At least I still retained that delight.

The rug felt scratchy on my back, and I needed to stand up. As I did, some of the other fellow's errant seed dribbled along my inner thigh, feeling cold and wet.

So, such an encounter illustrated this new life. My back broken, a passive bunny, receptive to the gooey fluid of long life from other men. Nevertheless, I can live like a wealthy noble. And I still have a mission, as prescribed by my guardian dragon.

As I cleaned myself and prepared for bed, I wondered if Lao Peng You had a mission as well. The Blue Dragon spoke to him, gave him a new name, and instructed him to pluck me out of my old life in its last moments, transmuting me into an Immortal. I could never reveal the nature of my assignment to him, and, in reverse, he could never reveal his to me. Sleep came as I considered this very peculiar arrangement.

Once again, standing before the bejeweled wall in Wu Chu, I contemplate my position. Separated from family–and my old life–by a massive structure that represents wealth beyond imagination. Each time I reach out to touch the wall, it moves away from me. "I am not worthy of wealth," I tell myself.

"It is sour," I hear a male voice say. "You can be worthy, if you apply yourself and follow all the rules."

I look around. No other person appears within my eyesight.

"It is bitter," says another voice, deeper than the first. "And your worthiness is part of all things around you, if you open yourself to it."

Again, I look, but I see no one.

"You are both wrong." Yet another voice. This one, while highest in pitch, still sounds like a man. "It is sweet. Do nothing and worth will come to you."

When I look back at the wall, three great gemstones sparkle in the sunlight. On the left, I see a ruby the size of my head, a giant emerald, directly in front of me and slightly above, and an opal like a large pomelo, off to the right.

"What?" I hear myself say without commanding any words.

"Tea," says the first voice, coming from the ruby.

"Life," says the second voice, from the emerald.

"No, no," says the third voice, the opal, "I thought we were discussing knowledge."

"Rice, perhaps," the ruby offers. "Rice is sour."

"Wine, maybe," suggests the emerald. "Wine is bitter."

"This is just like you both, to argue about nothing without end," countermands the opal. "And it is sweet."

"May I ask something of you?" My voice again, without instruction.

"Yes, my boy."

"Yes, my friend."

"Yes, please, ask us before we all end up dashed against the rocks."

Their discussion makes no sense to me, and I have no idea what I shall ask or whether their answers will mean anything.

"How will I know if I am doing the right thing?" The question comes from me without forethought.

The ruby blazes brighter. "Courage. Not doing the right thing demonstrates a lack of courage."

"You must learn to distinguish between what is right"–light shines out from the emerald–"from what is right for you."

Flashes of color spring from the opal, "There is a little bit of wrong in every right, and, conversely, a bit of right in every wrong. The goal is to balance the two in harmony with nature."

"You did not answer my question." I look at each of the three great gems again, but they remain silent.

Knock, knock. *"Huoban,* it is time for breakfast," chimed a cheery voice from outside. "Put yourself together and meet me in the courtyard."

I woke to the splendor of this royal suite, with its silk linen covered dragon-sized bed, and utilized its magnificent bathing facility with prolonged delight. As I dressed, I noticed my robe felt crisp and smelled of mulberry. One of the staff must have taken my garments during the night, cleaned, and returned them to my room without me hearing it. Oh, the benefits of presumed wealth.

In the enclosed plaza sat Lao Peng You, Marquis Pichan, as if holding court with the breakfast table. I observed no other people in the vicinity. Wisteria blossoms encircling the perimeter trailed down from above.

"Good morning, Baron Dongting," pronounced my *huoban*. "I hope you slept well and had fascinating dreams."

"Yes, to both, thank you. To you as well," I responded and sat next to him.

"Me, too!" His plate contained piles of delicacies, including some oddly shaped morsels I could not identify. He began placing bits of everything available on a platter for me. I recognized dried fish, steamed buns, and *zongzi*.

"What is in the *zongzi, huoban*?"

His face lit up as if he had just won a limit Mahjong hand, "A real treat, boiled duck egg." He placed the gustatory delights before me.

To my right on the dining table sat two shiny metallic utensils I could not identify. "What are these?"

"Ah," he bubbled. "Silver testers. If you wish to determine whether your meal has been poisoned, place the flat end into the dish. If the silver tarnishes, the food is foul, and you may not want to eat it."

"Ah," I replied. Something the wealthy and noble employed to protect themselves from the guiles of the poor and ambitious.

"However," he went on, "let them pepper our meal with *Gu* poison if they wish. It would have no effect on us." Food disappeared into his mouth with every gulping breath.

I tasted each exotic dish with guarded caution. The fish, oily and salty. Steamed buns, soft and gooey. *Zongzi*, slightly tart and most tasty. I took two more of them from the serving tray.

Do Immortals become corpulent? I wondered.

I realized my throat felt dry after ingesting all those delicious delicacies. As a servant passed, I requested, "Tea, please."

"*No!*" shouted Lao Peng You. "No tea for you!" His intense expression evoked terror. "More rice wine, please, my good fellow." He waved the waiter away.

I held my tongue until the server moved far enough so that he could not hear. "What is wrong with tea? Another impermissible?"

His chest heaved in quick breaths. I had not observed him exhibit such agitation. "This is the first time I had a chance to warn you," he sputtered. "Tea consumption counteracts the immortalizing effect of the seed."

Sex with women I could eventually learn to live without, but tea, an entirely different matter.

"Drinking tea makes you age and wither." His respiration returned to its normal rate.

"If we cannot drink tea, and river water is not fit for human consumption, what are we allowed to use to slake our thirst?"

He lifted his cup of rice wine as in a toast. "*Kan pei.*"

When we finished eating, he turned to me and said, "*Huoban,* I know I exhausted most of your funds last evening on our luxurious accommodations." Quite correct. "Today we shall seek out a Mahjong table here in Fulu and take advantage of the local capital."

"Yes." Mahjong seemed to be his solution to just about everything. "As you suggest."

We returned to our respective suites, and I prepared myself for the day ahead. I brought nothing with me other than the clothing I had purchased from Lao Peng You. Perhaps I should explore options for acquiring more suits for myself. I inquired with the house mother. She informed me their tailor would meet me in my suite.

Back in the room, I counted my remaining coins. Seventy-and-two silver, and approximately the same in copper. I would need to keep some for playing Mahjong later.

A tall, slender, middle-aged gentleman arrived a short while later. He carried the tools of his trade: a measuring device, scissors, needles and thread.

"Did you need something repaired, my lord?" he asked with the serious professionalism of an undertaker.

"No. I brought only this one suit with me, and I have need of another. Can you assemble something for me?"

He examined what I wore in the same manner a horse trader might evaluate a possible purchase, making a slow orbit around me. "Your fine cloth is very expensive and rare, my lord. I have nothing like it."

What would a *genuine* nobleman say to this?

"Is your best fabric… worthy?" Clumsy words, but I am not yet accustomed to addressing people in an inferior way who were once my superiors.

He coughed into his fist. "I have a few samples I can show you."

I nodded. The tailor left and returned with several sheets of fabric in his hand. One in particular caught my eye.

"Is that material made with cinnabar?" Woven into the cloth I saw threads of earthen red, reminiscent of the ore that caused my former demise.

"Why, yes, my lord." He smiled. "How observant you are. No one else has distinguished that before."

None of your customers ever spent thirty years digging that dreaded dirt out of the desiccated earth with their splintered fingernails either. "How much would a suit of that cloth cost?"

He placed the samples on a table, stepped toward me and measured my body. A few quick mental calculations led to, "Seventy-and-five silver, if you want it by the sunset, my lord."

My count tallied seventy-and-two, but I happened to see several wayward coins from last night's encounter under another table. "Seventy-and-five it is."

He smiled and nodded in response.

Sunset seemed like a long time away. "And I will throw in fifty copper if you can complete it by midday."

Following a deep and reverential bow, he concluded, "I shall return very soon, my lord."

I left the suite a while later with pride, wearing my newly crafted suit. Lao Peng You sat at the meal table, taking a midday repast. He gazed up at my cinnabar-encrusted clothing.

"An excellent idea, *huoban*. It suits you well. I grew weary of seeing my shabby old clothes on you." He returned to a bowl piled with dried fish, dried fruit, and green leaves. Perhaps the bellies of Immortals do not grow larger with excess food. At last, a benefit I can enjoy.

"It appears you have emptied your purse yet again." Along with the past and future, he appeared to have vast knowledge of the present as well. "You will win the first game with a special hand, thus securing your monetary needs for the rest of this trip." He indicated a seat next to him. "Sit. Eat. You will need your nourishment. We have a long day ahead of us." I sat despite lack of desire, partly because I wasn't hungry but more because of my shrunken funds. "Do not fret, my friend," he whispered, "I shall cover the cost of this meal."

Thank the heavens. Appetite multiplies when the food comes without charge.

"Waiter," he shouted, "another bottle of rice wine!"

Even though the sun soared high, I felt midnight knocking. My skin turned clammy as I brooded over costs for the trip so far. Expensive suites, expensive meals, paying men for the seed of our immortality, plus a new set of clothing. Money, money, money. Rich people cannot endure without a medium to maintain their extravagant lifestyle. They pursue this all-consuming greed like a snake attempting to swallow an elephant. Remove the money and the wealthy would surely fall. But I imagine it far better to live a long life in prosperity than to subsist in absence and insufficiency.

"*Huoban*, are you ready?" shouted Lao Peng You outside my rooms. I stood and opened the door to him.

"You are not yet ready," he scolded. "Pack up your belongings."

"Are we not returning to our suites after playing Mahjong?"

"No." He seemed unwavering. "After we fleece this village, the inhabitants might not continue to offer us safe lodging. If we do not mend our fence first, the sheep will run off for certain. Bring everything with you. Following the scheduled undertaking, we shall be leaving with all due haste." He walked away and stood by the oxcart.

The only thing I brought with me was the suit of clothes I had purchased from him. They say the sage does not hoard, but I am not yet a sage. I grabbed the old garments and approached our wagon.

"Get in," Lao Peng You commanded as he jumped up. I threw the clothes into the box and got onboard.

Off we went through the village, somewhat bigger than Wu Chu but not very different in its construction. At the top of a small mound sat a park with a few tall trees and a short table. We pulled up and approached two men.

"Good day," called one of them. His hair had started to gray. He looked comfortable and chubby. "I am Wang Ho and this is Li Dao." The other fellow seemed older but taller and thinner. They shuffled face-down Mahjong tiles around the table.

My *huoban* introduced us, "I am Marquis Pichan, and this is Baron Dongting." He turned to me and asked, "It is Dongting, is it not?" He looked to the other two. "We just met, and I want to make sure of presenting his title accurately."

I smiled this time, knowing the emergent deception. "Yes, my lord, I am known as Baron Dongting."

Wang Ho indicated the set of tiles. "Shall we roll the dice for positions?"

The outcome had Wang Ho as East, Li Dao as North. I sat South and the Marquis drew West. As we sat, I heard Lao Peng You's voice in my head, *You will win the first game with a special hand.*

We used the washed tiles to build our walls, and Wang Ho rolled the dice to determine where to break his. Following the initial draw, I had two Red Dragon, two Green Dragon, two White Dragon, two South Wind, one East Wind and assorted simple tiles. During the *Tai Feng*, Lao Peng You passed me more dragons and a South Wind. At that point, I only needed an East Wind to make a pair for Mahjong.

Play commenced. I drew and discarded through several rounds until my *huoban* dropped a tile on the table, calling out, "East."

Birds chirped in the trees. A chance ray of sunlight penetrated the clouds and illuminated the tile, outshining all around it.

"Call," claimed Wang Ho, doubtless for a set of his own wind, also the Prevailing Wind for this round. He reached toward the miniature treasure in ivory.

Lao Peng You's right toe dug like a dull dagger into my left shin. "Wait!" I blurted.

"Wait for what?" Wang Ho questioned. "I have a Pung." He pushed the other two matching winds over so that we could see them. "As there are only four East tiles in a set, you cannot have a triplet as well," he said, grabbing at his little delight from the table.

"Perhaps the Baron has Mahjong, Wang Ho," cautioned my *huoban*. "And according to the authoritative rules, his call would supplant yours."

The other player's expression warped from joy to disbelief. "Is this true, Baron Dongting? Do you have Mahjong?" asked Wang Ho.

Of course, I did. As masterminded by Lao Peng You. A magnificent hand full of honor tiles. Certainly, a limit hand guaranteed to fill my purse with many, many coins.

I pushed each tile over, one by one, to the amazement of the others.

"We are ruined," cried Li Dao.

"Impossible," sobbed Wang Ho.

"Delightful," exclaimed Lao Peng You. "I believe this winning hand with all the dragons is called *The Three Great Scholars*." He indicated each set with a clack of fingernail.

"A limit hand," wailed Li Dao.

"A limitless hand," bemoaned Wang Ho.

"Nevertheless," spoke my *huoban*, "We must make good to the Baron's turn of luck." He smiled and nodded a few times. The other players heaped piles of coins in front of me. I did not have sufficient room in my purse. Most of my wealth sat on the table, taunting its previous possessors.

Throughout the rest of the afternoon, I never had Mahjong again. When the sun fell below the line of trees, Lao Peng You had regained his losses plus a bit more. The other two players frowned like little gray clouds before standing and walking away.

"It is best we leave now," Lao Peng You whispered to me. "The faster, the fairer." We stood and moved without delay to the oxcart.

I looked over my shoulder several times, but no one followed us. Perhaps the two losing players went to assemble a mob for dealing with our appropriation of their former assets.

On the road back to Changshou Shan, with the village of Fulu behind us, I looked every so often to see if anyone pursued. I feared pitchforks, torches, and halberds, but no such army materialized.

When darkness prevented us from further travel, we stopped in a secluded copse next to a stream. We slept in the open cart, the stars and heavens watching over us.

"Hao Lan," a deep, resonant voice cries out. I stand in an open field. No one around me. "Look up."

Not again. Above me hovers Shen Lung, the Blue Dragon.

"My Lord," I bow in obeisance.

The Dragon chuckles, if dragons can, indeed, laugh. "You are an obedient servant, Hao Lan. You attend me well. How do you like immortality so far?"

Perhaps I should not mention my discomforts, but Shen Lung knows all, and withholding information from him could be detrimental.

"While I have quite enjoyed not dying from cinnabar poisoning, I have discovered two things in which I may not partake."

"You will find more than two obstacles as your life river runs its course, Hao Lan. Which two, in particular, concern you at this moment?"

I look down at the recently plowed earth. "Physical enjoyment with women..."

"A pleasure you had not undertaken before. I do not see how you could pine for something you never had." He flutters around my head like a personal tornado. "And what is the other?"

"Tea."

"Ah, yes, tea." The dragon descends and hovers so that he faces me. "Ever since Shennong inadvertently discovered that delightful infusion of dried leaves hundreds of years ago it has been a bane to us Immortals."

I look into his mesmerizing eyes. "Your Lordship is correct that I cannot miss something I had never had, but the beverage quenched my thirst every day. Surely you can see a way for me to drink tea again."

Shen Lung flaps his wings as if it helps him think. Dust from the barren field whirls up. "In the southernmost region of China, deep in the swamps of Guizhou Province, you can find a twisting vine orchid named Jiaogulan. An unusual plant in that it has two genders, male and female. If you dry and crush the leaves of the male Jiaogulan, you can steep them in boiling water and drink that. The local people refer to it as Dragon Longevity Tea. Do not get the wrong idea. It will not bring you or anyone else immortality. Quite the contrary. It is only Dragons and other Immortals who can consume it. We refer to it as Herb of the Immortals *for that reason."*

At last, a way to have my beloved beverage.

"Thank you, Lord Shen Lung."

"And how is your assignment with Lao Peng You progressing?" He glides up and hovers over me once again.

"With some difficulty, my Lord."

"Oh? What impediments have you encountered?" His tail flops down near my face.

"Lao Peng You prefers to live a luxurious life."

He glances down, and a smile reveals his colossal, sharp teeth. "As do we all."

My hands clench. "But his methods for acquiring wealth differ greatly from how I had been taught."

"I see." The Dragon twirls around. "And you do not like his methods?"

It feels as though he attempts to box me into a corner of logic. "It is not a matter of like or dislike, O Great Dragon. My concern is for the people from whom he extracts the wealth. I find the deception and thievery objectionable and unconscionable." After speaking out, my fists loosen.

"And that is troubling for you?"

"Yes, my Lord. I lived an honest life before I met Marquis Pichan."

"You had lived an honest life," he corrects me.

"True, my Lord," I acquiesce. Without Shen Lung and Lao Peng You, I would be dead.

"Please keep in mind, my young apprentice, that he has lived many hundreds of years. From his perspective, you are naïve, inexperienced, and provide no guidance for him. Do not expect Master Lao to be looking to you for example." His shimmering eyes stare into mine. "He will expect you to see him as a model citizen, one who wishes to perform a role you can emulate in time."

Difficult concepts for me to grasp together in harmony. Moving forward, I shall have to learn how to hold contra- dictory beliefs in my head at the same time, much like a koan. I blink to lessen the intensity of Shen Lung's pene- trating gaze.

"Hao Lan, I have provided you with three advisors to guide you along your way. Ask them to assist in deciphering your assortment of riddles."

Ah. So that is the source of my other reverie. "Are you referring to the trio of gems in my dream? I mean the one of the wall in Wu Chu?"

"Yes, indeed. They are wise and will present good counsel."

"Pardon me, my Lord, but they argue and disagree with one another like three roosters squabbling over one hen."

His flight pauses in front of me. "You must listen to what they say with wise reasoning so you can discover the path that best serves your wishes."

Most disturbing advisors. "Yes, my Lord. I shall make more of an attempt to use their sage assertions to my advantage."

"That is a good attitude, my little devotee." He begins to ascend, then halts, "If you want to have some innocent fun, ask one of them to tell you how the others would answer a particular question."

"Excellent counsel, Shen Lung. Thank you, my Lord."

As he flies away, he advises me further, "And, Hao Lan, do not complain so much!"

The next day as we trundled along through the verdant countryside, I decided to engage my *huoban* in a discussion.

"Marquis, you acquire and spend a great deal of money." His head turned to me. "I am not used to such affluence, and, while you have been extremely generous with me"–he nodded in agreement–"I have observed you appropriating wealth from others."

Lao Peng You grinned at my remark. "Yes, Baron, I do acquire a great wealth, mostly at the Mahjong table." His gaze shifted forward. "It is a game I have studied and can play in my slumber, if necessary." He smiled as if this had happened before.

"Do you not feel remorse for those you have beguiled?"

"Remorse? Beguile? Ha, ha, ha." This seemed to amuse him. "Words spoken like a Confucian scholar."

"I have studied the great philosopher, *huoban*. His teachings make much sense to me, and I believe the world could be fairer if everyone followed his rules."

Lao Peng You laughed so hard I believe I observed leaves on the trees shaking as we passed. "Hao Lan, those principles are for the commoners, the abject poor, a group neither of us belongs to anymore. Confucian principles ensure a stable society so that those of us with wealth and power can pursue our exalted lives without fear of unexpected upheaval."

While I am certain this concept makes sense to the entitled few, I come from the numerous destitute and found it difficult to accept. We rode on in silence for the next few *li*.

"*Huoban*," Lao Peng You broke the peace, "I want you to think of money as water. It does no good sitting in a reservoir. It goes bad, grows stagnant. When you accumulate it, you must use it to grow crops, make snow, feed streams."

So many water metaphors. Life is a river, money is water. Tea, however, is forbidden.

"In the future, many will attempt to redistribute the wealth of society in order to promote a sense of universal welfare."

I marveled at his knowledge of times to come.

"Some governments will take directly from the rich and give to the poor as they see fit. Others will want to centralize the assets of their country into a deceptively benevolent administrative system, giving the impression of taking care of all its citizens' needs."

These mysterious economic concepts confounded me. As far as I knew, our exalted Emperor collected taxes from his subjects to spend as he determined best.

"But the worst offenders will be those who engage moneylenders to maintain the appearance of generosity but do not collect adequate levies from its populace to compensate for such amenities."

If any of these schemes succeeded, the upper classes could attempt to smother the plentiful poor, and uprisings would result. Given what Lao Peng You has described, I would not expect any permanent money reallocation program to last very long.

"My goal is to free the water from its reservoirs and flood the countryside in order to grow the crops that sustain us all." He grinned and cocked his head like a sly rabbit with three burrows.

Selfishness for the sake of everyone's benefit. This did not follow the teachings of Confucius. However, I decided I would make every attempt to see things in new ways if it would assist me to maintain my association with Marquis Pichan. My life, my lives–both the old and this new one–appeared to be in his grubby, manipulative hands.

I must remember to ask Shen Lung how to distinguish the male and female *Jiaogulan* leaves.

4. Chrysanthemum

"*The wise find pleasure in it,*" *a familiar voice croons.* "*And sometimes it is sour.*"

"*Drop by drop it can fill you with goodness,*" *the deeper-sounding advisor adds.* "*And it is frequently bitter.*"

"*It is a flow,*" *the last sage chimes in.* "*Just go with it. Sweet, I say. Sweet!*"

I stand before the immense golden wall. Three gems sparkle as they attempt to dazzle me with their profound wisdom.

"*What are you discussing this time?*" *my voice asks.*

"*Money?*"

"*Enlightenment?*"

"*Pihua! And you are both full of it!*"

As before, they cannot agree on anything.

"*Shen Lung appeared in my dream. He instructed me to seek and follow your counsel.*" *My dream self speaks without me willing it.*

"*The Blue Dragon is only good for one thing: bringing the needed rain to our dry land.*"

"*Immortal beings transcend our reality.*"

"*Do not stand under him as he flies overhead.*" *The opal flames.* "*He excretes pihua excessively.*"

"*How can I believe the three of you when you cannot agree on anything?*" *When will I be able to control my own voice?*

"*We do not disagree,*" *the ruby states.* "*The others are merely wrong.*"

"*Agreement is not always necessary,*" *the emerald adds.* "*Knowledge permeates all things.*"

"*Pihua!*" *The white stone seems to be in a foul mood.*

"*Can you not even agree to disagree?*" *my image asks.*

"*No!*" *retorts the red gem.*

"*I already did,*" *the green jewel brags.*

"*If the three of us ever agreed on anything at all, our world would end in a blazing conflagration,*" *the opal contributes in a sardonic fashion.*

"*I would like to ask each of you a question.*" *My dream self pauses, and I realize, at long last, I can choose the words.* "*How would the other two answer if I asked them what this wall represents to me?*"

The ruby jumps right in. "*The Green One would say the wall is a part of all things and you must become one with it. The other stone, well, who knows, he is so unpredictable. He would probably tell you to avoid thinking about it and concentrate on doing nothing.*"

"*An astute observation,*" *the emerald remarks.* "*I believe my red friend would instruct you on how to address the wall correctly. Rules and proper procedures are very important to him. As for our cloudy white companion, I must agree. His randomness seems tantamount. You would be lucky to get a worthwhile answer from that one.*"

The opal flashes and sparkles. "*Ha, ha, ha. My two colleagues like to have fun at my expense, but, luckily for me, I don't heed their inconsequential words. The one farthest away*"–*referring to the ruby*–"*cannot see the wall for the decor, and my green neighbor would probably tell you the long, boring story of how the wall separated him from his prior life while he sat under a droopy banyan. So much talk, so many words, so little content.*"

I gather it is going to be difficult indeed to glean any kernels of wisdom from this trinity.

"I have a feeling"–I still control my voice–"that this wall divides my old life from my new life, but I am having difficulty identifying a home."

"The strength of a nation derives from the integrity of the home," the ruby chants. "Make your home where you feel most strongly."

"Your home is within you," the emerald advises. "You carry your home with you wherever you are."

I dread to hear what the opal might say.

"There is no such thing as home. Here, there, all the same. Be at home with that."

With one day left before we would return to Changshou Shan, our trail wandered through rocky hills reminiscent of Hunan Province and my beloved home town of Wu Chu. Sparse vegetation, short trees, parched mud. Not much in the way of resources. The kind of place you could only love if you dwelled there your entire life.

An idea struck me. "Marquis, have you been to Pichan? Have you actually seen it? Lived there? Know it?"

My *huoban* tilted his head away from me. "No, Baron. Why do you ask?"

"It strikes me as curious that you represent yourself as a noble from that region, yet you have no idea of what it looks like or what the people do."

"Yes, I suppose that is true." He tilted his head toward me. "What is your point?"

"Perhaps I am being naïve"–he grinned a slight bit–"But I believe it is important to appreciate where you have come from."

"To understand the future, you must first study the past," he quoted.

"I have heard that before, *huoban*." I glanced over at him, and his expression appeared melancholy.

"You wish to return to Wu Chu?" he asked. "It is best not to be seen in your home town at the present. Too complicated. Too many questions." He faced forward.

"No, Marquis. I wish to visit Dongting." Lao Peng You registered surprise with wide eyes. "You told me the barony was not too distant from Changshou Shan. We, certainly, cannot be far away."

He nodded, but I could sense he had other devices developing in his scheming mind. "Yes, perhaps a side trip to Dongting might have some value, indeed…" I pictured the cogwheels of his mind whirling on little pinions.

"It would mean much to me to get to know the area I intend to represent."

Eyes glassy as a still lake on a windless evening, Lao Peng You drove the oxen away from our original destination and onto a lesser-used path I could only presume ended at Dongting.

After a quiet interval, we passed a wide but shallow lake. I watched pale pink river porpoises swimming and dancing in choreographed frolics. We descended into a steep valley lined with white mulberry trees. A profusion of silk cocoons shrouded their leaves.

"Is this Dongting?" I could not believe the beauty of the region.

Lao Peng You nodded. His eyes moved side to side, and he scowled. I wished I had some idea of what he sought. He guided our cart toward the lowest part of the valley. An open, grassy area appeared to have appealed to him.

My *huoban* stood and gazed about. "I present to you Baron Dongting!" he shouted to anyone who could hear him. "Baron Dongting!"

I wanted to hide my face because I felt public approbation embarrassing. Knowing my own roots as more humble than any of the townsfolk here made my hands sweat.

"Meet your new Baron, people." Lao Peng You hawked as if I were a carnival exhibit.

Within the span of a few breaths, a group of perhaps fifty citizens approached the cart. Some brought gifts of silk or fruit. They reached up to greet me, smiling, welcoming me.

"Baron Dongting?" A high-pitched man's voice sang out. "*Baron Dongting*?" it repeated. "*I* was supposed to be the Baron of Dongting. Who is this interloper?"

The crowd parted and a tall, pale, round, lordly man stood glaring at me, his green and gold silken robes flowing with the slight breeze.

My *huoban* spoke up, fortunately for me, "I am Marquis Pichan, and I introduce to you, Hao Lan, the Baron Dongting."

Some people bowed in reverence. The tall, pale, round, lordly man did not.

"And who are *you*, my good sir?" Lao Peng You inquired as he piled gifts onto the cart.

"I am the man who was to be Baron Dongting until a scoundrel named Lao Peng You purchased the title before I could make my claim. Do you know the rascal?" Sweat dribbled from the large man's wide forehead.

A foot tapped my toe. I stood. "I am Hao Lan, Baron Dongting." I bowed. Probably not the best thing to do, but I could not think of anything else. "And whom do I have the supreme honor and pleasure of addressing?"

His pale, moon face reddened. If I knew how to drive an oxcart, we would have been rushing up the side of the hill, far away, fast as possible.

"Baron," he huffed, "I am Wang Yue." A fitting name for one who is tall, pale, and round. "You have my rightful title."

The crowd backed away. The full moon of a man stomped toward us with deliberate strides.

"This is your noble vehicle?" He pointed at the oxcart. "I would have expected someone as aristocratic and dignified as yourself to have a palanquin, a litter, at the very least a rickshaw." He guffawed.

"We came from Changshou Shan"–I pointed to markings on the cart indicating our point of departure–"where no such means of transportation could be found. The Marquis kindly procured this humble cart so that I could introduce myself and visit the good townspeople." I waved in small motions, the sort of way I imagined a nobleman would greet his subjects.

As my challenger approached with a threatening glare, I lowered my arm, not wanting to become the target of two-hand combat practice.

"When I am finished with *you*," he menaced, "you will be carrying *me* through the streets upon your ruptured back."

I groaned when my mind displayed the agonizing image of carrying this large fellow about.

"Gentlemen, gentlemen," my *huoban* attempted to soothe the situation. "There is no need for puffing of chests and thumping of... um... chests." He seemed flustered for once. "I believe I know of a peaceful way to settle this misunderstanding." His gaze rose to heaven. "If only there were a Mahjong table near by..."

Wang Yue smiled with nearly closed eyes. "Mahjong, you say?" He frowned at me. "Do you play Mahjong, *Baron* Dongting?"

Before I could verbalize an answer, Lao Peng You provided one for me, "Of course, good sir." He continued to sell me like so much bean curd. "Hao Lan is a master at the game." He beamed in my direction. "Unfortunately, there are only three of us present, and we sadly lack a fourth."

"I oversee the silk production in this region, and that is my home." Wang Yue pointed to the large house atop a mulberry-encrusted hill nearby. "Give me time to return with my servant and we shall use providence to settle this utterly despicable business." He indicated the grassy area. "Wait for me by that table."

Could it have been this fiber merchant's operation that Lao Peng You sought? With his Mahjong skills, the Marquis might soon have a source of income to swim in for a very long time. However, I had purchased the title of Baron–through my *huoban*–and felt I must fight for my honor.

After a short while, Wang Yue returned with an older gentleman, slouched from age, his long, white beard not far from touching the ground. He carried an ornate wooden box.

"This is my servant, Chang Hu." The elder bowed a slight bit, and his lengthy chin hair brushed the earth. "He will be our fourth player."

Chang Hu dumped tiles onto a table with thunderous clatter. Our host produced dice and proceeded to roll for position. He sat East, I drew North, Lao Peng You ended up West, leaving the servant as South. The crowd clustered about us to observe what promised to be an exceptionally exciting match.

In a Mahjong set most tiles–Winds, Dragons, Suits–are embodied in quadruplicate. Additionally, there are eight unique tiles, generally referred to as Flowers. Only four of them represent plants: Plum, Orchid, Chrysanthemum, Bamboo. The others depict Seasons: Spring, Summer, Autumn, Winter.

If a player draws one of these eight special tiles, he places it face up and draws a replacement from the back wall. Should one have the good fortune of obtaining each of the tiles in a set, called a Bouquet, values are redoubled and redoubled again.

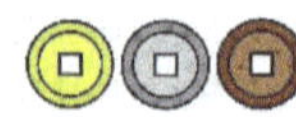

After the first round, each of us held our ground fairly well. No one triumphed or lost more than a few coins. By a curious phenomenon, I drew the Chrysanthemum tile every game.

Observing my *huoban* and Wang Yue in a constant match to scrutinize each other for fatal flaws drained my energy. I did not know how they managed to stay alert with all that grueling analysis and counter-assessment. It felt more like a lesson in the thirty-and-six stratagems of Sun Tzu.

As the sun set behind the Marquis, our host began to take more and more coins from us. When the last rays of light barely illuminated our tiles, Wang Yue declared a limit hand while sitting East. Each of us had to pay him double. Unfortunately, my exhausted treasury would not satisfy the obligation.

The tall, pale, round, lordly man looked over and down at me. "Baron–as I must call you for now–I believe your purse cannot cover your losses." He expressed the obvious. "However, I would call our debt even if you would do the honor of dining with me this evening."

"We would be delighted!" Lao Peng You responded before I could inhale.

Wang Yue glowered at him. "I did not invite *you,* Marquis. I wish to dine alone with *him.*" He pointed a short, stumpy finger at me.

My *houban*'s eyes opened like giant serving bowls. "But... but..."

"If you do not like my town, Marquis, I suggest you return to Pichan." He waved his hand toward the distance. "Immediately."

"A word with my associate first, if you please."

Our host chuckled. "Of course, ladies. Take your time."

Lao Peng You and I walked back to the wagon. "Hao Lan, be very careful with this cunning tiger. I do not trust him. He is quite devious."

A phrase I once heard echoed in my mind: *A snake sees its own reflection in the still waters of a bowl.*

"Be assured, *huoban*, I can take care of myself." He looked at me as if I were nothing more than a ripening child. "And, besides, are we not immortal? What can he do to me?" I suppose that might sound unsophisticated, but what benefit did immortality grant if you worried about harm in every moment?

"It is not you who is the object of my concern," he admonished. "Be very thoughtful about your actions. That is all I ask."

"Of course, Marquis. Of course."

I walked toward Wang Yue and his party. Together we strolled up the hill to his manor.

"Do you like octopus?" he asked.

I had never eaten that delicacy and desired to attempt new things. "It sounds delicious."

His terrace courtyard provided a view of the entire Dongting valley. A dining table with two chairs awaited us. We sat and Chang Hu brought us steaming bowls. I looked down at the fleshy tentacles, some with their suckers still attached.

"Eat. Quickly. It loses its flavor when it cools."

I tried to think of the delicious *zongzi* I had for breakfast in Fulu a few days ago as I popped a segment into my mouth. Again, I had to accept that it might not be the last objectionable and oozy thing I would attempt to swallow during my extended existence. Fortunately, the sauce had too much red pepper and it covered the taste of anything else.

"Delicious!" I quipped after getting the slimy bit down my gullet.

Wang Yue examined me with great interest. He clapped his hands and two servants appeared, cleared the table, and departed in an instant.

"My lord, is something wrong?" I asked.

"Not to my knowledge," he replied. "Hao Lan, you possess something I want."

"Yes, yes, I know. You wish to be Baron Dongting." I nodded.

"Not as much as another desire," he goaded. Devious indeed, as Lao Peng You had observed. Vigilance seemed warranted.

"And what might that be, sir? You took my travel money."

He interwove his fingers like a mechanical toy. "Superior to money, Baron," he addressed me, acknowledging my appropriated title. Yes, caution would be advised here.

"*Superior to money*?" I mocked. "What could be better?"

His gaze fell to the spot on the table where the bowl of octopus sat moments ago. "I had Chang Hu put enough *Gu* poison in your dish to dispatch an entire imperial guard unit. It appears to have had no effect on you." His eyes cut through my soul. "A test. You passed."

"I'm not sure what you mean, Wang Yue." Perhaps I did know but did not wish to give him that pleasure.

"I had the impression you might be an Immortal. And now I know you are, and that you can make me immortal as well." His eyes tightened to fine slits. "Is it too much to ask in return for forgiveness of your debt to me, and, of course, the title of Baron Dongting?"

Too much?? This man is more dangerous than a mountain of knives and a sea of fire. I tried to conjure up what Lao Peng You would do in this circumstance.

"Sir, you ask more of me than I can impart. What is it, if I may ask, that you believe I could do to bestow immortality upon you?"

He grinned and winked. "Did you not get the Chrysanthemum tile each game today? Was that too subtle?"

I had no desire to impregnate this man, but as a guest in his home, I felt it best to leave as quickly as possible without creating any further trouble.

"Alas, I am incapable of performing the act you request."

"Incapable–or unwilling?" He glowered. "There is a difference."

"Sir, Shen Lung, the Blue Dragon, came to me and presented a gift, the Peach of Immortality from the Celestial Queen Mother's garden." I spoke the truth. The dragon taunted me with that heavenly fruit. "I cannot make the same offer to you as I do not carry such a treasure." I had no desire to discuss the true nature of how one obtains immortality.

His mouth drooped. "I see. And now you and your minion, Lao Peng You"–his sidelong glance displayed shrewd understanding–"travel the countryside attempting to hustle people with your Mahjong incompetence?"

"Wang Yue, you are very perceptive about my traveling companion's identity; however, he is not my minion."

"Ah," he smirked. "He is merely your unassuming servant."

I discovered the duality of life presents many interchangeable couples: the master and the slave, the teacher and the pupil, the changer and the transformed. I felt it best not to converse or argue with him any longer. "Yes, you have reasoned well."

He nodded in apparent victory and glanced at me askance. "Would it interest you to repay your debt in another fashion?"

I must honor my obligation but could not determine this man's veiled objectives. "What do you have in mind, my good host?"

He dropped his trousers to the ground and tilted back onto the table, his legs elevated, chrysanthemum in full bloom. His magnificent silk coat opened and drooped to the sides. A mound of flesh rose from his spine in the shape of a volcano dome, complete with caldera at its summit.

In his exuberance, he must have forgotten that I told him of my inability to fulfill his desire.

"Alas, I am incapable of performing the act you propose."

"Incapable–or unwilling?" He sneered. "There is a difference."

"My little bird cannot fly, honored host. One of the unfortunate sacrifices we endure in return for immortality, I am afraid."

He propped himself on his elbows and sulked. It pained me to misrepresent the truth such as I had, but

I did not wish to divulge secrets nor share the seed of immortality with him.

"However, if you think it will do any good, you may perform the act upon me." Have I learned the art of trickery from Lao Peng You? Have I learned too quickly?

"Alas, Baron, I do not think that possible either. The gods did not see fit to provide me with a little bird big enough to discharge such duties." I followed his glance down to the place where another man would have a yumberry but saw only its pit.

"Wang Yue, I could provide oral service for you, if you think that is possible."

His smile gave away the answer. "Possible and desirable." He yelled for his man, "Chang Hu!" and lay back on the table.

The servant appeared, dropped his drawers, and began tilling Wang Yue's back yard. I cannot imagine how many times this conniving lord had employed similar deceits to obtain his delights from other victims. Chang Hu's great white beard rustled in the evening breeze, giving the appearance of clouds scurrying.

"Baron," grunted my host, "if you please." He nodded toward his south.

As I looked upon his shirtless abdomen for the first time, I realized it displayed a large tattoo fashioned like the Moon Rabbit. It took some self-control to suppress a laugh. It also took some hunting to find his little, little brother. Perhaps how a woman's *yinhu* might appear, an image I held in my head as I attempted to winkle out his longevity-sustaining juice with my lips and tongue.

Between his servant's barrage at the bottom and my suction at the front, Wang Yue did not last very long.

For all my suffering, he rewarded me with a mouthful of appetizing, soy-flavored liquid. Perhaps I could become inured to this after all. If each man tasted differently–and with a little good luck–my life could become a flavorsome banquet.

Before my host could follow me, I swallowed the nectar and ran back down the hill to the wagon.

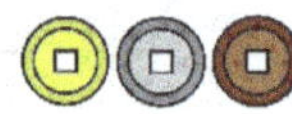

Lao Peng You sat motionless in the oxcart, as in meditation. When approaching footsteps gave away my return, he looked in my direction like a resolute night sentry. His face softened when he realized it was me.

"How was dinner with that fat rice bucket? May his children be born with hemorrhoids!"

I smiled at the concept of Wang Yue attempting to impregnate a woman. "There will be no issue from that one, you can be assured."

Lao Peng You's disgust shifted to alarm. "You did not give him the gift of immortality!"

Ah, I saw where the misunderstanding might lay. "No, *huoban*. Of course not. It is his lack of an adequately sized seed delivery apparatus."

We both tittered at the insult. I climbed up into the wagon, the Marquis lifted the reins and directed the oxen.

"Where are we going? It is late."

Without looking at me he responded, "We must flee. Wang Yue or his cronies will attempt to thwart us."

Thinking back on the day's events, I realized, "Hasn't he already thwarted us?"

"Yes." He nodded. "You reason well." He stared off into the darkness. "That son of a rabbit is too devious, even for my taste. I do not wish to encounter him ever again."

The image of Wang Yue's abdomen flashed through my mind. "He has a tattoo of the Moon Rabbit." I indicated its location with my hand.

Again, we both tittered.

"Marquis," I declared in a casual tone. "I wish to go on a voyage."

"Oh, you do, do you? Where are you planning to go?"

"Shen Lung visited me the other evening and we discussed the tea situation." I looked over, but he concentrated on driving in the near darkness. "He told me about a vine in Guizhou Province that can be brewed as a tea substitute. Have you heard of it?"

"*Jiaogulan.*" He nodded. "Herb of the Immortals."

"Yes, that is it. Have you tried it?"

"Of course. You won't like it," he snapped.

"Why is that, *huoban*?"

"It is an acquired taste and one that takes many, many years to acquire." He looked at me with an expression of parental concern. "You are far too young," the hundreds-of-years-old man who appears forty advised the thirty-and-five years old man. "I have some back in my suite. If you wish, I shall brew it for you to try."

"Yes, thank you very much. I would like to at least give this variety of tea a go."

Lao Peng You considered me with knitted brows. "Am I correct to assume that–when you test this infusion–if you like the taste of it–or believe that in time there can be sufficient acclimatization–you will want to make your way to the southern nether region to obtain this extraordinary herb?"

I took a few moments to decipher the trail of complicated reasoning through the jungle of his words. "Yes, you would be correct in assuming that." I smiled with self-satisfaction. "Even if I don't like it, I would consider sojourning south, just to see the country. I have never sailed on a sea vessel before, and I would like to try that as well."

"Squandering your fortune," he grumbled while shaking his head.

"Was it not *you*, my *huoban*, who advised that I start thinking of money as water? It does no good sitting still. Only when we spread it around does it achieve its full potential."

He faced forward without speaking.

"A vessel floats on water, money is like water. It seems a good balance."

Still no response.

"Is there a suitable agent who arranges travel at Changshou Shan?"

"If you decide to go on this foolhardy expedition, I shall organize the passage for us. We can sail down the Yangtze River to the Southern Sea."

"*We, huoban*? I don't remember including *you* in my plans." I wanted to purse my lips but held back.

"You are not ready to travel by yourself, my child. Who will coordinate your feedings?"

It sounded as if he saw me as his own sacred offspring. I could not determine whether I liked this paternal side of him. Before we met, I felt quite capable of taking care of myself.

"At some point I shall need to become independent from you, Marquis. Besides, I have already taken seed without your assistance."

He jolted upright with wide eyes. "From whom? Please tell me it was not that *wangbadan* back there in Dongting!"

Instead of speaking, I nodded my ascent of the fact he did not wish to hear.

"*Huoban!*" he cried out. "Taking seed from men like that could be –"

"Delicious!"

"No! He is a bad man!"

"With tasty seed." I recalled the sensation of fermented soy on my tongue. "It was the first time I enjoyed it. My apologies if it upsets you."

"I am not upset," he stated with upturned chin. "I just don't want you to be harmed by men like him."

"What further harm could he have done? He had my octopus saturated with *Gu* poison."

"Oh, no!" Lao Peng You wailed.

"It had no effect." I attempted to calm him by patting his shoulder.

"But now he knows we are Immortals."

"Sorry to inform you, Marquis, he already knew that. The poison test merely proved it." He averted his eyes. "Wang Yue may be a bad man, and the universe will dispose of him in its own time, but I learned how to take care of myself without you holding my hand and playing mother."

He blinked. "You are quite correct, Hao Lan. You must learn for yourself how to make your way in this evil world. I only wanted to make sure that no harm befell you unnecessarily."

"I appreciate your concern, Lao Peng You." We smiled at each other. "But when is it exactly that harm *would* be necessary?" I laughed, and he joined in.

"When we return, I shall make arrangements for you to sail to the southern wilderness. You can have your little adventure, if that is what you want. Do you prefer luxury class or economy?"

"Luxury, of course." I grinned. "If I have learned anything from you, it is that if you are going to do something exceedingly foolish, do it in the grandest way possible so that all may observe." I patted him on the shoulder again. "And, by the way, make sure you book passage for two travelers."

Even though darkness had fallen, I could feel him smile.

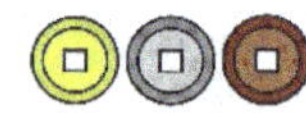

It was well after midnight when we arrived at Changshou Shan. The moon had set, and we made our way back to our rooms in dim light. We parted ways, and I fell onto my bed.

"Wealth and rank are desired by people, but they do not remain if they are not acquired in the right way."

"The real measure of your wealth is how much you'd be worth if you lost all your money."

"If your happiness depends on money, you will never be happy with yourself."

"Wealth is like a chrysanthemum. Its beauty only comes from those who appreciate its blossom."

"Wait!" says the first voice. "Who made that last argument?"

"Not me," the emerald chimes in. "Not my style at all."

"True though it may be"—the opal coughs—"you would never hear those silly words come from me!"

"Good night, gentlemen," I croon and walk away from the big, big dream wall.

5. The East Wind

Morning at Changshou Shan seemed a bit too quiet. On any other day, I would hear people bustling about, birds chirping, Lao Peng You banging on my door. This day started with none of those characteristic sounds.

For the first time in several sunrises, I woke up in a bed I had slept in at least once before. The lush mountaintop surroundings created a comfortable and restful atmosphere. After considering the benefits of remaining at the resort for a while, I decided to ask about staying on. In my new life, I had no other place to call home.

Following my morning ablutions, I approached the house mother to discuss leasing the room on a long-term basis. She informed me those lodgings only let by the week. If I wanted to remain for a longer period, I would have to rent one of the suites, but they all had occupants. As the two of us planned to travel south, I would have to deal with the situation upon our return. I headed to the food table.

There sat my *huoban*, munching on dried fish and boiled eggs. Beside him, an ornate pot with two matching cups.

"Good morning, Marquis." I bowed for no particular reason.

"Good morning, Baron." He continued chewing.

I sat next to him. "I hope you slept well."

"As well as could be expected." He returned to his morning meal.

"Is something on your mind, *huoban*? You seem distracted."

"What?" He looked at me while munching a spongy egg.

"Nothing." I took some cold rice and a bean cake. "Where is your usual flask of rice wine?"

"No rice wine this morning." He pointed to the pot. "Dragon Longevity Tea, as you requested."

My *huoban* poured a small amount into one of the cups and examined the infusion. "Not yet ready," he declared and emptied it back into the pot. "It takes a long time to steep properly."

"How long has it been?"

Lao Peng You glanced over at the water clock in the garden. "About half an hour so far."

"Half an hour? That is a very long time to steep tea leaves."

He looked at me with eyebrows elevated. "Why do you think they call it *Longevity Tea*? Never hurry a palatable potion. Besides, are you expected to appear somewhere this morning?"

One advantage of being immortal, I suppose, it provides an individual with abundant time. Patience develops into a virtue acquired over many seasons. It outlasts power and money in the long run. Or so I have read.

"Have you had an opportunity to inquire into our anticipated voyage?" I hoped he had made the best use of *his* time.

"Yes, of course. All done. Leave tomorrow."

"Tomorrow? How grand. For how many days are we scheduled?"

He scowled. "Who knows? We shall return when we return. You seem quite preoccupied with the future at the moment. Are you anticipating visitors?"

His mood felt rather foul this morning. I wonder if he had swallowed a bitter melon–or, perhaps, an opal–during the night.

"Thank you for booking our passage. I thought we would be going on a standard package tour with predetermined days."

"No." He went back to chewing again. "I chartered a small junk. No need for a tower ship. A cart arrives for us tomorrow morning."

"Is this expensive?"

"It depends on your definition of expensive, *huoban*. As you wish to explore the uncharted backwaters of our southern provinces, no *standard package tour* exists. Fortunately, I was able to locate a ship captain foolhardy enough to undertake this unwise mission."

"Thank you, Marquis. I shall pay whatever the cost."

"You will pay one-half of whatever the cost. I am splitting it with you."

"Of course, *huoban*, of course."

Lao Peng You poured from the pot again. "It is ready." He filled both cups and handed one to me.

This brew had infused for so long, the cup felt cooler than my own skin. Most of the time, one can smell the aroma of a steeped beverage, but this particular one had no discernible scent.

No need to wait. I took a sip to get a sense of its flavor. *Bleh!*

During my days as a miner, cinnabar powder would often drift into my mouth. It tasted gritty and bitter. If you add muddy, stagnant river water to that distasteful dust, it approximated what I experienced here.

Not wanting to give Lao Peng You the satisfaction of being correct, I swallowed without protest and sipped some more. He slurped his while observing me. Once I downed those first bits, I decided to finish the cup in one gulp. I set the decorative little container down.

"Did you enjoy your first taste of *Xiancao*, Baron?" His tone suggested I should not have.

"Of course. I found it quite –" Before I could finish the sentence, I cast up the entire contents of my stomach on the ground.

"Dear me," he consoled, although I found it difficult to imagine him sincere about it. "Some people do have that reaction. Did I mention it takes many, many years to acquire a taste for it?"

I heard a loud thwack on the table as Lao Peng You hit his cup to dislodge the tea leaves.

"Ah," he purred, "just as I would have expected." Without any further conversation, he stood up and returned to his suite.

When I regained my composure, I looked at the abstract collection of dregs. I had not received formal training in tasseomancy, but I saw a globe and a waterfall, signs of travel and prosperity. However, off to the side I recognized a definite triangle shape, which I could not interpret.

I banged my inverted cup and found the following: a baby, a flying eagle, a ball, and a horseshoe. My rudimentary skills decoded these as new life, good transcendence, desire for travel, and good luck during travel. All favorably auspicious.

Satisfied with the leaf reading, I returned to my room to ready myself for the day ahead. It figured that Mahjong matches would occur at some point. I counted a sufficient number of coins into my purse and secreted the rest in the room's security box. Given that we shall begin a long journey tomorrow, I am determined to fall asleep sooner than usual, especially as we arrived back here very late in the evening. Reading from *The Classic of Filial Piety* should produce weariness.

Knock, knock. "*Huoban*, it is me." Lao Peng You entered without consent. His furrowed brows imparted a sense of gravity. What could be the problem? Could he have concern for my health after attempting the noxious Longevity Tea?

"I am fine, Marquis. Thank you."

"Hmmm? Oh, yes, I am glad, but that is not why I am here." How comforting. His eyes shifted about, as if thinking or spying.

I studied his face for clues. Finding none, I pressed on. "What brings you to my room this morning, *huoban*?"

He stared at his feet. "I wish to consult you regarding our Mahjong partnership."

What could be so disturbing to him? "Yes, Marquis. What do you wish to discuss?"

"I believe"–he looked up to face me–"it is time to operate independently. We have been an amazingly good team and we have acquired greatly, but I wish you to function by yourself from now on and earn your own money. Is this arrangement acceptable and to your liking?"

Perhaps he had observed my game strategy development and offered a chance to demonstrate my competency. Perhaps he found a new confederate.

I nodded. "Of course. If that is your wish. You have brought so much to my life, and if our converged paths must now diverge, I cannot stem the flow of time's river."

"No, no!" he cried. "You have misunderstood me. I have no desire to dissolve our partnership, merely the subterfuge at the Mahjong table. From now on we shall each play for ourselves and let the tiles fall where they may."

Either I have had some positive effect on the old man, or he has–without doubt–found another confederate.

I felt I must ask, "Have you a new partner for your scheme?"

"Hao Lan, you are correct to be skeptical"–he snorted"–but I assure you I shall be operating alone, without an accomplice."

I could not wait to see what would happen.

That afternoon we played. Each of us won and lost many hands. However, by the end of the day, we both accumulated more money than we had brought with us.

At one point I sat East. During the game I acquired a triplet–a Pung–of East Wind tiles. This would score very highly for me, as East was also the prevailing wind for that round. Soon after, I had the fortune of drawing the Summer Flower tile. When I took a replacement for it from the back wall, I could hardly believe what I held in my hand! The fourth East Wind tile had come to me.

That completed a quadruplet–a Kong–of the prevailing wind, also my own wind. This would most likely be a limit hand for me, and I would collect a small mountain of coins from the others.

The rules of Mahjong dictate that if a player obtains a Kong without having to pick it from a discard, he must place all four tiles face up to show the others, but then turn the outside two face down to indicate its status as *concealed*, which scores twofold. He then draws a replacement tile to return his hand total to thirteen.

The faces of the other players soured when I displayed my good fortune. When I drew another replacement, it completed my other sets and gave me Mahjong. After we settled, the other two gentlemen left the table with nothing.

"*Huoban,*" the Marquis whispered, "I believe you have learned very well. Your brief association with me has been worth ten years of book study. Or perhaps you have a departed ancestor assisting with your play."

Could it be that difficult for him to believe I played well or had a stroke of good fortune? His inflated ego continued to swell with each sunrise.

As no one else waited to join us, we both returned to our rooms to rest. And, perhaps, count our earnings.

Soon I found myself tired and lay down on the bed. Moments later I fell asleep.

I stand on a small raft floating along a big river. The steep rocky banks rise almost straight up. Every so often a lone tree braves out from the bits of mud along the sides.

"I hear you are going on a little journey." The voice of Shen Lung, the Blue Dragon, rings out behind me, and I

sense the raft rise in the water. When I turn around, I discover his head looming over me, bejeweled eyes flashing with the rapid current of the river. He floats on his back, and I stand on his great belly, the foreboding tail serving as prow and rudder.

"News travels fast," I retort.

When he laughs, his belly moves up and down, similar to a carnival ride. Or an earthquake. He holds a zongzi in one claw and munches bites of it.

"Forgive me for asking, my Lord, but I thought dragons were unable to eat zongzi."

Another little quake as he laughs. "Whose dream is this, Hao Lan? Yours or mine?"

Yes, who is to say? *I consider.*

"In this particular dream, dragons enjoy zongzi. Is that a problem for you?"

Legend relates how the famous poet Qu Yuan's departed spirit created zongzi–triangular, stuffed rice cakes steamed in bamboo leaves–as a deterrent and safeguard to keep the river dragon from devouring him in the afterlife.

"No, my Lord, not at all. May I ask what is inside the zongzi?"

"Qu Yuan," *he replies, licking his giant lips with that dark, forked tongue.* "Look up, Hao Lan," *he instructs.* "I wish to give you a vision of what is to come."

Overhead I see what looks like a thin thread connecting both sides of the banks high above. "What is that, my Lord?" *I point to the delicate strand.*

"That, my son, is the Wushan Bridge. It allows people to travel to and from Chongqing across this long river."

"It is up so high, Shen Lung." *I strain my eyes to see it.* "People travel across that wisp in the sky without fear? It seems so tenuous."

"Like a spider's web, Hao Lan." He grins. "Thready thin, but iron strong."

I swallow with anxiety. "Even as an Immortal I would have apprehension about traversing it."

He laughs, and I bounce up and down again. "I assure you it is quite durable. By the way, I warn you, this is not the last time you will see that particular bridge."

"Will we be sailing along this waterway on our journey?" I ask.

"Yes, that, too." He snorts a great flash of fire high up into the air above. Charred ashes fall like gray snow. "But that is not why I have brought you here, Little One."

"My Lord." I bow. "I carry out your bidding."

"And you do it well, my son. Have you noticed any recent improvements?"

My mind ponders the last few days for a moment. "I believe my confidence level is developing daily, my Lord. Thank you."

"No, no, no!" he roars. "I refer to Lao Peng You. Have you noticed changes in his behavior?"

Now that he mentions it. "It was a great surprise that he allowed me to play Mahjong without his assistance. At first, I suspected that he had found a new, more compatible, confederate, but it does not appear so."

"It does not appear so…" the dragon repeats. "Yes, perhaps you have inaugurated my old friend along a new path." His tail turns a bit, and we shift right to avoid a set of rocks in the flow. "Did you enjoy your first cup of Jioagulan?"

My face could not conceal the disgust.

"It appears you have not yet acquired the taste."

"*My Lord, if that is tea for Immortals, I may have to give up entirely on the idea of ever enjoying the beverage again.*"

He chuckles and the belly bounces. "*Many people have a similar reaction to tobacco, another gift of the gods, but they eventually overcome the disgusting taste to enjoy its medicinal benefits.*"

"*If Jiaogulan has medicinal benefits, I would try it again, but Great One, the taste reminds me of cinnabar mine dust, not a very happy memory for me.*"

"*Cinnabar mine dust?*" *he shouts.* "*That is not how Longevity Tea is supposed to taste. How long did Lao Peng You allow it to steep?*"

"*Please be assured that he left the leaves to infuse more than the minimum time. I saw them sit for the span of twenty-and-five breaths, and he told me they had been steeping for half an hour before I arrived.*"

His eyes narrow, and the light refracting from their facets diminishes. "*I do not believe he served you Jiaogulan, Little One. It requires but seventy breaths of steeping. Any less and it is too sweet to drink. Any more and it becomes too bitter. If Lao Peng You spoke the truth, then it sat too long before he served it to you. If he misrepresented the time, then he served you something that surely was not Dragon Longevity Tea.*"

"*My Lord.*" *I bow again for insurance.* "*He also drank from the same vessel with no ill effects. I cast mine up after the first cup.*"

The dragon's head shifts from side to side. "*Did he tell you the name of this putrid infusion?*"

I try to remember what my huoban *said.* "*I believe he called it 'Xiancao,' O Great One.*"

His shriek shakes the whole river valley, and I almost fall from his great abdomen. "That is not Jiaogulan! Please keep in mind that he is hundreds of years older than you. He has had time to inure himself to many noxious substances in order to conduct his petty, noxious schemes. Lao was most likely attempting to dissuade you from the voyage you desire to take. One step forward, one step rearward. No advance."

The Blue Dragon flies upward, dropping me into the powerful river. At the crest of the gorge, he bellows a heaven-jolting noise, and rain begins to fall.

I pray that I can swim in my dream.

When I woke, my clothes felt damp and had a smell reminiscent of the *Dragon Longevity Tea* Lao Peng You served this morning. After changing into the suit I had purchased from him, I took the soiled garment to the launderer for cleaning.

At the food table sat my *huoban*, stuffing his face with delicate baked goods and piles of seafood. The sun appeared low on the horizon. Time for the evening meal.

After the discussion with Shen Lung in my dream, I had even more doubts about this scoundrel but knew I should not disclose my knowledge of his earlier deception. Once again, he had a plateful of oysters squirming in front of him.

"Baron," he greeted me between half-shells. "Won't you please join me for dinner?"

He has introduced me to several new and fascinating foods, but what will he entreat me to attempt next? Monkey brains?

"Marquis, I am planning to turn in early so that I shall be fully refreshed for tomorrow's voyage."

"Oh, yes, that," he muttered with a jiggly morsel in his mouth. "You still want to go? Even after you had that bad reaction to the Dragon Longevity Tea?"

"Oh, yes! More than ever."

His face shifted to a sour expression, and I could not tell if it came from a bad oyster or my unrelenting enthusiasm.

I enquired, "You did not cancel our booking, did you?" If he even made one in the first place.

"The cart arrives just after sunrise. Be ready." He picked up another shell.

I walked to the food table and chose a few bean cakes, some vegetables, and rice. When I sat next to Lao Peng You, he peered down his nose at my choices.

"Still eating like a peasant, I see."

"I enjoy these foods, *huoban*. I am certain my gustatory horizons will expand over the years to come. At the end of the day, I have all the time in the world, do I not?"

Every so often, I enjoyed taunting him just to see the variety of pained expressions his face could generate.

We sat side-by-side, each dining on our preferred meals until a thought occurred to me.

"Marquis, how shall we sustain ourselves on this voyage?"

He looked at me as if I had just asked his real age. "Do you mean to ask if they serve food onboard the boat I have engaged?"

"No, *huoban*. I am referring to our *special diet*, the one required by people like you and me." I winked for conspiratorial effect.

"Ah, the elixir of long life." He smiled. "I understand your concern." He picked up and swallowed the last oyster on the platter. "Hao Lan, one thing you will learn about travel upon water: If you confine robust and hearty men to a small vessel without women, they become quite agreeable to our specific requests." His laughter rattled the empty shells on the table.

Following our meal, I returned to the launderer to retrieve my cleaned suit. As I placed coins on the counter, my thoughts drifted to the concept of money and how much of it has passed through my purse since my association with Lao Peng You.

In my former life, I never possessed more than a handful. The stash in my locked box could feed the entire village of Wu Chu for a year. I could donate half of it to the nearest monastery and still have enough to live like a prince. This new wealth has brought comfort, but I could not be certain what other transformations it portended. Water can float a boat but sink it as well.

I went back to my room to pack a few belongings for tomorrow's adventure. Sometime about moonrise I lay down to sleep.

"Sir, if you please!" An older, wrinkle-faced gentleman sits in front of me, legs folded beneath him. He holds a beggar's bowl, full of coins, which he raises and lowers.

It appears we are on a street in my home village. I look around to locate the golden wall.

"Without charity, I am nothing," bleats the ruby. "Sour."

"True charity occurs only when there are no notions of giving, giver, or gift," the emerald counsels. "Bitter."

"*Because of frugality, one is generous,*" informs the opal. "*Sweet! Sweet! Sweet!*"

I turn back to the old man.

"*Please, sir, help me if you can,*" the poor fellow entreats. He does not look particularly undernourished, his clothing seems well-tailored, and he appears to have all his hair and teeth.

I search my pockets but find no coins to give.

"*How is it that I can assist you, my good sir? I have no money to donate.*"

He smiles, and it cracks his face. "*You do not under-stand. I do not wish you to give me money. I am not poor.*"

His appearance corroborates that.

"*I am confused. I wish to help you, but I am not certain what it is I can give you.*"

He emits a generous laugh. "*My friend, you can help by taking some of this burden from me.*" He holds up the bowl. "*I need to rid myself of this wealth before my wife returns from visiting her mother.*"

"*You wish me to take money from you?*" Impossible! Beggars do not distribute coins back to the wealthy.

"*Yes! Please help me. If she returns and I have but one coin in this bowl, she will not allow me to stir her rice pot.*"

This woman sounds exceptionally obstinate. How can a man's wealth ruin his woman's conjugal appetite?

"*I wish I could help you, my friend, but I am also replete with coins and do not require further wealth to satisfy myself, or anyone else.*"

He squints at me. "*But you do not have any coins now, do you?*"

True enough, but I see no good in taking coins from another when I do not need them.

"Please, sir, you must help me." He remains insistent. "Charity begins at my home, and my marital happiness will end without it."

Such a conundrum, perhaps another koan to wade through, with its deep logic and cryptic mysteries. If I take his money, I shall be unhappy because I do not need it. If I do not take his money, he will be unhappy because his woman will not engage in connubial interests.

To whom do I owe a greater responsibility to make happy? Ultimately myself, but a person could always make use of additional funds, especially when presented in such a forthright manner. If I can make another person happy, perhaps I should indulge his request. Even though it seems like an attempt to put out a fire with wood, I stoop to take coins from the bowl.

"It is unsuitable for the man who has all he requires to sustain his greed," the red jewel shouts behind me.

"Greed is an imperfection that defiles the mind," the green gem cautions.

"There is no greater disaster than greed," the milky white stone imparts.

With the three advisors in agreement for the first time, my dream world ends in a fiery cataclysm, as predicted by the opal.

This startling conclusion, due to my injudicious decision, brings on destruction. However, if Shen Lung controls these visions, I can rest assured this scenario will repeat itself some other night.

I rose before the sun, the flower of my heart in full bloom with anticipation and excitement for the day ahead. The food table had not yet been set at this early time of day. I strolled along the garden path and watched the sky slowly redden with the emergence of our great ball of fire in the sky. Like a giant dragon, it floated at a turtle's pace up from behind the mountains to the East, just the way it has for thousands of years before and will for thousands of years hence.

The beatific silence ended when kitchen workers began their morning chores. Wonderful smells wafted from the food table, and I walked there to see what I would want to eat. I chose some cold rice but avoided the *zongzi* for fear of what–or *who*–it might contain. Freshly caught fish in plum sauce looked appetizing as well. As I sat down, the Marquis graced me with his presence.

"All packed and ready to go, I presume," he said with a slight mocking in his tone.

I stopped chewing. "Of course. I woke before sunrise."

"No surprise to me." He moved to the food and filled a plate before returning.

"*Huoban*, I was wondering what they will have for a beverage on board our ship."

As he sat next to me, Lao Peng You responded, "Most crews drink bad tea or cheap wine." His head tilted before he spoke again. "Perhaps we should supply our own liquids." He nodded and continued, "Well reasoned, *huoban*. Let us procure a few barrels after we finish eating our meal."

We purchased six small casks of rice wine to take with us, hoping that we could acquire more along the way, if necessary.

Soon after, a medium-sized wagon pulled by two horses arrived. The driver asked after us and we hopped up, indicating our travel bags and wine barrels.

Once the fellow loaded our belongings, we proceeded along the winding path down the hill. My hands trembled with eagerness for the thrill of a mysterious journey. Lao Peng You sat still as stone while the extraordinarily beautiful display of tall trees and narrow peaks nestled in early morning fog passed by us.

An hour later we entered Wanshou, a city along the Yangtze River. My humble village of Wu Chu had but a few hundred residents. This town appeared to have thousands, more people than I had ever seen in one place. Tall stone buildings poked out here and there, and pillars of black smoke trailed up into heaven. Merchants screamed the names of their diverse wares: "Carp! Fresh carp!" "Honey! Sweet honey!" "Vinegar! Vinegar!" "Bam-booooo!" The air smelled of onions, body odor, and dead fish.

Our wagon stopped next to a wooden pier extending a dragon's length into the streaming water. The most beautiful boat I had ever seen moored at the end. *Tong Feng*, painted in large gold characters, adorned the prow. Its flanks appeared to be dark teak, and a tall stick stood in the middle with tree branches emanating from it. We jumped down from the wagon and walked toward the vessel.

Someone leapt from the boat to the pier and approached us. "I am Xin Yue, captain of this vessel. Are you my charter clients?"

My *huoban* might have nodded in the affirmative. I had no idea because I could not stop staring at this captain, the most exquisite woman I had ever seen. Not that I had seen many, but this woman's splendor exemplified loveliness for me.

Sharp jaw lines converged toward a tiny, angular chin. Large, dark eyes twinkled. Hair of liquid amber flowed from beneath the captain's hat. She appeared to be a few years younger than me, but you can never tell with women, so I have heard. Her long, buttery tunic with black trim nearly brushed the ground, revealing thick-soled shoes like the other sailors wore. Another duality: feminine and masculine in one person. If only I could plead my troth for her, but, alas, I could never consummate our potential love.

"Come aboard," came the order as she retreated onto her floating cloud upon the river.

Lao Peng You broke my reverie, pushing me toward the boat. He instructed the crew to bring our belongings aboard. The men had no shirts. They wore only long, black pants tied at the waist with a red silk sash that hung to their knees.

At the end of the pier, I bowed to Xin Yue before boarding her vessel. With my hand on my chest, I managed to croak, "Hao... Hao Lan," from my tense throat.

"Yes, yes, hurry now," instructed Lao Peng You, who had already hopped onto the boat.

I stepped over the railing with trepidation, never having been on such a water vessel before. The floor rocked and moved in an unpredictable pattern. My head wobbled, and I felt myself careen. Just as I began to topple, a strong pair of arms rescued me. This particular set of arms lurked beneath a buttery robe with black trim. I wanted to melt.

"Is this your first trip, Hao Hao Lan?" Her creamy voice pooled in my ears.

I smiled and nodded in my daze. "By the way," I managed to rasp, "It is merely Hao Lan, my lady captain." Perhaps I smiled too much.

"Yes, *xiansheng*. Hao Lan I shall call you." She struggled to raise me toward a vertical position, but my body remained flaccid and would not cooperate. Xin Yue turned to my *huoban*, "Is he going to be like this the whole trip? If so, I shall have to double the price."

Lao Peng You shrugged. "This man has never seen such beauty as the Yangtze before. Also, I believe this is his first water voyage."

Our fair captain leaned me against the railing. "Well, I do hope he gets his water legs soon enough. We cannot squander our time buoying him like this." She turned and pointed to a door at the rear of the boat. "That is your cabin." She walked away and barked orders to the crew.

"But where do *you* sleep?" As in my dreams, the questions erupt without me wishing them to.

The surprised expression on her face suggested she had never been asked that before. "The crew and I sleep below." She turned and resumed shouting commands.

"You mean this boat has a cellar?"

"Marquis!" she shouted, sounding exasperated. "Please instruct your traveling companion regarding the construction of a junk so that I can get the wretched thing down the river before he has me explain the entire scientific design involved in building such a vessel as well as the intricate principles of riparian commerce!"

My *huoban* guided me into our cabin. "There is another deck below this one. Room for cargo and two sleeping chambers. This room"–he pointed to our cabin–"is usually the captain's quarters."

I nodded and sat on the bed. It seemed more prudent to sit than to be jostled about by writhing of the boat. "And how does a beautiful woman become a ship captain? What a pleasant surprise!"

"You are giddy!" he accused. "The river air makes you irrational. Or are you smitten with that female pirate?"

"*Pirate*?" I screamed. "How can you call that epitome of beauty a pirate?"

"You are smitten," he intoned. "I label her that because she charges us two gold coins per day for this little trip. Robbery upon the water is called piracy; therefore, she is a pirate."

"One gold coin from each of us for every day we remain in her presence is but a trifle for the pleasures we shall receive in return. Besides, did you not say you had difficulty finding someone willing to transport us?"

My *huoban* gazed skyward, "I could think of many, many other, better, better ways to spend one gold coin."

Rather than arguing with an immovable rock, I gazed out the window at lovely little fishing villages and groups of domestic animals roaming the riverbanks as we passed. Other boats headed upriver, their crews working large oars to overcome the moving water's supremacy.

Time flowed by as I observed these new and diverse surroundings. Beyond the various settlements, I saw pastures and farmlands. After a while, I heard our golden-throated captain call, "Gentlemen, there is luncheon out on the deck if you choose to sit with us."

Lao Peng You–who would never miss a meal–and I exited the small cabin. It took a few steps on the rocking deck for me to learn the proper walking pattern. It reminded me of a crane wading in a muddy pond.

We joined the others at a table that just seated six people: the captain, her first mate, two crewmen and us. Of course, I wanted to sit next to the lady, but the crew surrounded her. In the center sat a platter of fish, presumably from the river, and a bowl of rice.

As we ate, the *Tong Feng* sailed into a deepening ravine. The sides continued to rise higher and higher. With the sun directly overhead, something familiar caught my eye. A slender thread spread from one bank to the other high above us.

Pointing upward, I asked, "Is that the Wushan Bridge?" They all glanced to where my finger directed.

"Why, yes, it is, *xiansheng*. I thought you had never taken a water voyage before. How do you know about the Wushan Bridge?" Her polished obsidian eyes gleamed, focusing my attention.

"Yes, Hao Lan. How *do* you know about the Wushan Bridge?" my *huoban* prompted me.

I cannot mention my dream of Shen Lung. "A friend described it to me once, and the distinctiveness of it appeared obvious straightaway."

Everyone returned to their meal except Lao Peng You, who glared at me as if I had withheld some significant secret from him. I looked down at my bowl as I chewed, wishing to keep the dragon hidden.

I passed the afternoon sitting by the rail looking up at the high cliffs as we cruised along the course of this mighty river. At irregular intervals, a bare tree or two struck out from the barren banks. The flowing water beneath the boat darkened as we glided eastward.

Dinner consisted of fish and rice. Still delicious, but if they continued to serve the same thing over and again, it might get wearisome after a while. Lao Peng You opened a cask of rice wine, and we shared it with the crew.

As we ate, several of the men looked at us from time to time. I could not tell if their interest came from desire, fascination, or curiosity. In our tailored silk suits, Lao Peng You and I probably gave the impression of two cranes standing amidst a flock of chickens.

I chose to focus my attentions on the lovely lady who shut out the moon and put flowers to shame. As the meal progressed, my curiosity grew. Even though I felt much like the overzealous dog stepping on a cat's paw, I inquired, "Pardon me Xin Yue, but, if I may ask, how does a woman come to be captain of her own vessel?"

For the first time since I gazed upon her gorgeous face, she smiled. Her lips parted just enough to allow the tips of her perfect teeth to gleam in the light of the setting sun. My chest warmed.

"That is a good story, *xiansheng*. Yes, it is unusual for a woman to be admiral of her own navy, but–unlike this vast river–my life has had a few unexpected turns."

"Whose has not?" interjected Lao Peng You.

"Indeed," concurred Xin Yue. "As it happens, this boat used to belong to my husband."

My heart dropped, crippling my soul.

"He was a happy and successful fisherman. We survived on the catch plus a few meager coins of profit from selling to others."

My *huoban* looked at me with what felt like concern in his eyes, as if sensing my grief.

"One evening, my uncle invited us to dine with him," she continued. "For the main dish, he served octopus, and my husband got very sick from it. When he died a few days later, I inherited his boat."

"*Octopus*, you say?" queried Lao Peng You. "It sounds like a very treacherous dish." He glared at me.

I ignored my *huoban* and rejoiced in relief. "I am sorry to hear about the death of your husband, Xin Yue." What a creamy smooth name. It melted in my mouth.

"Thank you, Hao Lan. This set of unlikely circumstances has allowed me to subsist tolerably on a simple living and provide fish to my village. But when this distinguished gentleman"–she indicated the Marquis–"requested a charter boat, I saw the opportunity to increase my earnings, and here we are." She raised both hands above her head, framing those auburn locks and caressing the heavens. In my eyes, she became more and more lovely.

When darkness began to envelop us, the crew lit lanterns. Ahead I could see a great city with many, many lights.

"What is that place?" I asked.

"Wuchang," Lao Peng You responded. "Capital of Hubei Province."

"We shall dock there for the night," announced Xin Yue. "It is too dangerous to sail the Yangtze in the dark. River pirates." She stood. "Gentlemen, I bid you good evening." She went below deck, and I followed her willowy form with my disheartened eyes until she disappeared into the darkness.

"Shall we?" The Marquis indicated our cabin.

The two of us returned to the little room. I felt too aroused to fall asleep right away. Xin Yue revealed she had no husband and owned her boat. She would make a wonderful wife. *Alas*, I thought, *not for me*.

Through our window I watched the buildings and lights of Wuchang approaching. *Tong Feng* steered into an area with many piers, and we pulled up to one of them. The first mate interacted with a local fellow dressed in unfamiliar clothing. His outfit did not fasten closed in front. Instead, it crossed in the manner of a robe, and the dull, gray fabric did not shine like silk. He kept his long hair in braids beneath a simple, dark skullcap.

I could hear them speaking, but the expressions made no sense. Their conversation sounded more like frogs croaking in a well. Up until that moment, I had only heard our common language, but this dialect sounded peculiar and completely different.

After a short while, I grew tired of looking at all the strange sights and decided to sleep. I reasoned I should save some energy for whatever adventures tomorrow might deliver.

"I congratulate you, Hao Lan." Shen Lung greets me from above. I stand in the plowed field again, but this time, light rain falls. "You have managed to destroy my golden wall." He bellows a loud laugh. I seem to have a knack for amusing Immortals.

"O Great One, I am not sure to what you are referring." My clothes feel damp.

"Ha, ha, Little One. In your last dream, you encountered a beggar man, did you not?"

"Yes, my Lord, I did. He attempted to give away his coins so that his wife would allow him to stir her rice pot."

"And what happened?" he roars.

Yes, what happened? "I endeavored to reason through the difficulty. Should I act to please myself or should I act to please another? I decided that it is better to please others because in doing so I please myself." I smile because I know I did the right thing.

"No!" the Blue Dragon erupts. "Never please others before you please yourself!"

I tremble at his outburst and bow several times in rapid succession. "My sincerest apologies, my Lord. I believed I was only following the great teachings."

"Stupid teachings!" He whips round and round, making the rain spiral as it falls. "Did I not provide you with three wise men to impart their learned counsel?"

"Yes, my Lord, you did, but I have difficulty grasping their wisdom. They contradict each other constantly. I find it challenging to decipher their confusing words."

"That is because you are not paying attention!" He blows a great flower of flame that singes some of the water droplets, making them hiss and steam. "Because of your inability to reason well, the three of them agreed without intention, thus annihilating one another."

This dream is just as impenetrable as the other. Many, many words but very little understanding.

"Hao Lan, life will present the same lessons to you over and over until you can resolve them correctly." The dragon flies around so that his giant, multifaceted eyes are on the same level as mine. "Not always in the same form, mind you." He blinks.

"So it would seem, my Lord." I really don't know what to say.

A small grin replaces the grimace. "I know you don't know what to say, Little One." One of his shaggy eyebrows rises. "You needn't say anything." His head tilts a bit. "At times, silence is louder than words. Silence is a true friend who never betrays. Silence is an empty space, and space is the home of the awakened mind. Silence can be a source of great strength." He ascends above me.

I step aside–in case of pihua–*because he sounds much too much like the gems in the golden wall of my other dream.*

"Keep in mind, my servant, that answers to questions do not always solve the problem at hand."

He flaps his wings and disappears into the dark sky. It concerns me how I dread a dream dragon more than a clay figure fears falling rain. I follow his upward trajectory, and my eyes flood with droplets.

6. Imperial Jade

The boat's gentle rocking provided superior sleep–following the dream–to any night the last few years. With few expectations, it turned out I might enjoy travel by boat much more than I had anticipated. Perhaps I shall do it more in the future.

Through the cabin window, I saw we drifted again, no city in sight. I had hoped to go ashore and experience life in Wuchang, but I believed more opportunities to taste a big city might present themselves before this voyage ends.

As I opened the door and stepped onto the deck, I breathed in the brackish air. When I observed the crew, I coughed it out and stopped thinking about salty water, or anything else. They moved in slow, bizarre motions, holding their arms straight out, making fists, and hopping about on one bent leg. Had they turned into *Jiangshi* overnight? The fright in my face must have been obvious because Lao Peng You placed a hand on my shoulder.

"They are performing *Taijiquan*, their morning ritual."

"Are they possessed?"

He laughed with hand over mouth. "No, *huoban*, they execute this routine every morning. A series of coordinated movements designed to maintain and improve mind and body."

Xin Yue, along with her men, gyrated and punched the air in synchronized rhythm. As before, I could not take my eyes from her. At times, she noticed me looking at her, and I had to turn away for the sake of propriety and modesty.

"Why did we leave Wuchang so early?" I asked.

"We want to reach Moling before nightfall. It is the last city before we go into the open sea. Perhaps you and I shall be able to go ashore while the crew replenishes supplies." Lao Peng You smiled with narrow eyes.

He said *Moling* and *ashore*, but I heard *Mahjong*. Perhaps we need to earn more coins to help pay for this delightful charter.

"Are you hungry?" I was not sure what he suggested. He could have referred to breakfast, or he could have meant the seed of men. "We saved some fish and rice for you, just in case." Lao Peng You pointed to a small pot near the rail.

Fish and rice, fish and rice. I wanted to go into this Moling if only to get some food other than fish and rice.

I spent the remainder of the day resting in our cabin. If I stayed out on deck too long, my gaze gravitated toward Xin Yue, and that would have been most frustrating for both of us. Along the sides of this river, I observed many farms with both animals and crops.

The Yangtze continued to widen, and eventually we arrived at the largest population center I have ever seen. Both banks contained rows and rows of houses, buildings, temples, shops, and shrines. The sight of so many people and structures caused my heart to race. Behind us, the sun began to touch the hills, and the crew prepared for docking.

Lao Peng You snuck up behind me. "Ready for an evening in Moling, my boy?"

I did not care what we did, I just wanted to experience life in a big city. My chest tingled with each breath of the salty and invigorating air. Our boat bumped the pier as we approached. We stepped to disembark.

"Wait!" shouted our captain. "Before you leave, remember to be back by dawn. We set sail shortly thereafter."

"Dawn?" I questioned.

"Captain," my *huoban* responded, "if we do not return by dawn, presume us dead and revert to your riparian life." He started to move over to the dock.

"Wait!" shouted the captain again. "If you are planning to be dead, then you must pay up now for the voyage so far. Four gold, and while we speak of money, please add some coins to help pay for additional supplies. The two of you eat more than planned."

I looked sidelong at Lao Peng You, knowing where most of the food had gone.

"Here is four gold from me, my lady," he said as he put the coins into her exquisite hand, pausing after each one, as if they might have been drops of his own blood.

I fumbled in my coin purse and found the same. "And four from me as well." As I placed the gold in her hand, our skin met for the first time. I had hoped it would unleash the fireworks I felt when I brushed up against men when the hunger struck. Alas, her most flawless flesh only felt cold and far away to me. She appeared to have no reaction either.

Ah, me...

The Marquis led me through the web of streets, turning down narrow alleys and up grand boulevards. My neck strained from turning to look at each new building or group of people.

Eventually we stopped in front of a squat green structure labeled *Moling Mahjong Club*. He knocked on the large bamboo door, and a small spyhole opened. An eye peeked through the aperture.

"Marquis Pichan and guest," he announced.

I heard the latch click, and the great portal opened to admit us.

"Five gold each," said a mechanical voice. We both presented coins from our purses. The host led us to a room with countless tables, men sitting around them, and a cloud of incense smoke. I had a difficult time breathing, given the fresh river air we had the pleasure of inhaling the last two days. I tried not to cough. Even if I did, the sound would have been inaudible under the constant loud clacking of tiles.

Our guide sat us at a table with two other gentlemen. One lanky and grey, the other young and corpulent.

"Marquis Pichan," my *huoban* bowed, "and Baron Dongting." He indicated me, and I bowed as well.

The older gentleman introduced himself as Lord Nanhai, the other one called himself General Sima. It appeared we graced the company of noble gentlemen. Lord Nanhai started the dice roll and we took our places.

Over the next hour or so, we played many hands in many rounds. We each accumulated enough gold coins to cover the rest of the journey and provide lavish food for the *Tong Feng* crew. Servers visited the table and provided us with dried fruit, crunchy baked goods, and glasses of wine between rounds.

As midnight approached, the host announced, "Last hand." Most of my tiles came from the Bamboo suit. I also had a set of Green Dragons. General Sima discarded the Eight Bamboo I needed. I claimed it for Mahjong, and the other players groaned. When I put the hand up, they all stared at it with full-moon eyes for some reason I could not grasp.

Without realizing it, I had accumulated a winning hand consisting solely of green tiles: the dragons, Pungs of Bamboos and a pair of Two Bamboo. It looked ordinary enough to me.

"Imperial Jade," sighed Lord Nanhai. "I have not seen that hand in many, many years."

I happened to sit East that game, and they all had to pay me double. By the time the other players settled, I could barely lift the purse.

Lao Peng You touched my arm. "Let us go quickly, *huoban*. Sloth will prove costly." He stood and addressed the others, "Thank you, gentlemen for the most enjoyable evening." He made a slight bow. "Until next time."

We struggled to move toward the door, but so many others attempted to leave at the same time. It took us a while to make our egress.

Once outside, the Marquis strode at a brisk pace back the way we came. When we entered a narrow alleyway, four large and brightly clad youths stood in our way.

"Where are you going, gentlemen, at this time of night?" inquired a very tall fellow. His head towered over us. "In a hurry now?" In his right hand he held two sticks connected by a chain. He twirled one of them and passed the other from hand to hand.

"Impressive," Lao Peng You remarked. "Now let us pass before your mother's little bird leaves the nest." He attempted to walk around them, but they let out a collective gasp and huddled closer to prevent our passage.

"How dare you! You do not *know* my mother," the tall one cried.

"Do *you*?" the Marquis quipped in response.

The boys circled around, sneering at us and grunting.

"Your purse seems very heavy, Big Brother," the offended fellow taunted me. "Let us lighten your burden for you."

He reached out for my winnings, but before his left hand got within an arm's length of it, Lao Peng You's right leg flew up to it, and I heard a distinctive crack.

"Owwwww!"

"Who is next?" my *huoban* invited.

One of the other boys, this one about our height, but more muscular, closed in on us. Just as he got to the same proximity, the Marquis levitated on one foot, twisted full circle around in the air, kicking the aggressor in the face, again with a distinctive crack.

As he landed, Lao Peng You grabbed my hand. "Of the Thirty-Six Stratagems, running away is best. Let us go!"

We scampered back toward the boat, and after I had caught some of my breath, I asked, "How did you learn to do that?"

He looked back and said in a casual manner, "I shall teach you when we have some free time, but for now, please run faster."

The bag of coins felt like an anchor, slowing my pace. As we reached the boat, Xin Yue stood on deck snuffing the lanterns. "I didn't think I'd see you boys until morning. Did you have a good evening?"

I could not speak, only huff and pant.

"Adequate," Lao Peng You responded as we entered the cabin. "Goodnight, *huoban*. I am quite tired. Sleep well."

I lowered my purse to the floor, still breathing in heaves. The bed, while small, induced quick slumber.

"Sir, if you please!" An older, wrinkle-faced gentleman sits in front of me, legs folded beneath him. He holds a beggar's bowl, full of coins, which he raises and lowers.

I feel the great gold wall against my back, but I look over my shoulder to make sure.

"Without charity, I am nothing," bleats the ruby. "Sour."

"True charity occurs only when there are no notions of giving, giver or gift," the emerald counsels. "Bitter."

"Because of frugality, one is generous," informs the opal. "Sweet! Sweet! Sweet!"

I turn to face the old man.

"Please, sir, help me if you can," the poor fellow entreats. *He does not look particularly undernourished, his clothing seems well-tailored, and he appears to have all his hair and teeth.*

This feels very familiar. The Blue Dragon informed me lessons would be repeated until I behaved correctly. In the previous version, I believed taking the old man's money would help him with his wife.

The gems all accused me of being greedy. Agreeing on a topic for once, utter destruction ensued. This time I intend to act in a different manner.

"Sir," I proclaim, "I shall not take your coins."

The man stiffens and lurches as if I had added frost to his snow. "Why would you take my coins? I am but a modest beggar."

Apparently, this situation differs from the last. "Do you not need someone to empty your bowl so that your wife will let you –"

"My poor wife died years ago! Why do you persist in upsetting me so?" He weeps in soft sobs.

This time, the man does not want to give up his wealth. A distinct change from the previous dream. I search my pockets but have no coins once again. Not knowing how to proceed, I turn about and approach the wall.

"If you please, I need your guidance," I say to the stones.

"He who knows all the answers has not been asked all the questions," the Red One imparts.

"To walk safely through the maze of human life, one needs the light of wisdom and the guidance of virtue," the Green One contributes.

"As you discover yourself," the Milky White One concludes, "you will find inner guidance."

And I feel no better off for asking them. Banging my head against the wall might be more helpful. Perhaps, then, I could provide my own advice.

Shen Lung instructed me I need to please myself before pleasing others. In this situation, the beggar would be pleased with a donation. I would be pleased to give him some money but have none. Again, a conundrum with no obvious solution.

I return to the old man, "Sir, I wish to make a donation but have no coins. Is there any other way I could help you?"

A smile crosses his wrinkled face. "You just did."

With a puff of smoke, the beggar transforms into the Blue Dragon. "Very good, Hao Lan. One step forward." He leaps up into the sky. "Keep up the good work!"

The next few days blurred together. Once we reached the open ocean, my stomach churned as much as the turbulent waters upon which we sailed. I spent most of the time in the little cabin like a sick duck, casting up my guts or, if I was very, very lucky, sleeping. I do not remember much about that part of the voyage.

One morning we pulled into a calm, fragrant harbor. The air smelled a bit sweet, perhaps due to the profusion of lotus blossoms floating around us. A wide bay encircled the boat, and I could see jade green hills once more. I went out onto the deck.

"Well, look who has joined the living!" quipped Xin Yue. "I was worried for you, *xiansheng*. Feeling better today?"

I could not determine if she enjoyed poking fun at me or if she felt concern for my welfare. Because I preferred the latter, I presumed she intended that.

"Yes, thank you. Where are we?"

She spread her arms out to indicate. "This is the mouth of the Pearl River. From here we head inland to Guizhou so you can find your precious *Jiaogulan* leaves."

I turned to Lao Peng You. "You told her the purpose of our voyage?"

He shrugged. "No harm. Besides, I have found that if you tell the rickshaw driver where you wish to go, you usually get there faster than if you do not."

The crew must not have begun its morning exercise routine because they all sat at the table eating fish and rice. For the first time in a few days, fish and rice sounded good.

On both sides of the river, I saw dense groves of tropical plants, much like I imagined a jungle would look. Thick vines wrapped around slender trunks of plant stalks. Huge, green leaves blocked the sunlight, filtering the rays with their giant hands.

Because we did not have the flow of water behind us, the crew had to row against the powerful current.

I asked Lao Peng You, "Should we not assist them?"

He responded, "Stop thinking like a peasant. This is what we pay them for."

I supposed his attitude correct, but I reasoned we could save some money by speeding up the pace of the boat. A while later, the tide came in behind us, and we moved along faster.

That evening I began to feel weak. Different from how the rocking and pitching of the boat affected me. No urge to heave.

I spoke to Lao Peng You once we were alone in the cabin. "*Huoban*, I do not feel well, as if I am in the jaws of a tiger. My head is light, and I can barely hold my eyes open."

He nodded. "It is the hunger, Hao Lan. You need to take the seed of man."

So, this is the sensation. Yes, I had better enlist the aid of one of the sailors. "Who is amenable to us here?"

He shifted his eyes left and right before responding. "The first mate belongs to Xin Yue, as one would expect. The tall sailor is mine. You will approach the shorter one. If you prefer privacy, I shall sit outside on the deck for a while."

Privacy? My body shivered. Would he have sat with us counting his hoard while we performed the act? I could not imagine another observing my intimate encounters, already challenging enough *without* an audience.

My immediate pangs of hunger spurred me. "Is the fellow out there?"

Lao Peng You looked through the door. "Yes, he is. Shall I ask him to see you?"

I felt my limbs tremble. "Does he know the purpose of the requested visit?"

"You worry too much, Hao Lan. Of course, he knows. He has been patiently waiting for you to feel better. Instead of wasting your efforts on the captain, perhaps you should turn your eye to the crew instead." He exited onto the deck.

A few moments later, the sailor entered and closed the door behind him. He displayed a nervous smile and glanced down at the floor. I motioned him to me. From the lump in his pants, I could tell he was inclined to participate in our endeavor without question or explanation.

His hand went to the back of my neck, and as soon as our flesh connected, uncontrollable urges ignited within me. I yanked the bright red sash, pulled the trousers open and swallowed his little brother faster than a flying dragon. Like a suckling babe, I lapped and slurped. The young man grunted and gasped. It had probably been some time for him because within a few moments, my mouth filled with a sticky substance that tasted like river water. I felt better at once, and, I expected, so did he.

The crewman did up his pants with a grin, retrieved and retied the sash, bowed, and went back on deck. The Marquis walked in straightaway.

"That did not take very long, my friend." He grinned.

"The boy experienced urgency as well, it would seem."

"Sometimes it is good that those with similar needs can find each other." He gazed at me with downcast eyes, and I felt he looked upon me as he would a pile of his treasured gold coins.

"I am tired. Perhaps I should get some sleep," I said before lying down and closing my eyes.

"Feeling better now?" Shen Lung's voice resounds in my ear.

Wind buffets my face and stings my eyes. I cannot see the dragon at first, then I look down. "Aaaaaaaaahhhhhhh!" I scream in fright because I am hundreds of chi *up in the air.*

"Be still, Little One. I have you."

Between my legs I can feel the warmth of an unfamiliar body. "Aaaaaaaaaaahhhhhh!" I scream because I have never been hundreds of chi up in the air, especially on a dragon.

"Hao Lan, either you stop screaming or I shall let you drop. Then you will most certainly have something to scream about."

I try to gain my control. Short, quick breaths. Close my eyes. Deeper breaths.

"And you were doing so well..." he mutters.

After the thirteenth long exhale, I regain my composure. "I am better now, thank you, my Lord. I apologize for the outburst. You startled me."

"It appears that ocean sailing does not agree with you either."

I rest one hand on my belly. "No, it does not."

"Your boat voyage is almost at its end. You will soon find what you seek, plus a surprise I have hidden for you."

"A surprise? A good surprise?"

He chuckles, which makes his body shake. I grab for his hide. "A surprise is neither good nor bad. It is what you make of it."

Again, he reminds me of the opal. "Yes, my Lord. I shall keep that in mind."

"Hao Lan, I have a very special assignment for you. Something that only you can do. Do you believe you are ready and capable?"

"I serve you, Shen Lung, who have saved me from my old life and given me immortality." I bow my head in reverence.

He grunts, and we climb higher. The wind force intensifies, and I begin to sweat.

"The Emperor needs to hear a message, but he will not suffer it from me."

My eyebrows raise. Perhaps from the rushing air, perhaps from my surprise. "And you believe he will receive it from me? You are great and I am small."

"The greatness of the Emperor is exceeded only by his own self-value. Our illustrious Qin fears death. The desire to live forever absorbs his thoughts. His advisors have convinced him an elixir of immortality exists on Zhifu Island guarded by the giant sea monster Kun."

"Kun really exists? I thought he was just a myth, my lord."

"True, Little One. Mere pathetic propaganda. The emperor's circle of confidantes has presented false counsel to get him away from the palace so that they may murder him in secret."

Blinded by his own ambition. I wonder what the three illustrious gems in the golden wall would have to say about that.

The dragon turns a glittery eye to me. "Before he departs on this spurious unicorn hunt, he needs to uncover his advisors' plan."

I find it difficult to believe the emperor would grant me an interview. "And how may I assist you, Shen Lung?"

"I wish you to give him this message: Zhao Gao calls a deer a horse."

"Zhao Gao calls a deer a horse?" I echo.

"Yes. Zhao Gao calls a deer a horse. Have you got that?"

"I think so. Zhao Gao calls a deer a horse." An enigmatic phrase, but it is not my task to understand, only to perform. "But how will I get near enough to the emperor to deliver your words? No one can get close to him. I have heard he is very well guarded."

The dragon faces ahead and nods. "You have heard correctly, Hao Lan, but I shall provide you with a means to meet him so that you can impart the message."

"How will you do that, my Lord?" The Blue Dragon, who appears capable of performing many miracles, requires my assistance. I shall need to reevaluate my self-worth.

He chuckles. "That, my friend, is the surprise. Be patient. All will be revealed."

"But what if he does not believe me? He will surely go to his doom."

"He will not believe you. And he will most assuredly go to his doom. That is certain."

"Then why should I attempt to enlighten him with these words if they will not do him any good?"

Shen Lung stops flapping his wings, and we begin a steep descent. My breathing stops. My heart pounds. About a hundred chi *above the ground, he flexes his back and I pop off.*

Before I could start screaming again, he admonishes, "You have much to learn, Little One. Try not to complain so much."

In my freefall, I gaze down to the approaching green ground below, screaming with all my might.

Thump!

I woke with a start. Still in the bed of the cabin on the junk.

"Did you have some bad dreams?" Lao Peng You asked with one arched eyebrow.

"Hmm? What?" I struggled to rouse myself and make some sense of the situation.

"You screamed like a little lass bitten by a big snake and muttered something about a horse."

Zhao Gao calls a deer a horse, I recalled.

"Yes, just a bad dream. Where are we?"

He pointed out the window. "We just docked in Guizhou. Gather your things. We are going to harvest *Jiaogulan* leaves." He grabbed his satchel and stepped out onto the deck.

I stowed my belongings in my own bag and followed him. The boat sat tethered to a small, rickety wooden pier that had not been mended in years. Tall marsh grasses surrounded the waterfront. No buildings adorned the shore as in other places, just tropical greenery. I hoped to find a city in the vicinity.

"Just a moment," the lovely sea captain declared. I halted near the railing. "Will you perform the honor of paying me for this portion of your journey?" Her outstretched palm spoke to our purses.

Lao Peng You blinked slowly. "We shall settle with you when we return… later." He took a step.

Xin Yue positioned herself between us and the pier. "It is quite possible you may not return as expected. It is a dangerous place you seek." Once again, her palm appeared.

"And how much does the woman sailor want from us?" my *huoban* asked.

Even the furrowed brow on her ivory forehead could not diminish the beauty. "Five gold… each."

I slipped several fingers into my purse and brought out the coins. Lao Peng You snatched them from my hand, added them to his and dropped them one-by-one onto the expectant palm of the sea seductress.

She stepped aside. "Marquis, when shall we expect your return?" Xin Yue inquired as we stepped onto the wobbly dock.

"The Baron and I plan to be gone most of the day. I should imagine we shall return shortly before the sun is set."

The lady captain's eyes doubled in size, and she smiled at me in a grand way I had not yet experienced. "A *baron*, you say. Why did I not know this before?" She winked at me with the hint of a blush.

"Yes, well," I muddled. "It's not a big thing..."

"Of course, it is," she cooed. All of a sudden, this handsome woman took an interest in me. Why did I not mention the title before?

My *huoban* introduced us using our formal titles, "I am Marquis Pichan, and this is Baron Dongting." We each made a small bow for effect.

"Dongting!?" she shouted. "*Dongting*!?" she screamed. Xin Yue glared at me, hands on hips, any trace of romantic interest gone. "My favored uncle, Wang Yue, was supposed to assume the title Baron of Dongting."

"But, but, but, but..." faltered from my forlorn mouth.

"You are the stupid egg who snatched his rightful title away from him!"

"But, but, but, but..." continued the sad barrage.

"Get off my boat!" Her finger pointed toward the jungle behind us. "Get off my boat! Go away! Go far, far away! Never want to see you again!" She turned back to the crew. "Cast off! Cast off!"

I observed the shorter sailor looking in my direction as he untied the tether. He shed a slight tear as the junk drifted downriver.

The Marquis and I stood on the remote shore of this river, many *li* from any civilization with little hope of ever returning.

I attempted to stare a hole through his head. "Did you not know who she was? Did you not know how she might react? Did you not know this would happen?"

Lao Peng You shrugged. "*Pihua* happens," he quipped before hiking off into the jungle.

Not wanting to be left behind, I ran along the path he created. "Where are we going now?"

"To find your precious tea leaves, *huoban*."

"Are you not concerned about our abandonment?" I squeaked.

"Tut, tut. Come along. We shall let the breezes blow us where they may. For now, the *Jiaogulan* harvest awaits."

My heart pounded, my breathing quickened. I could not understand how he could be so nonchalant in this desperate and dangerous situation. Until such time as we find our way, I must rely on his unfounded confidence.

"What does the plant look like? How will I know when we find it?"

"*Jiaogulan* is a twisting vine with five jagged leaves on a stalk. The female plants have black berries. We want the male plants."

Lao Peng You led us through the overgrown vegetation without hesitation, as if he had been in this location before. After about a *li* or so, we came to a clearing with a small bog in its midst. I noticed around the perimeter several climbing vines with five-leaved stalks.

"Is this it, *huoban*?"

He examined the plants with his critical eye. "Yes, I believe this is *Jiaogulan*. Good job. Leave the female plants."

We worked for hours, plucking leaves and filling the bags we had brought with us for this task. My fingers felt numb after a while from the constant pinching and pulling.

"Marquis, how will we return home?"

"Baron, you worry too much." Even though I could not see his face, I sensed his eyes rising to the top of their sockets. "Something will turn up. If not, we can always walk."

"*Walk*? That would take years, and we don't know where we are going."

"And years we have, my friend."

I glanced around at the forest beyond the clearing, and I thought about the approaching darkness of evening. "What sort of wild animals live in this jungle?"

He turned to me and smiled. "Nothing more dangerous than you and me." His response gave me little comfort.

With our leaf-stuffed bags, we started back toward the little dock, my *huoban* leading the way. The added weight of the *Jiaogulan* decreased my walking speed, and the sack obscured the view of my feet.

The balance of the bag shifted unexpectedly, and my right foot slipped from solid ground into the marshy bog. I attempted to pull up on the leg, but my knee disappeared before the downward motion halted. Sweat dribbled across my face and down my neck.

Lao Peng You just kept walking away. I watched his bright silk tunic disappear into the foliage and imagined he had no awareness of my predicament. Should I call out to him, he would most likely chide and scold me for getting caught in the muck. Not sure I wanted him to discover my dilemma, I attempted my own rescue.

A stroke of fortune for me, one foot rested on solid ground. I placed the bag nearby and pushed down on my left leg as hard as I could. The sludge held my other foot firm, sucking it down even further with each attempt. When I wiggled and wriggled my ankle, the mud separated, allowing me to bring the wayward foot back toward the surface, but at a very slow pace.

Just as I could see my right knee again, the top of the foot struck something solid from below. Trapped. I shall spend the rest of eternity in this forsaken wilderness. On contemplation, I realized one consolation, it is more beautiful than the cinnabar mines of Dong Ping.

"Hao Lan!" I heard Lao Peng You call out for me in the distance. It took him long enough to realize my absence.

With one last struggle, I popped my foot out of the mire. Accompanying the limb, a solid object about the size of my two fists together landed on top of the bog just beyond my reach. As slime dribbled away, the sun's rays illuminated a gleaming green stone within, and I caught sight of a large jade trinket with intricate carvings.

I searched for something to help me retrieve it and picked up a dried fallen tree branch about as long as my arm. Steadying myself on solid ground nearest to the shiny object, I reached out with the bough and scooted the jade across the murky surface. Once it got close enough to the firm soil, I dropped the wood and stepped toward the stone, careful not to repeat my silly mistake.

Leaves rustled nearby. Lao Peng You must have traced the route back to me. Before he could get to the clearing, I reached out and rescued the jade, stowing it in my bag just as he appeared from behind a bush.

He pointed to my soiled right leg. "*Huoban*, what happened to you?" His concern sounded somewhat sincere.

I could not wrap this fire in paper. I resigned myself to sharing the misadventure with him. Most of it.

"My foot got stuck in the mud. It took me a while to extricate the errant limb." I grinned like a fool.

He squinted at me. "Please be more careful about where you place that foot from now on."

"Yes, *huoban*."

My eyes scanned the terrain ahead as we walked back to the dock. The sun melted into the Western horizon, and it would soon be dark. Birds resting on nearby branches chirped.

I would not want to sleep in this remote location among all the potential wild animals. Even as an Immortal, there might be pain involved, and I have had more than my first lifetime's share of pain.

The cloud of birds took flight against a golden sky, erupting in a squawking racket for a few moments followed by complete silence. I felt a gust of wind behind me, and a bellowing trumpet, louder than any flock could manage, split my ears.

7. Winds and Dragons

Two yellow dragons perched on tall plants behind us, shrieking while staring down in our direction. I couldn't help thinking they saw us as potential dinner.

Yellow dragons signify the Emperor. Perhaps we had encroached on royal land, and they functioned as border sentinels. I had no idea how close Guizhou might be to the Imperial Palace in Xianyang. Our esteemed country is very, very large.

Lao Peng You gazed up at the mighty beasts and angled his head from side to side, as if attempting to make sense of the situation. When he nodded, the screeching halted. The creatures' golden tails swished back and forth, lopping off parts of other nearby plants.

"How did you do that?" I inquired.

"Do what?"

"Get them to stop making that racket."

"Oh." He waved his hand with indifference. "I had not noticed."

I glanced up at our great visitors and then at Lao Peng You. "Are you able to communicate with dragons?"

He looked thoughtful for a moment, then responded, "I am not certain if I would call it communication, but I can hear and understand some of their thoughts. Shen Lung is the only one with whom I have ever really conversed."

"Why are they here, do you think?"

The Marquis looked up into their lizard-like faces before replying. "I believe they have come to retrieve something for the Emperor."

I hoped he had no knowledge of the stone in my bag. "What could that be?"

"I am not sure." He scowled. "Do you have any idea what it is that His Eminence might want?" His squinty eye scoured my countenance.

It could be the hunk of jade that found me in the bog, but I did not want my *huoban* to acquire knowledge of it. "I have never met the man. What insight could I impart? You see before you but a humble cinnabar miner from Dong Ping. Does the Emperor drink *Jiaogulan*?"

The two dragons launched upward, beckoned us with their wings, and headed in the direction of the rickety dock.

Lao Peng You scrutinized me one more time before he started walking back toward the river. "Come. Let us not keep them waiting, *huoban*."

We reached the end of the path. The dragons floated in the water on either side of the unstable little pier. Their shimmering eyes followed our movements.

The Marquis climbed onto one of them and stared at me with a resolute eye. "Hurry, Baron, we must not keep the Emperor waiting."

Between the uncertainty of the dock and the daunting yellow beasts, I froze in terror.

"What is the matter? Have you never ridden a dragon before?"

Not in my waking life, to be sure.

"Just hop on," he instructed. "Nothing simpler."

I had not even sat atop a horse or an ox before. This will be a big step up.

After a few tentative tries, I managed to get my footing and threw myself up onto the dragon's scaly back. Its head turned to me, nostrils flaring as it sniffed at the mud-encrusted right pant leg.

"Phew!" the creature snorted.

The beast did not smell much better.

The two mighty monsters leapt up together, and we rose about one hundred *chi* above the jungle below. I observed greenery in all directions. Every so often I would glance over at Lao Peng You, who sat as if posing for a portrait, and perching upon a flying dragon had become as commonplace as eating rice.

A while later, the great beasts slowed and began to descend. Tall pyramid-shaped pagodas peeked up out of the luxuriant vegetation. Ornate buildings became visible, and they looked like a set of giant boxes, one ringed inside the next, with the largest pagoda pyramid in the center. Perhaps the dragons had transported us to the imperial palace at Xianyang.

We landed in one of the square courtyards near the middle. Lao Peng You slid down the side of his dragon, and I imitated his action. Once we both stood on the tile-paved courtyard, our transports leapt up and flew off. I glanced at my *huoban*, but his widened eyes focused behind me.

When I turned to discover what seized his attention, I saw three large men in royal guard outfits running toward us. They carried halberds in their studded, leather-gloved fists. Their polished metal helmets with black bull horns gleamed in the fading sunlight.

My first instinct told me to run from them, but on reflection I reasoned that within a walled courtyard, the chance of escape seemed slim. I tried to stand with a carefree attitude, similar to what the Marquis displayed when confronted. His frozen face suggested the approaching men terrified him.

"Halt!" the first one yelled.

This confused me as we stood unmoving. Motionless.

"You are prisoners of the magnificent Lady Xing."

"Halt!" the second one commanded.

More confusing because we had not moved.

"You are prisoners of the glorious Lady Xing."

"Halt!" the third one shouted.

Even more confusing because we still stood in the very same spots.

"You are prisoners of the celebrated Lady Xing."

It appeared we had become prisoners of some very remarkable and significant woman named Xing.

The first guard lowered his halberd and pointed its tip at me. "I am taking *you* to the delightful Lady Xing."

The second guard lowered his weapon and pointed it at Lao Peng You. "I am taking *you* to the enchanting Lady Xing."

The third guard swung his blade around. "No, *I* am taking them to the charming Lady Xing."

"But it's my turn!" the first guard whined, turning his blade to the third guard.

The second guard hit the first guard's helmet with the shaft of his halberd. "No, it is my turn! You brought the prisoners last time."

"No," the first guard shouted. "It was him." He swung his blade toward the third guard.

Lao Peng You appeared to be stifling a laugh. I found it difficult to believe these fools had been assigned to guard our Royal Emperor. While they argued over who was going to take us to the mysterious Lady, we walked away.

"Halt!" yelled the first guard. "*I* am taking you to the most excellent Lady Xing."

"Halt!" shouted the second guard. "*I* am taking you to the most exceptional Lady Xing."

"Halt!" barked the third guard. "*I* am taking you to the most admirable Lady Xing."

"Stop it, all of you!" came a scratchy voice from behind us.

We paused and looked back. Lao Peng You set his bag on the ground, but I held onto mine.

The guards bowed with respect. A stately and dignified woman wearing flowing, fluttering, and glittering gilt robes sauntered toward them.

"Get up! Go away!" she commanded. With one wrinkled hand the shade of aged ginger, a long, curved, red lacquered fingernail pointed.

"But, beloved Lady, *I* am in charge of the prisoners," the first guard whimpered. "I was bringing them to *you*."

"No, they are *my* prisoners, cherished Lady," the second guard protested.

"I saw them first, treasured Lady," the third guard whined. "*I* was just bringing them to *you*."

She glanced at us, the intruders whom these guards attempted to terrorize, with a scowl. "They are not your prisoners!" she instructed. "They are my guests. Now, go protect the palace from any *real* intruders."

The three men bowed a few more times and huddled off to some secluded spot. I imagined they would wait with vigilance for the next unannounced infiltration, allowing for yet another opportunity to please their beloved Lady.

"I apologize for the rudeness of our welcoming deputation." She approached us and bowed. Tiny sparkling jewels adorned the black lacquered comb of her cochineal-dyed wool hairpiece. However, it could not be overlooked that a troupe of lice crawled throughout the wig.

"I am Lady Xing, consort to the Emperor." Streaks of light from the setting sun revealed how she tried to hide her advanced age with too much face powder. Her cloudy and sagging eyes scanned our faces. "I have been expecting you. Please follow me."

She walked toward a gate at the side of the courtyard. Lao Peng You and I looked at each other for answers but found none. He picked up his bag and we followed the woman.

Once we passed through the gate, we stood in a small garden with flaming torches and stone benches. She indicated that we should sit.

"Welcome, gentlemen." She beamed a girlish smile. "You will meet with the Emperor tomorrow, but this evening, I shall be your hostess." The coquettish look she gave me suggested a desire to function as less of a hostess and more like a concubine. I considered it a blessing how my inability to satiate a woman might assist me in this situation.

"If you please, Lady Xing. I am Marquis Pichan, and this is Baron Dongting. How may we serve you?"

She glanced at me with such craving that my turtle retreated back into its shell. "Shen Lung has apprised me you have a special gift for the Emperor. The honored dragon requested me to entertain you tonight and bring you to meet His Excellency in the morning. You will present your gift to him at that time."

The Blue Dragon informed me the Emperor had become obsessed with attaining eternal life. Lao Peng You and I possessed the power to bestow immortality upon him. I hope this is not the *gift* Lady Xing suggested. I have never been inside another man's backyard, and I would not wish to begin the practice with our Great Emperor.

"Pardon me, my Lady," the Marquis spoke. "You have mentioned we have something that the Emperor desires. Can you be more specific, please?"

Her outburst of childish laughter penetrated my soul like a lightning bolt made of ice. She sat next to me on the bench. I would climb back up a dragon on fire just to fly out of this apparent trap.

Lady Xing eyed my pants. "He wants what you have in your sack." She reached out with one of her long fingernails, almost touching my egg basket.

I brought my knees together as if attempting to crack a walnut.

Lao Peng You jostled his bag. "*Jiaogulan* leaves, my Lady?" he suggested.

She laughed again, and my blood ran cold. "I think you know what I mean, Marquis." The Lady turned her oozy gaze to me and stood. "Follow me, gentlemen."

We pursued our hostess through a series of great, tethered bamboo gates and towering halls. Along one of the corridors, she opened a set of tall doors into a chamber about the size of our entire charter boat, the *Tong Feng*.

"Here is your room for tonight. Please make yourselves comfortable. I shall return in a while to escort you to the evening meal."

My *huoban* and I stepped with kitten feet into the ornate chamber, one fit for a prince. Or two. Lady Xing bowed and exited, closing the doors behind her. A metallic scraping sound caused us to look at each other with dread. Lao Peng You tried the door, which appeared bolted from the outside, as I had feared.

"*Guests?*" he questioned. "I think not."

"What should we do, *huoban*?" I deferred to his wisdom, never having been held prisoner in a palace before. I imagined this might not be his first–nor his last–time.

"*Do*? Why we shall do as instructed, of course," he affirmed. He glanced around the room in the same way I imagined a burglar sized up potential plunder.

"Of course," I responded for lack of anything else to say.

If we have been imprisoned, I could not think of a more pleasant place to be confined. The walls all but disappeared behind a collection of decorative trappings: carved cinnabar dragons, gold Buddha figurines, silver bowls, copper poetry disks. I couldn't imagine how Lao Peng You planned to fit all of this into his one bag.

"By the way," he confided, "I know about the jade piece."

My heart skipped a beat. After everything I did to keep it from him. I should not have been surprised. "You do? How so?" Well, he knew more about it than I. "What exactly is it?"

"The stone has a long and curious history. It disappeared a few years back. The Emperor has had his minions searching for it on mountaintops and river beds."

"But how did you know I have it?"

He pursed his lips. "The manner you have been carrying your bag suggests it has more than just leaves in it. At one point, when we stood next to each other, I felt the jade through the fabric, recognized the shape, and knew it at once as the Imperial Seal."

"*The Imperial Seal*?" I repeated.

"Yes. I shall explain." The Marquis continued, "Bian He found the original rock in Chu Shan. He offered it to King Li, whose royal jeweler determined it nothing but a plain stone. King Li had Bian He's left foot cut off."

Gulp. That King Li was not one to mess with. You would think a gift bearer might be treated with more gratitude. My right hand went to my gaping mouth.

"After the king died, Bian He offered the stone to the rightful heir, King Wu, and again the royal gemologist concluded the piece a mere boulder. King Wu ordered the fellow's right foot cut off."

Yikes! Another man you would not want to cross. My left hand rose to cover the other. These kings did not appear to look kindly on their adoring subjects.

"When King Wu died, Bian He unwisely considered offering the piece to the new king, Wen. During presentation at court, Bian He's tears of blood caused much dismay among the assemblage. King Wen ordered his jeweler to crack the proffered rock open. They discovered a glorious natural jade inside. It became such a prize that our current Emperor offered fifteen cities for it, but Wen would not accept the bargain. Eventually, Qin conquered the region and took the cherished jade for his own. He ordered these words carved into it: *Having received the Mandate from Heaven, may our Emperor lead a long and prosperous life.* The Emperor designated it the Imperial Seal."

I did not realize I had stumbled onto something so great. To me, it appeared a pretty trinket that had trapped me in the mud.

"And now you have been chosen to find it and return the treasure to its royal owner. Well done, Hao Lan. Well done."

The flat tone of his voice suggested a lack of enthusiasm regarding the way things transpired.

He parted the curtains on one of the beds. "Is the other adequate for you?"

A pad of nails in this most luxurious chamber would have been quite welcome. "Yes, it is fine."

"*Huoban*," Lao Peng You started in a familiar, unctuous tone. "I wish to discuss our Mahjong game with you, if that is acceptable."

"Of course." Although I had my justifiable suspicions. "If there is something you wish to discuss, by all means."

He sat on the edge of his mattress. "I have been thinking about our last few sessions. Ever since we agreed to terminate our secret confederacy, the game has not been as enjoyable for me."

Probably because I have been doing most of the winning, and he preferred to possess the largest pile of coins at the table.

"I am saddened to hear of that, *Huoban*," I said in a futile attempt to mollify him. "Our Mahjong play has brought me many hours of pleasure." Not to mention untold wealth that I would have never imagined possible a season ago. As I continued to drink from this well of riches, I felt it best not to forget who dug it for me. "What can I do to relieve you of this unhappiness?"

"It is not that I am unhappy," he rejoined, "but having a partner in the game heightens the satisfaction for me, and you are a most superb partner, indeed."

A most superb partner, indeed. As long as I pass him the wind and dragon tiles. "But is it not unfair to the other players if we act in concert clandestinely? Surely the heavens look unfavorably upon our gains acquired through deceit."

"What concern do I have for other players? They will soon be dead." He waved the notion away. "As I see it, we are assisting the national economy by distributing their wealth to the needy, rather than allowing the former owners merely to pass it along to their undeserving offspring." This self-serving, subjective redistribution of wealth seemed to be a recurring theme for him.

"There is a certain logic to that reasoning, my *huoban*, but what about those who do not participate in the national economy, our overlords?" I pointed skyward.

His head dropped. "At one time I cared deeply for our associates above, but over the last few centuries I have begun to realize that their stewardship is not as pristine as they would have us believe." He turned away. "With time, I have arrived at the conclusion that it is better to please oneself first and allow others to find happiness in their own individual ways."

That sounded rather familiar.

"Marquis, I have heard your words, and it gives me much to consider. Please grant me the time to meditate upon these points before responding to your request."

"Yes," he groaned and faced me once again. "But what if we are at a table and the eye of fortune has shut upon us. Perhaps we should have some pre-arranged signal–a particular sign, if you will–to indicate we resume the confederacy immediately."

That could come in handy. But what kind of sign can we devise that would not alert the attention of others?

"Might I suggest this?" He touched his ring finger to the center of his head.

"Would that not attract suspicion, *huoban*?"

"Ah. Perhaps you are correct." He lowered his hand and gazed at it. "Do *you* have any ideas?"

Lao Peng You liked to shuffle and play with his coins at the Mahjong table, which I found quite annoying. However, he could do as he wished with his money, even if that included spending it on lavish clothes and gratuitous delicacies.

"Marquis, I believe a more subtle gesture might be to make a small stack of coins in your hand: one gold, one silver, one copper." I demonstrated the action. "That is not out of the ordinary, and I believe it would not draw attention."

"Yes!" he decried. "Simplicity itself, my boy." He displayed a grin more hearty than I had observed in a while. "I shall place a stack of one gold, one silver, and one copper coin in my hand if I believe we need to work together."

We nodded in synchronicity.

My mind blinked. "But what if *I* wish to be the one to receive the honor tiles? Perhaps *I* might find myself in a position where *I* need to win a hand." I doubted this occurred to him.

"Yes, I can see that," he muttered, but I did not believe him. "If you perform the same act of stacking three coins, I shall then pass you the tiles. Yes."

I wished I could trust him.

Both our heads turned toward the scraping sound of the bolt outside.

A tall, well-appointed gentleman opened the chamber doors. "If you please, Baron, Marquis." He waved at us through the frame. "Lady Xing awaits you in the dining hall."

We looked at each other and shrugged, again in synchronicity. The man strode away, and we followed him through halls and doors until we arrived in a chamber the size of a small mountain. In the middle stood a long dining table, Lady Xing at one end, and two place settings on either side of her. She rose and motioned us to her.

"Baron, Marquis, how nice to see you again." Her gaze followed me.

"My Lady," crooned Lao Peng You. "How nice of you to –"

"Yes, yes." She swatted her hand at him. "Sit down, please. Baron, you will be at my right." Lady Xing indicated the position with one of her long fingernails then smiled at me, her caked powder cracking.

"Yes, Baron," my *huoban* taunted, "sit at the lady's right. Don't disappoint our hostess." I sensed him giggling inside.

Once our hostess sat, we took our appointed spots. Servers approached from all sides with delicacies I could not decipher. Some smelled like fish, some like roasted root vegetables. Everything appeared delicious. After Lady Xing filled her bowl, the Marquis and I took our share. I could feel a decrepit set of eyes linger on me the whole time. Before I could lift a piece out of my bowl, I observed our hostess pick up the silver tester–as best as she could with those implausibly long fingernails–and touch it to each of the foods in her bowl.

"Safe, as far as I can see." She smiled at me like a mother protecting her only child. I hope her timeworn eyesight is adequate to detect a subtle difference of tone in the silver, just in case. Although, it would not matter much to the two of us.

Servers poured rice wine into golden goblets.

"*Kan pei,*" she chimed as we raised our glasses together.

"*Kan pei,*" we responded before taking a drink.

Lady Xing stared at my bowl. "Baron, I see you have not partaken some of my specialty dishes. The oysters"–she pointed to a platter of shells, a quarter of its original total rested in Lao Peng You's bowl–"are one of my particular favorites." She slopped her leathery tongue around bright vermillion lips in what I assumed she fancied as a suggestive gesture.

I cleared my throat. "The Marquis favors oysters, my Lady. Having dwelt in a land-locked region, the fruit of the sea is unfamiliar to me."

"I have made every attempt to educate the Baron on finer dining, but –"

"Yes, yes," she hushed my *huoban*. "Perhaps you would like to try some of my famous llllloooonnnngggg beans." She ran one of those bony fingers up the inside of my left leg with a smile intimating sensuality I could not fathom. "Or perhaps some… turtle would be more to your liking." She grinned, once again cracking her face powder.

"Lady Xing," I stumbled, "it all looks so delicious, but if you would pardon me, I need to worship the Purple Maiden. Where is the chamber for such things?" I looked about for an obvious portal, but none seemed the correct one.

She clapped her hands, and a woman servant approached. "Shinu, show our guest to the pot hall."

I stood and followed the handmaiden to an alcove off the main chamber. She indicated the entrance, bowed, and backed away.

"Thank you," I said as I entered the room. It contained lines of pots and papers, each with its own cubicle for privacy. Never had I seen such opulence before. I chose the one closest to the entrance, removed my trousers, closed the door, and sat down.

Just as I finished my business, I heard footsteps on the tiled floor outside.

"Baron," beckoned the Lady. "Are you in here?"

It might have been better to remain silent, but I imagined she would have gone to each cubicle in turn until she found me, so I decided to speak. "Yes, my Lady."

I heard the rustle of fabric, and the door of my cubicle opened. Before me stood the exposed and sagging flesh of a great-grandmother, her pallid steamed buns dangling in frayed fishing nets. "Baron," she purred. "At last, I have you all to myself."

There seemed like no better time to inform her of the situation. "Lady Xing, I must confess that–as lovely as you are–my little bird does not fly, and I would be unable to satisfy you."

"Your bird does not fly?" she echoed. "Are you like Zhao Gao, the Emperor's eunuch?"

So that's who Zhao Gao is.

"No, my Lady, I have all the parts with which I was brought into this world. However, I have been cursed. The little bird can no longer fly."

"I see," she mused. "There are other ways to satisfy a woman." She licked her overly bright lips with her overly aged tongue while she paddled her silver haired chicken with a nail tip. "Are you a gambling man, Baron Dongting?"

"The Marquis and I play Mahjong, my Lady."

"Mahjong?" she responded in ascending tones. "Yes, we shall play Mahjong this evening, Baron. If *I* win, you will submit to my will and perform erogenous acts upon my sumptuous body. Should *you* somehow win–which I sincerely doubt–I shall allow you and your friend to return to your room untouched. Agreed? Good."

She fastened her robe and departed.

I wished I had known telling a woman you could not perform adequately would intensify her desire.

Back at the table, the Marquis continued to stuff his face with epicurean delights. The Lady's empty seat confused me.

"Where is our host?" I asked.

"I thought *you* would know," he mumbled through an oyster.

Footsteps on the tiles announced her return. We stood until she sat down again.

"Gentlemen, it has come to my attention that you both play Mahjong, a game I enjoy favorably." Her gaze rested on my lips. "I hope that you would honor me by playing a few rounds before we retire for the evening."

"My Lady," Lao Peng You began, "we have had an arduous day, and I believe –"

"Yes, yes," she interrupted him. "I shall have Shinu lead you to the game room." She started to leave.

"But, my Lady," I attempted, "there are but three of us, and Mahjong requires four people to play."

"Shinu is educated and can join us," she responded with a wizened glare.

"But, my Lady," I tried again, "our coin purses are in our room. We have no money to play with."

She had begun to mince away but turned back. "I shall provide a small sum for you to use during the evening. See you soon, Baron." Our hostess disappeared into the shadow of an arch.

We stood and followed Shinu through a door and down a hall. In the next room, Lady Xing sat at a silk-covered Mahjong table. The tiles appeared to be made from white jade, very valuable looking, indeed. A set fit for royalty. She patted the seat on her right and glanced at me.

We sat and rolled the dice, with our hostess taking East. On the first draw, she had an entire bouquet in her hand, and I began to wonder about the fairness of play here. After the second round, Lady Xing had most of the coins, and sweat dampened my robes.

"Is it too hot in here, Baron?" she inquired. "Shall I have the curtains opened for you?"

"No, my Lady, the temperature is fine." I attempted to smile.

"I wonder what could be making you perspire so," she said, smirking.

With the few coins I had left, I took one gold, one silver and one copper, stacked them together and showed it to Lao Peng You. He produced a flat smile.

On the next hand, he passed me all the honor tiles he could so that by the beginning of play I needed but a North–my own wind that game–for Mahjong. Lady Xing sat East and discarded first.

"North Wind," she declared.

"Mahjong!" I wheezed in relief.

"Blessing of the Earth," sighed Lao Peng You.

"Indeed," I agreed. The Earth had certainly blessed me with a special bonus for completing my hand from the first discard.

Lady Xing stood, and we followed. "Baron Dongting, as East, I would owe you double for your limit hand with Blessing of the Earth win. As you can see, I do not have sufficient coins. The evening is yours to do as you see fit. I shall see you in the morning to escort you to His Highness, the Emperor. Good night."

She walked away from us through another shadowed archway. Shinu ushered us back to our chamber. This time, no bar scraped across the door from the outside.

"*Huoban,*" the Marquis quipped, "I did not expect *you* to be the one who called for our collaboration again."

Instead of explaining the whole situation with Lady Xing, I decided to say, "Sometimes one must please himself instead of giving pleasure to others. Good night, Marquis." I hopped into my bed and fell asleep with a small, respectful smile.

Once again, I stand before the big gold wall.

The red gem starts, "Good fortune may forebode bad luck, which may in turn disguise good fortune."

The green jewel continues, "The fool waits for a lucky day, but every day is a lucky day for the industrious man."

The sparkly white stone concludes, "There is no such thing as good fortune, bad fortune, or luck. Things are... or are not."

Perhaps there is a message here for me, but I am not certain as to what it might, or might not, be. I could, however, ask them about my mission from Shen Lung to see if they have any suggestions.

"I must convey a veiled message to the Emperor regarding a member of his retinue."

"The message must not be heavier than the messenger," posits the ruby.

"A message from far away is preferable to a dispatch from nearby," the emerald adds.

"Every message has a bit of truth and a bit of untruth," the opal advises.

Once again, I am stymied by their responses. "One of his most trusted advisors schemes against him."

The red stone counsels, "When plotting revenge, dig two graves."

The green gem imparts, "One can never truly know what one does not know."

Not to be outdone, the opal states, "Deception is only as clear as the muddy waters it swims in."

"I am not sure I understand the message I am to give."

"You hear, you forget. You see, you remember. You do, you understand. Sour."

"To understand everything is to forgive everything. Bitter."

"If you understand yourself you are illuminated. Sweet!"

Sometimes I am not sure why I even bother.

8. The Big Joker

Upon awakening, it took a few moments to recognize my location. I had never slept in a bed surrounded by curtains before.

"Baron, are you awake?" The Marquis's voice rang out from across the chamber.

"Yes, *huoban*, I just woke." The plush mat cushioned my body like a cloud, and I stretched my limbs to hasten my consciousness.

"Did you sleep well? Any dreams?"

I had no desire to inform him of my ongoing nightly adventures. "Some dreams, yes. Why do you ask?"

He coughed. "I had the most fascinating reverie, and I wish to share it with you."

I might not have been able to comprehend everything this early morning, but he seemed resolute about relating his sleep time adventure. "Please, do tell me." I could, at least, hear the words, even though I might not comprehend.

The fabric parted. Lao Peng You climbed upon my bed and sat cross-legged. "Good morrow," he beamed.

"Good morrow," I repeated.

"Today we have an audience with the Emperor. Are you excited?"

I did not know how I felt about meeting our ruler. Part of me thought it would be a grand experience, but another part remained fearful, knowing I had a duty to perform that might get us both into big trouble.

"*Excited* is not the word I would use. More like… apprehensive."

"Emperor Qin is a most imposing fellow, but he has a human side as well," he said as if he had many encounters with the man. "You should not worry. I shall be with you."

I could take some solace in that, never having met anyone so important before. Lao Peng You must have. "Thank you, *huoban*. It comforts me to know that."

"Indeed," he affirmed. "Now, let me tell you about this fascinating reverie."

"Yes, please." I arranged the silken pillows to make myself comfortable.

He cleared his throat the way a lecturer would before starting the day's lesson. "In my dream, I stood watching three blind men near an elephant. Each touched the beast and reported his finding. The first landed a finger on the pointy tusk and said, 'This is a spear carrier.'"

How curious.

"The second stood near the beast's flank, reached out, and stated, 'This is a wall.'"

I thought that bit funny: the poor blind man thought he touched a wall, and it was, in fact, an elephant. I knew that walls did not feel like elephants. Lao Peng You has an unusual sense of humor.

"The third blind man pulls the tail and says, 'There is a rope dangling here.'"

Of the three, this one's assessment made the most sense to me.

"The first man asks, 'Where do you think we are?' The second says, 'I believe it obvious. A spear, a wall, and a rope. Gentlemen, we have all been here before.' 'Yes,' adds the third man, 'the Emperor's dungeon.'" Lao

Peng You glared at me as if I had something to add to his story.

"Interesting," I suggested.

"*Interesting*, indeed," he agreed. "I find it odd that today we are to visit the Emperor, and I had this dream. What do you make of that?"

"I hope it does not mean we end up blinded and locked in the Emperor's dungeon with an elephant."

The Marquis laughed. "Baron, you never cease to amuse me."

The door to the chamber opened with a scrape.

"Baron, are you in there?" called Lady Xing.

Time to meet our Emperor. "Yes, my Lady. However, I am still abed." I hoped this did not sound like an invitation to join me.

"Very good. I have brought some things for you, which I shall leave on the table."

Things? Nothing embarrassing, I feared.

"Thank you, my Lady. May I inquire as to your gifts?"

"Of course," she murmured. "I took the liberty of having your suit cleaned. You do not want to have an audience with the Emperor wearing muddy garments." Her voice sounded even and business-like.

"Thank you, my Lady. Very kind of you."

"Also," she continued, "I am leaving an empty box for you to conceal your gift to the Emperor. It is probably best not to have it on view during our excursion to his chambers."

"A wonderful idea, Lady Xing. I shall prepare myself now."

"Excellent, Baron. Shall I wait for you here?" she asked with a hint of eagerness.

I sat in a curtained bed with my *huoban*. It might have looked odd for both of us to leave together. Also, I believed she might have had an ulterior motive.

"Thank you, but please allow me a few moments of privacy."

"Of course," she sighed in crestfallen tones. "I shall wait outside."

The door scraped closed, and I peeked through the fabric to make sure she had not remained. "All clear," I announced and stepped down.

Lady Xing had placed my suit on the table by the door, cleaned and folded. Next to that, a cochineal lacquered box a little larger than the jade piece. Inlaid gold strips formed an intricate, interweaving border pattern. Soft fabric lined the interior.

Lao Peng You climbed down from my bed. "I believe that woman is fascinated with you."

I glanced at him with slightly raised eyebrows. "I believe you might be correct, Marquis." Then a thought occurred. "It might be me… or it might be something I possess."

I retrieved the Imperial Seal from my bag and studied the ornate inscription: *Having received the Mandate from Heaven, may our Emperor lead a long and prosperous life.*

"Priceless," whispered Lao Peng You while eying the green stone.

"Perhaps," I mused, "but valued highly by one particular person."

"Get dressed, then. We do not want to keep that one particular person waiting."

The Imperial Seal

Lady Xing stood outside our room. Her demeanor seemed more demure than last evening, but when she saw the lacquered box in my hand, her gaze snapped to it like a south-pointing lodestone.

"You have the gift for our Emperor?" she queried.

I nodded.

"May I see it?" Her eyes opened in question.

My first impulse advised against displaying the gem, but I concluded she might not present us at court without it. I lifted the top a bit to give her a peek at the prize. Her eyes opened even wider. I closed the lid.

"Gentlemen." She waved her hand to point the way, the long, gangly fingernails like misleading signposts.

We followed the Lady through a few doors until she stood at the top of a wide, descending ramp.

She pointed for us to proceed. The Marquis and I took a few steps, then looked back to see if she followed us. Lady Xing trailed a few paces behind, a curious change in protocol.

The ramp sloped downward and curved so that we stood about a *chi* below the floor above. Rows of torches lined the walls of the cavern where we stood, illuminating a fantastic subterranean world of hills and trees.

A lavish barge, like a royal palanquin, sat tied to a mooring before us. The river on which it rode looked like no other I have ever seen or heard of. The shiny surface rippled in the torchlight.

"Be careful," Lady Xing advised. "Do not touch the mercury."

I had never seen so much of the liquid before. Metallic, silver, and watery, most likely refined from ore of the mine where I had worked in my previous life.

"Do you think it dangerous, Lady Xing?" the Marquis asked.

"No, not dangerous," she responded. "However, the Emperor does not wish any of it to disappear inadvertently, either on your clothing or skin. It took him many, many years to acquire."

I sighed.

She stepped onto the barge and beckoned us to follow. Four bare-chested polemen stood at the corners. I tip-toed over with utmost caution, fearing any contact with the undulating liquid metal. The boat remained steady as I placed my foot on it, unlike on water. We moved to chairs under the canopy at the center, and the Lady bade us to sit.

Once the three of us had taken our places, the polemen conducted the palanquin along the fluid path.

"Lady Xing," I remarked, "this is an amazing feat of engineering. A river of mercury?"

She nodded. "The Emperor designed this large map, a replica of his vast territory, complete with waterways. We follow the path of the Yellow River and shall arrive at the Emperor's undisclosed location shortly. Please enjoy the ride." Her gaze followed along the banks and sometimes the bare chests of the polemen.

Artificial hills and artificial trees lined the artificial river. While beautiful in design and construction, this caused me some concern. Did our Emperor possess sound reason if he chose to leave the world above to live amid his own personal version with simulated scenery below?

After a while, we pulled up to another dock. Once the polemen secured the boat, we followed Lady Xing onto a stone path leading to a large metal door. She knocked, and a small, eye-level panel opened.

"I have the Emperor's guests," she announced.

The whole door swung open, and we followed her through. Three attendants stepped forward with long strips of black cloth. They moved toward us, holding the bands up to each of our heads.

"What is going on?" the Marquis demanded.

Lady Xing raised a hand, her long, curvy fingernails pointing in several directions. "We are to be blind-folded so that we do not know the exact location of the Emperor. These servants had their tongues removed so that they are unable to tell anyone. If you prefer not to be masked, you may choose to have your tongue cut out. However, I suggest the blindfold."

My *huoban* and I looked at each other with unspoken questions. I realized the only way to meet the Emperor had to be *his* way. Lao Peng You and I submitted to the blindfolds.

Once the attendants tied the cloth, someone took my hand. One of the mute servants, I presumed. They led me along a meandering pathway. When we stopped, I had no idea how far we walked or where we might have been. When the attendant removed my blindfold, I saw what I could only imagine as a throne room. The

Emperor's great chair, atop a small ziggurat of stairs, filled the view. Gilded with gold leaf and silver plate, the decorative seat looked large enough to hold a giant. A huge, silk-covered, brocade pillow occupied its center. Two well-appointed men with short, gray beards stood on either side of the throne.

"Show obeisance, please," Lady Xing commanded before placing her face on the floor before the throne platform.

The Marquis and I prostrated ourselves in the same manner on the woven grass mat. Heavy footsteps ascended the stairs, and the chair creaked.

"Lady Xing," a deep voice boomed and echoed. He sounded tall and impressive. "I appreciate your service. Please remove yourself."

She stood and toddled away.

"Pichan," he continued, "how curious to see you once again. Staying out of trouble? I would wager not." He laughed in a staccato style. "Please follow Lady Xing."

He rose and walked out.

"So… you are Hao Lan, Baron Dongting," the voice bellowed. "I hear you have something for me. Is it in that box you have brought with you?"

I began to look up, but a silent hand pushed my face back to the floor. Instead, I nodded in answer to his question. I felt the box removed and heard light footsteps on the platform.

"Ah! My wayward Imperial Seal. Where have you been hiding?"

A foot nudged me. "I found the jade piece in a bog along the Pearl River in Guizhou Province, my Lord."

"Fascinating! Tales I heard spoke of the jade vanishing somewhere into the south. I had begun to wonder if we would ever find it again. Were you hunting for this particular treasure, Baron?"

"No, my Lord. We went to gather *Jiaogulan* leaves for tea, and I accidentally got stuck in the mud. My foot fortuitously dislodged the stone from the muck."

"*Jiaogulan*? Tea of the Immortals?" His voice elevated in pitch. "Whom do you serve, Hao Lan?"

A question I did not know how to answer. If I explained my assignment from Shen Lung, he might have his royal guards cut me into little immortal pieces. If I did not answer the question, he might have me thrown into the royal dungeon for eternity.

He who knows all the answers has not been asked all the questions, a voice in my head reverberated. Perhaps I should just convey the message from Shen Lung and hope for the best.

"Zhao Gao calls a –"

"*Zhao Gao*?" he questioned. "You work for that eggless grandson of a sea turtle?"

"No, my Lord, but I wish to inform you: Zhao Gao calls a deer a horse." There I had said it, my mission completed.

"A *deer*? A *horse*? What kind of nonsense is this?"

I heard coarse whispering but could not understand the words.

"Ah, that is the loyalty test he administers to potential subordinates. Now, I understand. But you have not yet told me for whom you gathered the *Jiaogulan* leaves. That beverage is only enjoyed by a select few."

"Yes, my Lord. I serve one of the Immortals who prefers not to be identified." I figured that might have been the only way to be honest yet not divulge my true loyalty.

"Ah, yes, the Immortals. Of course. Well... one cannot serve two masters." His thunderous laughter reverberated from every wall. "There. I feel ten years younger. By the way, I do not envy your predicament."

More whispering.

"Hao Lan, I appreciate your returning the Imperial Seal to its rightful owner. How much ransom do you request?"

I did not want any money, as I already had more than I knew what to do with. This disclosure completed my duty, and I just wanted to get out of there.

"August Emperor, I do not wish monetary compensation for performing an act of filial piety."

He chuckled in his staccato manner again. "What? No desire for wealth?"

"No, my Lord."

"You puzzle me, Baron Dongting. You have returned a precious royal treasure. Do you not believe I owe you something valuable in return? Might there be something else you desire?"

I could think of nothing material to ask for. It has been said that the journey itself comprises the reward. However, I thought of one thing in particular I would like, if possible.

"My Lord, could you provide transportation for myself and Marquis Pichan back to Changshou Shan? We play Mahjong there as therapeutic treatment."

"Mahjong? *Therapeutic*? How quaint. That game is for swindlers and miscreants."

"Yes, my Lord. You have reasoned well."

"Well, if that is what you wish–and it is truly important to you–I shall instruct my yellow dragons to return you both to Changshou Shan."

Ugh... dragons...

"I cannot decipher whether you are astoundingly wise or astoundingly foolish to ask for so little in return for so valuable a prize."

Heavy footsteps descended the platform. *"Zhao Gao calls a deer a horse,"* the Emperor mused. "I must consider what that could possibly mean."

I felt a tap on my shoulder, and one of the attendants indicated that I should stand. They led me to the room where Lady Xing and Lao Peng You waited in silence and flashed a sequence of bent fingers to the Emperor's consort.

"Follow me," she said and walked away.

Again, they blindfolded us and led us along a twisting pathway. We walked up another curving ramp. At the top, the servants removed the cloths. We stood in a different tiled courtyard. The sun hung midway to noon. Two yellow dragons sat staring at us.

An attendant brought our bags and helped us mount the beasts.

"Baron, Marquis, I bid you a safe trip." Lady Xing smiled, turned, and walked away. Just as she was about to slip around a corner, she looked back at me and winked.

Thoughts of spending any more time with that aged matron propelled me to fly away with these detested, mighty beasts. The dragons launched up into the sky, and we glided over fields and woodlands. I gripped the hide of my transport with my one free hand for fear of falling. My *huoban* stared directly ahead. Neither of us uttered a word. A while later, the malodorous creatures landed at our mountain retreat.

The courtyard clock indicated midday on our return to the hilltop where I first met Lao Peng You. Moisture on the leaves suggested overnight rain, and everything smelled flowery sweet.

Once we dismounted, the dragons flew away. No one took much notice of our conveyance, as if this kind of thing happened every day.

"I do not know about you, Baron, but I am quite hungry, having had no morning meal. Let us see about satiating our hunger." He started off toward the food table, carrying his bag of leaves in one hand.

"Marquis, I don't have much of an appetite after that flight. I am going to my room for some rest."

"As you wish, *huoban*. Perhaps we shall play Mahjong later. I feel like I might need some seed soon." He walked back and handed me his bag before heading off to the dining area.

It had been a few days since our last encounter with men. Perhaps I should consider finding a source of seed as well. So many things to think about as an Immortal.

Back in the room I dropped our bags on the floor, laid some of the leaves on the bed to dry, and took out my extra set of clothes. I forgot to ask if *Jiaogulan* required special preparation before we could make Dragon Longevity Tea. Some varieties required roasting, some preferred smoking, and some must ferment. I shall have to consult Shen Lung during our next encounter.

"Hao Lan!" The angry voice outside my chamber sounded like the Marquis. "Hao Lan!"

I opened the door and observed Lao Peng You stomping in a state of disconcerted percolation I had never witnessed before. "What is it, my *huoban*, that has caused you such distress?"

His breathing slowed from gale force to bracing breeze. "I went to my suite only to find another person's belongings there!"

"Oh, my. Have you asked the house mother about this?"

"Yes! She said a wealthy man appeared yesterday and wanted all the suites for himself, including mine. Knowing I was away, she packed up my belongings and rented it to him, even though I had paid for a month in advance!" He paced in a haphazard pattern, huffing and grimacing.

Procuring a deluxe suite for my own long-term use appealed to me. I no longer had a home, nor a town to call home. Even though I have become the bogus Baron of Dongting, I did not believe I could live there, even with all its innate beauty because of Wang Yue. One of the towns along the river might be nice at some point, but for the moment, I wished to stay at Changshou Shan a while longer to establish myself as a veteran player and accustom myself to this immortal life.

"What can we do, *huoban*?" I presumed any assistance I could give him would also advance my own desires.

"I hear the unfortunate trespasser sits at the Mahjong table right now." He pointed toward the courtyard. "Let us proceed there to have a look at the squatter."

"Yes. We must rectify this upsetting situation straightaway."

I closed the door behind me and hurried to walk alongside Lao Peng You as he marched toward the playing area. Three men at the table I recognized from previous games. However, one person sat with his back facing us. He seemed very tall, very round, and very pale. A high-pitched squeal of laughter disclosed his identity.

"Wang Yue!" the Marquis accused as he strode toward the players. "How dare you usurp my living quarters! Surrender them at once!"

Rotating slowly, much like the full moon, Wang Yue revolved to face us. With his tunic open, the Moon Rabbit tattoo came into full view.

"Ah, Lao Peng You. I wish I could say it was pleasant to see you again, but that would be a patent falsehood." He turned to me. "*Baron* Dongting. A veritable delight. Perhaps we can make some time later to reconnoiter." A wink suggested his desires. Even though I found him disgusting, his seed had been the most tasty so far. However, I did not wish to repeat that experience. At least not so soon.

"I paid for that suite a month in advance. You have no right to occupy it," the Marquis charged.

Wang Yue pointed toward the lodgings. "That room stood unoccupied when I arrived. Apparently, you and your companion hired my niece, Xin Yue, for transport to the nether regions of our great realm for some paltry leaf-collecting expedition. When my niece returned without you, we all assumed you had died."

Ah, Xin Yue. Why must you be Wang Yue's niece? You possess such beauty, like the new moon against a darkened, cloudless sky. And just like the moon above, my destiny dictates I must admire you from afar.

"Hao Lan, I hear she abandoned you once she discovered your true identity. Lao Peng You, I thought I had seen the last of you. How did you ever get back here? And–more to the point–why ever did you even bother to return?"

My *huoban* balled and relaxed his fists a few times before responding through gritted teeth. "That–you ugly *piyan*–is all of my business and none of yours."

Wang Yue feigned offense. "Tut, tut, little man. There is no need for insults. We are all gentlemen here." He displayed a manufactured smile.

"You are occupying my suite, sir," the Marquis charged. "Vacate it at once."

"When we arrived at this sanctuary, given your sad, unfortunate fate, it was thought that you might never return. Your complaint should be with the house mother, not me." He turned back to the table and resumed playing.

Lao Peng You's eyes roamed the table. "I see that someone will be leaving soon. I shall take that seat, and then you and I shall play for the honor of my suite." His face reddened.

"Marquis, do as you wish. If we play at the same table, it does not need to be for blood. Mahjong is supposed to be a therapeutic game. That is the only reason for my stay here. Does this mountain retreat not impart a healthful air to *you*?" The hint of a smile tainted his rhetorical question.

An inflamed expression on my *huoban*'s face gave the impression he might blast off the surface of our world without the assistance of fire medicine.

I touched his trembling hand. "Please, come for a walk with me."

"Yes, Lao, go with your toady. Come back when you are ready to behave in a more civilized fashion." His sparrow-like laughter penetrated the hillside.

Grabbing his elbow, I guided my indignant friend toward the garden path. Once in the presence of flowers and lily pads, Lao Peng You seemed to decompress a bit. "I absolutely loathe, hate, and detest that man! I never wanted to see him again, and here he is, sitting at my table, eating my food, and sleeping in my bed!" He stomped in small loops.

"*Huoban*." I used tender tones in an endeavor to sound calming. "We shall prevail with time. As Confucius said: In any game between power and patience, bet on patience."

He halted. "You are quite correct, *huoban*, even though you quote that pathetic, old, inebriated harebrain. When did you get to be so wise for one so young?" He scanned my face as if meeting me for the first time. "Patience is our secret weapon, is it not?" He grinned that malicious half smile of his. "Yes. Let us return to the Mahjong table and teach that bottomless rice bucket a little lesson." Off he went back the way we came. I scurried after him.

Just as we arrived at the table, Fa Sha stood up. "Once again Wang Yue, you have managed to empty my purse, moths and all." He blinked his one remaining eye and walked off with slumped shoulders.

"Ah, Marquis," the big, pale man proclaimed. "We now have a seat for you at the table. I hope you have brought sufficient coins to defend your honor." He indicated the recently vacated seat. "I find it regrettable we have but one open position. Your auntie will just have to observe for now."

No simple shaded insult like that could provoke me. I believed I possessed insufficient ego or self-value to take offense at such gibberish.

As my *huoban* sat, a tender young girl came to the table with a pot of tea and one cup, which she set before the large fellow.

"Thank you, Tian Mei." Wang Yue smiled at the pretty youth. "Gentlemen, this is Tian Mei, my new servant." He motioned for her to leave.

"*New servant?*" balked Lao Peng You. "What happened to your old servant, Chang Hu?"

"Ah, Chang Hu," the full moon of a man sighed. "Poor fellow ate some poisoned octopus and died."

This seemed all too familiar. "You did not feed him the same octopus dish you prepared for me, did you?" I needed to ask because if he had, that would indicate a deliberate murder.

"Horrors, no, my friend." He attempted innocence. "I fed him the octopus dish he had prepared for *me*. It was a test. He failed. Shall we begin?"

I stood near the table and watched Lao Peng You play Mahjong with his nemesis, Wang Yue, for the honor of occupying one particular suite at this resort. The Marquis would not be able to execute his usual ploy of having me feed him honor tiles. For most likely the first time at Changshou Shan, he had to rely on his own skills and talents.

The coins moved back and forth, sometimes my *huoban* won, and sometimes Wang Yue. Sweat formed and beaded on the forehead of both men at different times. Each had acquired and lost a modest fortune. At one point, it appeared the man with the Moon Rabbit tattoo neared the end of his funds. The Marquis needed but a simple pair to win.

"Mahjong!" Wang Yue declared. He pushed the concealed hand face up to display his victory.

One of the tiles looked unfamiliar. I had never seen such a thing before. Two little pictures looked like a lotus flower and a floating candle; the inscription read *One Hundred Uses*.

"What is that?" questioned Lao Peng You, pointing at the strange piece with an accusatory finger.

"What is what?" responded Wang Yue with feigned ignorance.

"That unusual tile. What is it, and where did it come from?" The Marquis picked it up and handed it to Wang Yue.

"Oh, this," he attempted nonchalance. "The Big Joker. It can represent any other tile you want… except for Flowers or as part of a pair. Have you never seen one before?"

"Not in *this* set. One hundred forty-and-four various tiles I have witnessed on this table, but never one like that." He stood, yet his full height did not reach that of the seated Wang Yue. "You are attempting to cheat us!"

"Cheat, sir?" came the reply. "*Cheat*? That is the charge of a whimpering, feeble loser. Pay up and be gone!"

"I refuse to accept your explanation." The Marquis plucked the Big Joker from Wang Yue's flabby hand, slammed the tile onto the table, and pointed at it. "You inserted your own piece into the hand and expect me to accede to your duplicity?" His face flushed with fury.

The unwelcome visitor from Dongting glanced down with half-lidded eyes. "We could ask the Arbiter to settle this dispute, if you prefer. He could banish either of us, never to sit at this table again." Wang Yue smirked at my *huoban*. "However, I feel it only fair to warn you, he is my nephew, Tu Yue."

With a fiery scowl that could boil water, Lao Peng You sat and shoved all his coins across the table. He jumped up like a cornered dog and scampered away without even looking at me. I followed him because he had no place to go, and I feared he might choose my accommodations as a convalescence cave.

He headed to the garden instead. My clumsy and uneven footsteps reverberated throughout the otherwise quiet setting, heralding my presence.

"That big, fat cheat called me a cheat! I have lived for generations upon generations and never encountered the likes of *him*." He paced in small columns and rows. "You and I are going back to that table, and we are going to exhaust his coin purse until there is not even one speck of dust in it!" His trembling finger pointed toward the area we had just left.

"Huoban..." Again, I attempted to function as calming agent. "That man did a very bad thing, and he upset you very much, but I do not believe today is the day to reap your crop of vengeance."

His eyes opened wide.

"Remember, patience must be the ultimate winner of this contest. If we go back there now, he will be exceptionally vigilant, and he might even inadvertently uncover our clandestine maneuvers. Please, let us approach this mountain-sized obstacle one stone at a time. Eat, sleep. Tomorrow we shall be well-rested and better prepared to strike."

"My *huoban*, once again you speak with the voice of reason." His typhoon respiration reverted to near normal. "But where shall I sleep tonight?"

I did not want to let this man out of my sight for fear he would return to the Mahjong table in another unsuccessful attempt to take down his archrival. "You may sleep in my room, Marquis. The floor looks quite comfortable."

He nodded his assent. We walked to the food table and grabbed some bowls of rice. I heard the wheels turning and the gears grinding inside his continuously plotting cranium as we ate.

Later, we returned to my room, where he fell asleep on my bed after brushing the dried leaves away. The floor felt much less comfortable than I had imagined.

"Well done, Hao Lan, well done." Shen Lung sits next to the golden wall with the three large gemstones. "You have completed this assignment." He smiles at me.

"But what about the Emperor? Is he going to die at the hands of Zhao Gao?"

"Yes, he will die on Zhifu Island from an overdose of mercury."

"Then, he will be murdered by his own men. I thought if I gave him the message, he would understand they were trying to poison him."

"Little One," the dragon purrs, "The Emperor received and understood the message. He realized how Zhao Gao plots to murder him. That is why he will take the mercury. He believes it will convey immortality upon him, thus, making him immune to any poison his ministers might offer him."

I feel like an accomplice to an assassination. "But did I hasten his demise by giving him the message? I do not wish to believe my actions may have killed our Emperor."

The Blue Dragon looks down at me with the concerned expression of a caring parent. "Your performance had no effect on the actions of the Emperor. Had he not received the message, he would take the mercury all the same. This way, he knows the identity of his real enemy before he dies."

I feel a bit better, but it may take a while before I can fully accept not having any responsibility. My mind generates several questions I feel compelled to ask. "Shen Lung, if I understand correctly, the Emperor craved immortality."

He nods.

"Lao Peng You and I could have bestowed immortality upon the Emperor."

He nods again.

"Why were we not instructed to impart the gift of longevity? Did the Emperor even know he was so close to that which he sought?"

The hint of a smile crosses the great dragon's face. "Many times, we are so near to whatever we seek without knowing it. Wild-eyed men tend to be blind to that in front of them, and sometimes it is difficult to believe what we value so highly can be right within our grasp."

"Did you not wish us to make the Emperor immortal?"

"No, indeed not. Qin Shi Huang was a great ruler who united many warring tribes. However, he became drunk on his own wine, and it is time for him to relinquish the reins of a government he created."

Sometimes I fail to recall how the gods control our fates.

"Do you have any further interrogatories for me, my little servant?"

Indeed, I do. "My Lord, I thank you for the gift of the Jiaogulan leaves. How are they to be prepared? Do I need to roast or ferment them before steeping?"

"Little One, the gift of Jiaogulan is that it is ready to use directly from the bush. Fresh or dried, steep for no more, and no less, than seventy breaths. There is no need to do anything else. Any more questions?"

"No, my Lord. I thank you for your generosity." I bow in reverence.

"So sour," I hear a familiar voice, "to swallow your own poison."

"Ever so bitter," another voice, "to discover your own mortality."

"It is the sweetest thing," the third voice rings out, "to comply with fate."

9. Catching the Full Moon from the Bottom of the Sea

Despite the floor's firmness, I slept rather well. However, I woke to the face of Lao Peng You staring down at me from my own bed.

"It is about time you woke up," he chided. "I was worried you might sleep away the whole day. Come on, we have much to do if we want to pluck the flowers as they bloom."

He hopped off the bed and opened the door.

"Are you not coming with me?" he asked. "I wish to take my morning meal."

I did not feel hungry, nor did I consider myself quite ready to leave my room, let alone start the day. I brushed some of the *Jiaogulan* leaves while attempting to prop myself up. Perhaps I should make some tea.

"You go ahead, *huoban*, I shall join you in a little while."

"As you wish." He left so fast, all I saw was a blue blur. Through the door I heard him mutter to himself, "And to think I waited all that time for him. Hmmmph."

I grinned.

From the floor around me, I collected a fistful of dried leaves. They did not smell particularly enticing, nor did they smell like regular tea. My curiosity swelled to taste this new brew. Perhaps it would become something I could drink in place of my beloved hot relaxing beverage.

Outside the room, I saw people walking about headed in different directions, all looking like they had business somewhere. It seemed quite busy this particular morning.

At the food table, I found the Marquis with a bowl full of delectable-looking delights. When he saw me approach, he paused his munching.

"It is about time you appear in public. Half the day is already gone. If we wait much longer, all we will gather are twigs."

"I shall return shortly. I want to get a pot of hot water for these leaves."

He returned to his meal. I retrieved a teacup and teapot from the kitchen. With a measure of reverence, I crushed the leaves and placed them in the pot. I counted my breaths to measure the steeping period.

An unusual aroma arose. It started out sweet but tempered with time. I placed the pot on the table where Lao Peng You sat. After seventy breaths, no more, no less. I poured a cup and inhaled the steam. It smelled slightly bitter, slightly sour.

"You are actually going to drink that stuff?" he interrogated.

"After all the trouble of chartering a boat, spending days at sea, sick with churning bowels, crawling through a beast-infested jungle, nearly getting trapped in a voracious, sucking bog, flying on a most terrifying dragon, almost getting devoured by a ravenous old hag, having an audience with our esteemed Emperor but encountering only his voice, and flying back here on a dragon again?"–which did sound like a bit of trouble when I thought about it that way–"Yes!"

I drew in a small mouthful and gave it a taste. Not bad. Not good. Not tea.

"I do not know how you can drink that stuff. I find it particularly unpalatable." He continued to devour dried fish and imbibe rice wine.

"While it is not the most flavorful of teas, it is not objectionable, unlike whatever noxious potion you served me before. What was that?"

The wrinkling of his brow suggested I asked a question for which he had no idea of the answer. "Whatever are you talking about, *huoban*?"

"Before we left, you served me something you called *Jiaogulan*, which I am quite certain was not. What was it?"

The Marquis swallowed and averted his gaze. "I am not quite sure, but I told the practitioner you had been suffering with an intestinal impasse for at least a month." His eyebrows raised. "Feeling better now?"

Sometimes I felt like snatching a large boulder and smashing his skull with it. However, if it were not for him, I would be poor and alone–and dead. I shall attempt to endure his shameless behavior so long as it does no permanent harm to me or others around us.

"As far as I can remember, I did not feel badly at all, and certainly not constipated. For what purpose did you serve me that emetic herbal concoction? Were you attempting to dissuade me from going on the boat voyage I so desired?"

His eyes wandered away. "There may be some truth in that."

I began to think if I intended to wait for an apology from this man, it would take longer than the generations upon generations he has lived so far.

"Baron, I believe it is time for your *meal*." He winked as if he were speaking in riddles that I understood, which I did not.

"My meal, Marquis? I believe this tea sufficient for now." I took a sip.

He stared at me. "No." Another wink. "Your *meal*." He indicated his mouth then his bottom. "You seem a bit drained."

A young man from the kitchen stepped forward.

"This is Daniao. I believe he is willing and can provide what you need." He nodded to the fellow, who then approached me. "Perhaps he can join you in your room and prepare a special meal for you." A smile.

Ah. I got what he suggested with all the subtlety of an ox with a cart. I downed the rest of the *Jiaogulan*, a taste for which I hoped to develop over time. There have been quite a few things I have had to develop a taste for these past few weeks. This tea should prove to be much easier than most.

I turned the cup over and knocked it on the table. The leaf pattern signified an open window. If only I had some idea what that might portend. I shall have to make an endeavor to study tasseomancy a bit more.

I stood and walked back to my room. Daniao followed a step behind, in the manner of a loyal servant. Once we had both moved inside, I closed the door. Because this practice remained fairly new to me, I had some trepidation as to how to conduct such unfamiliar business.

"Um, I, er, please, uh, what do you...? Oh, I am not sure..."

He seemed to know what to do because his hand went to the back of my neck. As before, the skin contact initiated a surging desire within me to consume his seed. I observed a familiar bulge and knew what I must have. Before he had a chance to tell me what he wanted, I had his pants down and his little bird in my mouth. I could only guess he had not had an opportunity for release in a while because after just a few repetitions he delivered the goods. And so much of it. Not a bad-tasting man. I might have to consider having him prepare a *special meal* for me again.

Daniao pulled up his trousers, gave an appreciative bow, and left. And I felt much better as well.

"*Huoban, huoban,*" came the call from outside. "I just saw the man leave. Are you ready?"

"Marquis, please come inside if you wish to discuss personal business."

He entered and shut the door. "Most indelicate of me to be sure. I want to get started at the table as soon as possible. May we go now?"

"Not yet." I held up my hand. "We need to discuss some strategy first. Our opponent is quite skillful, deceitful, and shrewd. If we do not plan, we shall surely fall into more of his diabolical traps."

"Yes, I can only presume you have reasoned well, my friend." He sat on the bed. "What did you have in mind?"

Actually, I had not thought about it beforehand, but it seemed prudent not to rush into things without having had some opportunity to draw up battle plans together. "It is my belief if we attempt any sort of collusion, Wang Yue will sense it immediately."

"Yes. True. What can we do to assure my–I mean *our*–winning?"

At least I knew where his loyalties lay.

"I have heard that if you are planning to inflict revenge, you should dig two graves first."

An expression of surprise filled his face. "And what is that supposed to mean? I am no gravedigger! That is the kind of thing we pay poor people to do."

"No, no. It is a moral, *huoban*. It means when you attempt to extract revenge, you frequently do more harm to yourself than the target of your anger."

"Ah, like a deflected arrow that flies back and hits the shooter instead of the intended objective."

"Something like that." How can someone who has lived as long as he has never heard that expression. Of course, I reminded myself, Confucius had said it.

Sometimes it amazed me that this fellow could know so much, be so smart, yet be so blinded to his own shortcomings. Did not Shen Lung make a similar assessment of the Emperor's arrogance?

"*Huoban*, let me suggest that we do not approach Wang Yue with our usual strategy. I believe he is too formidable of an opponent, unlike the other men here. He has a goal, which I think is to shame you for purchasing–in my name–his assumed barony away from him."

"Yes, you may be correct." He gazed off through the window. Feathery clouds perched atop one of the other mountains nearby. "How do you suggest we proceed?"

While my level for strategies could not approach Lao Peng You, I knew of an age-old ruse the servant class used with their masters for millennia. "My recommendation–should you choose to entertain it–is that we lose to Wang Yue."

"Lose to Wang Yue!?" his former calmness gone. "I reject your recommendation. It is not my desire to lose anything more to that *wangbadan*!"

I felt it might have been difficult to explain, given his penchant for reacting before contemplating. "Please try to be patient and listen to the entire plan before passing your judgment, *huoban*."

He reassessed me with a squint. "I shall endeavor to give you my full attention, should you choose to speak with more reason and logic. Please proceed."

"Yes. Thank you. It is my belief if we start by losing to Wang Yue, it would further inflate his ego."

"Any more inflation and his ego will explode!" He puffed air and pulled his hands apart in demonstration.

"He will consider himself the better player, as he believes he is."

"But that is not true!" Lao Peng You slammed a hand on the mattress. "*I* am the best player! You know that I am!"

This man's self-absorption will be the death of him. "It will provide a false sense of confidence because he considers himself–whether true or not–the best player around."

"Which he most certainly is not!"

"Most certainly." I paused, waiting to see if he might rant further, but no. "And when it looks like he is just about to prevail, we launch our attack."

"Attack! Yes!" He leapt up with arms and hands in position to do battle with ruffians and hooligans.

"Attack, yes, but a subtle attack. We do not want him to become suspicious. We win some and then lose a little, win some and lose a little. If we continue that pattern, he will most likely not get suspicious because he believes–whether true or not–he is the superior player."

"Which he most certainly is not!" Lao Peng You squawked.

"Which he most certainly is not, but if we can maintain this tactic, we shall erode and exhaust his resources eventually."

His eyes darted about. His eyebrows raised and knitted. His chin jutted and subsided.

"I am partial to your plan," he said at long last, "but not entirely. I wish to have a dramatic finish to this fellow. I can only hold on for so long before I shall want his fat, blubbery head in a bowl. Fireworks optional."

"If that makes you happy, *huoban*."

His eyes illuminated. "When I sense he is ripe for the final blow, I shall remove my hat and fan myself with it. I do not believe he will interpret that as a signal. When I do this, pass me all the honor tiles you can. Yes, that will do nicely."

Something about this strategy did not feel quite right. "*Huoban*, I believe if you win with a hand full of valuable tiles, Wang Yue will have every right to be suspicious. Might there be another option?"

He took a moment to ponder. "I think the terminals–ones and nines–would generate little suspicion, and I can pass you the winds and dragons."

"Agreed. But not until the last hand. To minimize his suspicions."

"Agreed."

Later that morning we both sat at the table with Wang Yue and Fa Sha, who seemed to have produced a new pile of coins out of somewhere unseen.

"Gentlemen, what a pleasure," greeted our object of play. "And when I say gentlemen, I am referring only to Hao Lan and Fa Sha. The other person I find too despicable to be recognized as a gentleman." He pointed in the general direction of Lao Peng You, whose eyes steamed and popped.

"Wang Yue," responded Fa Sha. "If today is to be anything like yesterday, I imagine I shall be here only for a short while, even though my purse is fully restocked." He blinked his one remaining eye.

"You are a worthy competitor, Fa Sha," Wang Yue smirked, "and worth every last copper coin that you will surrender to me." He laughed his sparrow laugh. Lao Peng You cringed at the chirpy sound.

"Shall we start?" I suggested in hopes of giving my *huoban* something to focus on other than the immediate annihilation of Wang Yue.

We rolled for positions, and I ended up West to Wang Yue's East. Fa Sha sat North and Lao Peng You South.

For the first few rounds we each did well, even though my *huoban* and I attempted losing to Wang Yue. Could he have been employing the same strategy? I would think not. He did not like to lose. Ever. Perhaps Fa Sha assisted us to get back at the round fat man no one liked. I did not notice any obvious clues.

Around the fifth round, our adversary began accumulating more and more of our coins. At one point, he came close to finishing us off. Lao Peng You and I looked at each other and knew it was time to begin the second phase. As planned, we won some back, then lost a little bit, won some more, lost a bit more. By late afternoon, we had accumulated most of Wang Yue's wealth, and he had but a few coins left. The usual joyful expression on his face started to curdle, suggesting frustration with his inability to command the fortunes of the table.

Wang Yue called for Tian Mei to prepare a pot of tea for him. As the servant left the table, Lao Peng You doffed his hat and flapped it about.

"Baron Dongting," my *huoban* called, "is it not a warm day?" He fanned himself with fury.

"It is rather warm," Wang Yue responded, wiping his circular brow.

"Not you! I was speaking to Hao Lan, the *real* Baron Dongting, not you, you turtle-less *wangba*!"

"Gentlemen," inserted Fa Sha, "if you wish to compare the size of your little brothers to settle this feud, please do so now so that we may return to the game at hand. I shall close my eye if that is what you decide you wish to do."

I smiled at Lao Peng You as we began the next–and most likely last–game. Wang Yue sat East, but West, my wind, prevailed this round. Following the *Tai Feng*, when I passed all my one and nine tiles to Lao Peng You, I had a hand full of dragons and winds.

The game seemed longer than a twisting melon vine, with no one claiming tiles and no one calling Mahjong. I began to sweat with disbelief. Eventually, we got to the last undrawn tile. If no player won on this one, we would have to throw our hands in and start all over again.

Just as Lao Peng You reached for that final piece, Tian Mei returned with the tea. My *huoban* peeked at the face of the tile and smiled. He turned up the One Dot. I could only hope this meant he had triumphed.

"Mahjong!" he cried out. "Mahjong! Mahjong! Mahjong!" he taunted Wang Yue as he revealed a hand full of ones and nines. "All Terminals! The win comes with the very last tile–which just happens to be the One Dot–thus, I am Catching the Full Moon from the Bottom of the Sea!" He waved the piece around like a red lantern in a storm. As Wang Yue sat East, the rules dictated he must pay double.

"Lao Peng You, as much as I hate to say this: You have won. I shall vacate my suite immediately." Wang Yue stood, knocking the pot of tea to the ground with a crash. Tian Mei bent down and picked up the shards.

"Wang Yue, please. I have changed my mind. I no longer desire the suite."

The big moon of a man looked as surprised as an unexpected total eclipse. "If you... do not wish... my suite," he countered, "what exactly is it... that I can give you... to satisfy my debt?"

Lao Peng You smirked like an imp and pointed down at the young servant.

"Tian Mei!?" Wang Yue exclaimed. "You want Tian Mei? That is not possible! Please choose something else. Impossible!"

My *huoban* continued to brandish his devilish smile. "Do you want to be known as a welsher, Wang Yue? If you do not comply with my wishes, your name is defiled, and you might as well relocate yourself to the land of the banished Banana People. What say you now, *wangba*?" Lao Peng You crossed his arms across his chest and leaned back in a typical Marquis Pichan posture. My old friend had returned.

"But this is not... You said..." the tall, round man sputtered. "I thought we..."

"I would not give even a single millet seed for what you thought! If you do not comply with my request, I shall spread the word throughout the region of your unwillingness to make good your Mahjong debts." Lao Peng You glared at his vanquished nemesis and hissed, "Is that what you want?"

"No, no! But tell me: Why Tian Mei?"

My *huoban* glanced toward the servant with bland indifference, as if looking at discarded laundry tickets. "No reason. Will you grant my request or no?"

"Yes, yes, of course. How silly of me." Wang Yue pulled Tian Mei up by the shoulders and pushed the dainty creature toward Lao Peng You. "Tian Mei, meet your new master, Lao Peng You, Marquis Pichan. Best of luck to you both." He took a giant step toward his rooms.

The servant looked after the deflated, waning moon with a tilted head.

I called out, "Wait, please, Wang Yue." My turn. I pushed the tiles over. Even though I did not win, I still had very valuable tiles, sets of dragons and my West Wind. "I believe you also owe me something as well."

Lao Peng You's laugh reverberated around the playing area. Fa Sha spittled and choked.

"Baron," Wang Yue stammered as he returned to the table, "I have nothing left to satisfy you." He bowed, which I did not know was possible for someone of his stature. "*You* have my rightful title. *He* has my servant. What else would you ask from me?"

I stared at the man who made my life uncomfortable, Lao Peng You's life frustrating, and everyone else's life around him unbearable. After a protracted breath, I responded with as much calm as I could muster, "Your rooms, sir."

Wang Yue ran off on his stubby legs. We heard noises in the suites across the garden, and a few moments later a cartful of belongings rolled down the mountain making creaking and banging noises. Tian Mei's face followed the departure.

"I would suggest a thorough cleansing first, Baron," my *huoban* suggested.

"A good idea, Marquis; however, that is to be your suite again, as it was yours before. I shall select another. Any suggestions?"

He posed in thought for a moment and replied, "I think the one facing the garden is lovely."

"The garden suite it will be."

Lao Peng You glanced down. "Thank you, Baron, you are most generous."

"Thank you, Marquis, without you I am nothing."

"If you two bunnies are finished complimenting each other," Fa Sha complained, giving us the evil eye, "can we get back to the game, please?"

Hearty laughter erupted all around us.

That evening Lao Peng You and I ate a sumptuous feast as Tian Mei stood to the side, observing. I even tried some of the unappetizing tidbits he regarded so highly: slimy chunks of river eel, some sort of foul-smelling orange fish from the ocean, pickled root vegetables. However, I would not touch the one thing I had resolved never to eat again: octopus.

"Huoban…" I waited until he came up for air between gulps of seafood. "What made you choose…?" I nodded toward Tian Mei.

Lao Peng You's head swiveled to his latest acquisition and back. "In all my years, I have never had a personal servant. Now, at my advanced age, it seemed prudent to obtain someone to assist me with my daily activities. This one is as good as the next, but in my heart, I believed removing the child from the clutches of that overblown bag of moldy rice might bring comfort to us both."

Tian Mei smiled at me and nodded. I smiled back without thought. Something in that glance I could not explain told me it would be wise to employ diligence and caution in the times to come.

After dinner I moved my belongings from my old room into the suite facing the garden. It seemed very pleasant, and I could gaze out into the foliage at night, especially when the moonlight proved generous. I sat well into the evening, sipping a cup of *Jiaogulan*–in hopes of acquiring a taste for it–and contemplating my new life so far.

So many things have happened that I would have never predicted for the son of poor Hunan farmers. The boy who scraped his life out of a cinnabar mine and nearly died because the dust and fumes decimated his nerves. The man who became an unintentional Immortal, who played Mahjong for sport, and sought the seed of mortal men to maintain his longevity. The Immortal who visited large defensive walls, took boat trips to lands unknown, met with the Emperor himself, and flew on dragons. In my dreams, I deliberated with a large, blue dragon and three sparkling gems of wisdom. A life worth living, indeed.

I tapped the overturned teacup on the table to dislodge the leaves at the bottom. The pattern resembled an elephant. As I was not sure what this meant, and Lao Peng You recently had a dream involving an elephant, I left my suite and walked across the way to his.

"Marquis," I made a light rap on the doorframe. "May I ask a question of you?"

"What is it, Baron? I thought you were asleep." He sounded annoyed. Perhaps he had a gentleman visitor. Once the door opened, I saw Tian Mei scrubbing the floor.

"My tea leaves formed an elephant. Are you aware of what the interpretation might be?"

"Yes. It means you are a huge imposition upon everyone around you. You smell bad, produce much *pihua*, and you like to spray water everywhere. Tasseomancy is for fools! Now, let me be." He slammed the door.

In a perplexing way, it warmed my heart to have the old Marquis Pichan again. Feisty, annoying, greedy, self-absorbed. I strolled back to my suite with a gentle smile.

This new bed appeared large enough for two people. I wondered if someone else would ever share it with me. I knew I would sleep well tonight all alone. It had been a day of grand adventure.

"Sour, I say." The ruby chants, "sour, sour, sour."

"Bitter, you know," the emerald counters. "Oh, so bitter."

"Sweet, sweet, sweet, sweet, sweet!" the opal sings.

And I am once again standing in front of the golden wall.

"What trees grow on the Chungnan hill?" the red jewel asks. "The white fir and the plum."

"How will you find enlightenment?" the green gem poses. "Study at the Plum Village."

"Where was I born?" the milky white stone riddles. "Under a plum tree, of course."

It seems like plums will be the theme of tonight's dream. Everyone enjoys a good plum.

I feel something hit me in the shoulder from behind. Looking down at the ground, I spot a ripe plum and pick it up. Not so surprising, given the topic of conversation. When I turn to look where it came from, I spot a lone tree on a small rise. Its branches bend with the weight of the purple fruit. Three men sit underneath with their backs to the trunk.

"Tall and slightly rounded. It is the leg of an elephant," the first man says, "I am quite sure of that." A few years younger than me, a red tunic covers his hearty body.

"No. Flat and sturdy. It is a house," the second man says, "Of that I am certain." This fellow, a bit older, wears a green shirt and looks somewhat chubby.

"You are both wrong," the third one says, "A sharp point pokes at my back. It can only be a large rock, nothing else." His white jacket matches his white hair, and he appears underfed.

This feels like a story within a dream within a dream within a story. I walk up to the tree.

"I hear footsteps," the first man announces. "Perhaps another elephant."

"Yes, footsteps," the second says, "of the giant who lives within this house."

"No, the footsteps are of a lion who wishes to leap upon this rock," counters the third.

"I was chased here by a lion," the man in red proclaims, "and now I am enjoying the view."

"How can you enjoy the view, Yi?" the man with the green shirt asks. "You are blind. We are all blind. I was led here by a friend."

"I was born under a rock," the white-haired fellow adds, "totally blind, and I have no idea how I got here."

"You are blind if you study without thinking, Sen," the first man preaches.

"With or without sight, we are all a part of the great cosmic consciousness," the second man professes.

"Hear me, Er, out of the myriad things, everything appears," the third man imparts.

"Gentlemen," I say. *"May I be of assistance?"*

"Who speaks?" the youngest one asks. *"Is it the elephant? The giant? Or are you the lion whose footsteps Sen heard?"*

"None of those," I respond.

"Is it someone within the house I am leaning against?" the middle-aged man inquires.

"No, sir, I am not in a house."

"Then you are perched like a lion atop this great rock behind me looking down on us?" the eldest poses.

"Not at all. I am but a traveler who has happened upon the three of you."

"Is my back up against the leg of an elephant?"

"Or is it the wall of a house?"

"It is a stone I am leaning on, yes?"

So here is the pit of the fruit. Do I answer the blind men's questions with the truth and dispel their disbeliefs, or do I perpetuate their various inventions? They all perceive the same thing, but each one experiences it so differently, much like the three blind men in Lao Peng You's elephant reverie. In his dream, no one informed the blind men that they were, in actuality, touching different parts of an elephant, not within the Emperor's dungeon as they surmised.

The three blind men before me sense the same plum tree and arrive at different conclusions. Perhaps today's lesson demonstrates that each of us perceives everything differently and we must learn to be tolerant of others' viewpoints. Or maybe I need to start listening more to what those around me are telling me. Am I not hearing their messages clearly? Or could it be that without order, chaos follows? The infinite number of possible interpretations feels overwhelming.

"You are thinking about this much too hard, Hao Lan." I catch Shen Lung's booming words but cannot see him.

"Do you gentlemen hear that voice?" I ask the blind men.

"What voice?" Yi responds.

"I only hear your question," Er asserts.

"What was the question?" Sen asks.

"They cannot hear me, Little One. I am only intervening to let you know that, while I appreciate your innumerable thought processes regarding the situation, this is much simpler than you might expect."

"Thank you, O Great One," I respond.

"Who is great?" the first blind man asks. "Is it me?"

"Which one of us?" the second blind man asks. "Is it me?"

"He said, 'O Great One,'" the third blind man states, "O meaning nothing. I believe he is not addressing the three of us at all."

"By the way," Shen Lung's voice reverberates in my head, "they can hear you if you attempt to speak to me. I recommend you just listen."

That sounds like a good idea, given the propensity for these three men to prattle and ask peculiar questions in a seemingly random and baffling fashion.

"I suggest you think about a plum," the blue dragon advises. "The fruit, its color, its texture, its contents. Let that image guide you."

"Distinguished visitor, are you hearing voices?" the man in red asks.

"Do you hear voices frequently?" the man in green questions.

194

"I hear voices all the time," the man in white states. "Leave the fellow alone. He is only trying to help us."

"He is not doing a very good job so far," the first man, Yi, accuses. "I am still blind and leaning against the leg of an elephant."

"How good of a job can one man do?" the second man, Er, queries. "He is only a man."

"Will we be home in time for dinner?" the third man, Sen, demands to know.

"So, is it an elephant behind me?"

"Or is it a house?"

"It is a rock, is it not?"

I consider a variety of thoughtful answers. Finally, a response becomes clear in my mind. "Yes."

"Yes? What does that mean?"

"Yes? Do you mean to say that we are all correct?"

"Yes? Are you crazy, young man?"

"Yes," I restate with certainty.

"We cannot all be correct," the first man argues.

"It is either an elephant, a house, or a rock," the second man asserts.

"How can it be all three?" the third man asks.

"All right, then," I reply. "I change my answer to No."

"Do you mean that none of us is correct?" Yi asks.

"No."

"Are you trying to tell us we are all wrong?" Er inquires.

"No."

"Are you crazy, young man?" Sen probes.

"No." I look at the juicy plum in my hand and walk away.

"I hear footsteps. Where are you going?"

"Yes, where are you going, and why are you leaving me here with them?"

"Are you leaving us here to die, and without dinner?"

I take a bite of the delicious fruit. "This plum is delightful," I declare as I continue to walk down the little hill back toward the golden wall.

"A plum?" I hear a voice behind me. "Where did he get a plum?"

10. Plum Flower

I woke to gentle knocking at my suite. Following a few moments of groaning and grumbling, I left my very comfortable bed and moved to the door with justified apprehension, expecting Lao Peng You to look quite annoyed that I had slept half his day away. Then I realized the knocking had been polite and could not have possibly been him.

Tian Mei, the servant my *huoban* had won from Wang Yue, stood outside. She hid her face and held out a cloth sack to me. I took the bag; it felt very light. Tian Mei bowed and shuffled off to Lao Peng You's suite. I could already see the advantages to *me* of him having assistance.

The sack contained *Jiaogulan* leaves, presumably the ones the Marquis brought back from our trip to Guizhou. I already had quite a collection, and the supply could last me a month, or maybe more, if I made judicious use of the tea. Perhaps I could procure a container from the kitchen in which to store the leaves.

Once I had prepared myself for the day, I left the suite with a handful of *Jiaogulan* and walked to the food table. It did not surprise me to see Lao Peng You sitting there with a bowl full of fish. He barely looked up as I passed by on my way to the kitchen.

Daniao came to greet me with an eager grin. "How may I serve his lordship this morning?"

I cringed, not knowing if I would ever get used to people from my own former social station addressing me in such a noble manner.

"Daniao, I need a few things. First, some hot water for my leaves." He reached over to a table full of pots and cups, placing one of each on the surface next to me.

"Thank you."

"How else may I serve you, master?"

I looked at his innocent face, thinking of how hard he worked for such meager pay. There must be some way to reward him that did not involve extracting his seed for my own self-nourishing needs. While I am not attracted to him the way I would be attracted to a woman, such as the Moon goddess sea captain Xin Yue–regrettably, the niece of Wang Yue–I imagined most women would find him handsome.

"Master?" he prompted.

"Oh, yes. Sorry," I must not dally. My *huoban* most assuredly awaited my return so that he can plot our day, which I envisioned included more time at the Mahjong table. "Do you have a container I may borrow in which I can store my tea leaves?"

He sniffed at the fading sweet aroma of my *Jiaogulan*. "My lord, our kitchen has many, many varieties of the great beverage for your enjoyment. There is no need for you to provide your own."

While Daniao behaved in a pleasant enough manner, I did not wish to discuss the intricacies of an Immortal's life with him. As a consequence of the developing affinity I felt for him, and his willingness to cooperate, I hoped to continue utilizing his supply in the future.

"Thank you, my good man, but I require a special blend that comes only from Guizhou Province. I have a limited supply in my room and wish to store it for more carefully measured usage."

He darted into the storage area and returned holding a chest-sized ceramic container with a lid.

"Here you go, my Lord. I found this empty one in the storeroom. Please use it in good health." He handed the urn to me.

"Thank you, Daniao. Perhaps we can take a walk in the garden together some time." His eyes flinched and flitted about. Had I embarrassed him? "Is that not allowed?"

He bowed his head. "We are not permitted to socialize in public with guests. I am sorry. I would have very much enjoyed walking with you in the garden." He turned and withdrew into the kitchen. I could only hope I did not damage our budding friendship.

With the urn under one arm, I carried the teapot and cup out to the table and sat next to Lao Peng You.

He gave me a quick glance then resumed his chomping. "What is that odd vessel?"

I placed it on the ground next to me. "A tea storage urn. I plan to keep the rest of the *Jiaogulan* leaves we collected in it. Oh, I want to thank you for having Tian Mei deliver your share."

"Those leaves mean nothing to me. You seem to enjoy that putrid concoction. May it bring you health and long life." He resumed his meal then halted with the tail of a fish drooping from his mouth. "Wait." The protruding fins danced as he spoke. "Did this once contain tea leaves, *huoban*?" He pointed at the pot as he chewed and swallowed.

"I imagine it did. Why?"

"Because you need to remove the previous contents thoroughly before storing your leaves. What if there are some stray tea particles lodged somewhere inside? It could prove harmful to you."

I had forgotten that regular tea is anathema to Immortals. But how can I clean it out without exposing myself to the old leaves?

"If you have no objection," the Marquis continued, "I shall have Tian Mei perform a complete scrubbing before you place your precious Dragon Immortality Tea inside. Does that meet with your approval?"

Again, another benefit of having a mortal servant.

"Yes, my *huoban*, a most excellent suggestion."

He clapped his hands three times and the youth appeared from their suite. "Tian Mei, take this container and clean the inside most carefully. I do not want any tea particles remaining when you are finished. Do you understand?"

The servant nodded, picked up the urn and took it elsewhere.

"*Huoban*, did you instruct Tian Mei not to speak? I would have thought a verbal acknowledgment would have been required."

He smiled before responding, "Hao Lan, I have received a most wonderful gift. This obedient one is mute and does not utter a word."

"I see," I said. A servant who does not speak. What advantage this deficit provided I could not be sure, but if it made my *huoban* happy, all the better. While I still harbored apprehensions about this young person, I did not wish to beat the grass and alert the snake.

After crushing the leaves in my hand with reverence, I dropped them into the water. Seventy breaths later, I poured my *Jiaogulan* before it steeped too long.

"Let us discuss our day," the Marquis pronounced. "Are you ready to resume our Mahjong partnership? I am most eager to play."

As much as I enjoyed being part of his team, I felt the need to spend some time by myself, reflecting, meditating, rejuvenating. Besides, I possessed more coins than I required to maintain this lifestyle for at least a dozen years.

"Would you be offended if I did not join you at the Mahjong table today, *huoban*? I would like to take care of a few personal affairs on my own. Perhaps we can rejoin tomorrow."

I expected some wrath, some finger wagging, some condemnation for not complying with his plans. Much to my surprise he answered in a subdued voice, "If that is your wish. Who am I to order you about, Baron?" He grinned. "I shall have Tian Mei deliver the container to your suite. May you find the solace you seek today."

Did the gods remove Lao Peng You and substitute this mild-mannered imposter? Perhaps he had plots and plans that did not involve me. I should just be grateful and move ahead.

"Shall I expect to dine with you this evening?" he asked.

"Of course. I believe I shall finish my business by late afternoon."

I sipped at my *Jiaogulan*, and he absorbed his meal. Having sampled a few cups of this substitute, my taste buds had begun to become accustomed, and I shall soon be able to enjoy it.

With the tea gone, I tapped the cup on the table. The leaves suggested a seashell, and I knew better than to ask Lao Peng You for assistance with interpretation.

He stood, looked down at the soggy pattern before me and said, "At one time our people used seashells as currency. Later, they compressed tea leaves into coins. Perhaps this means you will collect more wealth soon." He started to walk away, paused, and turned back. "Or perhaps you will merely be picking up seashells along the shore. Who is to say?" He withdrew into his suite.

As I sat in contemplation, I felt a tap on my shoulder. I looked up and beheld Tian Mei. For the first time, my eyes witnessed the bottomless pupils directly. In the faintest of instants, I experienced a peculiar connection, and it felt like burning lava flowed within my ribcage. Tian Mei seemed different. Before I had a chance to determine what this strange sensation might have been, the incredible link ended with a blink.

Tian Mei indicated the storage pot, presumably cleaned with no residual tea. I attempted to initiate eye contact again, but the servant looked away, probably embarrassed by this intense encounter.

When my heartbeat slowed, I pointed to my suite. "Please put the jar in my room, Tian Mei. Thank you."

I waited until the servant disappeared into Lao Peng You's rooms before re-entering my own chamber. I wished I could better understand the spark of this happenstance. Perhaps I could contemplate the feeling further while on my solitary walk.

The garden at Changshou Shan extended for several *mu.* Only one path led to it from the central courtyard along the meandering stream with the mossless stones. About a *chi* beyond the adjoining roundabout walkways, three paths diverged, each leading to different natures. The first followed a trail of iron-rich red dirt. The middle path led to a green wood of tall, slender trees. The last rambled through a quarry of white, craggy rocks. A granite bench stood under an ancient gingko in the center of the crossroads, and I decided to sit a while in deliberation before choosing a path.

For most of my life, I woke up in the morning, went to work in the mine, came home to sleep and repeated the pattern the next day and the next. Throughout that ascetic time, I studied the Confucian principles on which our society operated to perpetuate itself according to orthodox beliefs. My current mentors have opened my eyes to new and different ways of thinking. While these innovative views may not conflict with those prior, I would like to use these newfound tools to supplement the ones already in my satchel, not just replace the old.

"Hao Lan." The voice of Shen Lung calls. I must have fallen asleep on the bench while meditating upon my pedestrian life.

"Yes, master," I reply.

"I have another task for you to perform."

"I live to serve you, my Lord. Instruct me as you will."

Up in the sky, no dragon hovers. In fact, I see nothing, as darkness fills my vision.

"You are hearing me directly even though I am not in your vicinity. Stop looking."

"Yes, O Great One." I close my eyes to minimize the curiosity.

"That is better. I shall need you to concentrate fully," the voice booms. *"This is an assignment only you can perform. When I have finished describing it, once you have realized what I am commanding you to do, you will inquire of me why I do not ask another."*

"If that is your desire, Shen Lung, I shall inquire why you do not ask another."

"No, you misunderstand!" His tone becomes dark. "You will think this task more fitting for someone else, and you will ask me why I have chosen you instead of another."

"Of course. I understand you, now."

"Be silent for a while as I describe my request." He pauses for a breath. "Hao Lan, I require you to bring someone into the community of Immortals."

My mind bursts with myriad questions, but he instructed me to be silent, and I shall still myself as best as possible.

"In the next month or so, we will banish one of the current members and require a replacement."

So many uncertainties, but I must remain silent.

"You will play Mahjong this afternoon. During one of the games, you will turn up the Plum Flower tile. Look for a person in the vicinity eating a plum. That will be our candidate for Immortality. At your first opportunity, we want you to approach this person and explain the process. Allow the candidate to weigh the issues, and if the person answers in the affirmative, administer the gift. And, above all, do not mention this to Lao Peng You. He must not learn of your assignment. Do you understand?"

He asked me a direct question and I suppose I may respond.

"I am to play Mahjong later today. When I receive the Plum Flower tile, I shall look for someone eating a plum.

You want me to approach that person at my first opportunity and explain about the life of an Immortal. Should the candidate choose to accept the invitation, I am to administer the gift."

"And…?"

"I am not to inform Lao Peng You."

"Yes, I believe you understand the instructions quite clearly."

"O Great One, you were correct that I do not consider myself fit for the task as I have never given the gift before. Can you choose someone else? I am concerned it might not be possible for me to fulfill this role."

The voice explodes inside my head. "Are you refusing to follow my instructions, Hao Lan!?"

"Of course not, my Lord. I wish to abide by all your commands. My fear is that I have not yet pleasured myself in this fashion, and I may not be able to function as you request. What if I am incapable? I do not wish to disappoint, Shen Lung."

His laughter pealed. "Oh, Little One, you never cease to amuse me."

It appears I have a gift of making other Immortals laugh without intending to do so.

"I have faith that when the time arrives, you will perform as if you have done this all your life. Ha ha ha."

While I still retain my doubts, I do not wish to anger the dragon further. "Yes, my Lord."

"So far, you have served me quite well. Go forth, be a clever bunny, and stop complaining so much."

When I opened my eyes, I saw a white leveret perched on the other end of the bench. It seemed tame, and its over-sized brown eyes peered at me with human-like curiosity. Its twitchy little nose moved in a hypnotic rhythm. How odd to encounter this creature when Shen Lung had moments ago given me the order to *be a clever bunny*. Having yet to decide which path to pursue on my journey of discovery, I resolved to follow the leveret along whichever road it chose.

We stared at each other for a few moments, then it leapt down. I stood up. It hopped back the way I had come, toward the courtyard. The other paths would have to wait for yet another day.

I lost sight of the little hare as I rounded the last bend. At the gaming table I saw Lao Peng You, Fa Sha, and two gentlemen I recognized from the Mahjong Club in Moling, Lord Nanhai and General Sima.

"Ah, Baron Dongting," my *huoban* called out. "Please join us. Fa Sha was just about to leave."

"I was?" questioned Fa Sha, blinking his one remaining eye several times.

"Yes, you were." The Marquis stared at him with lowered brows.

"Oh, yes," Fa Sha burbled. "I just remembered I have something else to do with... someone else... somewhere else... at this particular moment." He collected his coins and stood. "Gentlemen." He nodded with a glare for Lao Peng You.

"Baron, you remember Lord Nanhai and General Sima from the club in Moling?"

"Yes. Welcome to Changshou Shan, gentlemen. Is this your first visit?"

Lord Nanhai smiled. "I believe I came here once many years ago when I needed to spend some time away from my loving wife."

"This is new to me," the General said. "The Lord suggested we enjoy the therapeutic atmosphere this restorative mountain imparts."

"What the General is saying," Lord Nanhai interpreted, "is that he needed to spend some time away from his loving wife."

We all laughed, and I sat down.

"I have no money with me as I did not anticipate playing today."

"Not a problem. I believe I possess the correct medicine for this symptom." Lao Peng You clapped his hands three times. Tian Mei appeared. "Go to the Baron's suite and bring his Mahjong coin purse." The young person disappeared. Again, the servant proved handy.

"We can wash the tiles and build our walls while we wait," my *huoban* said with a wink in my direction.

I am not sure if I wished to perpetuate our previous subterfuge upon these two gentlemen. We used it with them in Moling, and I had concerns they might uncover our strategy if Lao Peng You started winning with hands full of honor tiles again.

Tian Mei appeared as if out of nowhere and dropped my purse on the table. Before I could get another look at that captivating face, she moved to the corner of the gaming area, eyes glued to the ground.

The General sat East this round and rolled the dice to break his wall. We all drew tiles and set our hands. Those with Flowers drew replacements, and we performed the *Tai Feng*. I chose not to pass Lao Peng You any winds or dragons and felt a scowl coming from his direction. Sima began by discarding a Four Dot.

I sat South. The next tile, oddly enough, turned out to be the Plum Flower. My eyes rolled up to the heavens as I thought: *Are you in a hurry, Shen Lung?*

Sweat beaded on my neck as I looked at the others around the table. I feared either Lord Nanhai or General Sima might have been the candidate, as they had made an unforeseen journey to Changshou Shan. Neither man held a piece of fruit. I scanned the area for someone with a plum as I placed the tile face up, but no one possessed such a treat.

I drew my replacement tile, the Spring Flower, with its motif design of a servant. Looking around again, I spotted Tian Mei cowering in the corner nibbling on a large, moist, purple, fleshy, ripe plum.

Oh, no!

Of all people. Tian Mei! The servant girl. Shen Lung wants me to administer the gift to Lao Peng You's new assistant. Misfortune never comes alone. I understood why Shen Lung said I would question his choice of me as gift giver. It made much more sense for the Marquis to administer immortality.

After a few deep breaths and a bit of reflection, I acquiesced because the Blue Dragon has godlike plans for us that we cannot always understand. What should I do?

"Baron, are you still with us?" Lao Peng You jostled my arm, jarring me out of my internal philosophical quandary.

"Yes, pardon me. I am suddenly not feeling well." I placed the tile on the table and drew a replacement.

"Do you need to go back to your rooms?" Lord Nanhai asked.

"You do appear ashen," the General observed.

My mind turned to rubbish. "I... uh... but... uh..."

The Marquis clapped three times. "Tian Mei, escort the Baron back to his suite."

I jumped up like a cornered dog before the young servant could get near to me again. "No, no. I feel able to get there by myself. I shall join you all for dinner." I grabbed my purse and scrambled away.

"Fa Sha!" The Marquis shouted. "Fa Sha! Where did you go?"

Once back in my room, I flopped onto the bed, heart beating like hummingbird wings. Sweat dampened my suit. I could not determine how to still myself. This latest development tested my resolve, my mettle, my faith.

The one person I could ask for help, Lao Peng You, must not learn of my obligation. I would need to sift through this pickle of a predicament on my own. It brought back memories of sailing the Southern Sea on our way to Guizhou. With the boat rocking and pitching, I could only hold on and wait for my world to calm down. Perhaps that strategy would prove successful in this situation as well, like dripping water wearing away a stone.

I noticed the bags of *Jiaogulan* leaves across the room. Next to the door stood the ceramic storage vessel. As an exercise, I decided to put the leaves into the big jar one at a time, instead of just dumping them all at once from the bags. I pulled one sack over to the bed and repositioned the vessel so that I could sit and perform my meditative task. Each leaf appeared as a miniature world, its jagged edges cut a sharp distinction between itself and everything else.

"*Huoban*," roused me from my focused, tranquil preoccupation. "Are you feeling better?"

I stood and went to the door. Lao Peng You entered and strutted about, examining the room, its nature, and the various objects within.

"Very nice, Baron. I believe this is the first time I have ever been in this suite. It suits you well."

"Thank you, Marquis. I believe I am feeling a bit better."

He looked into the jar. "I see you are squirreling away your leaves for another day. What a clever bunny you are." He smiled, but I did not wish to consider the subject of cunning rabbits at the moment. The expression on my face could have signaled distress. "Are you unwell again?"

I looked at him and wished I could explain everything but knew I could not and must not. I would need to find a way to relate my concerns without sharing the details. "Shen Lung appeared to me earlier today and presented a most difficult and puzzling assignment."

"Ah, Shen Lung, the big Blue Dragon." He nodded. "If he saddles you with complex missions, you must have impressed him quite favorably indeed."

I wished that statement could be as reassuring as intended. "Yes, he has confronted me with a most challenging task, one I am not sure I can accomplish."

"And that has you worried. I understand." He patted my shoulder. "I, myself, have had a great number of difficult undertakings to complete, but please keep in mind, if he did not think you capable, he would not have asked."

If only his testimonial would prove true.

He licked his lips and scratched at an ear. "I came by to see if you might be ready to eat."

The mention of food caused my stomach to grumble. "Yes, *huoban*. A meal sounds like a very good idea."

He and I walked to the food table together. We ate with the visiting Lord and General. Conversations ranged widely regarding politics, religion, military strategy, and–of course–Mahjong.

After the sun set, I grew tired, excused myself and returned to the suite. Once I finished putting all the *Jiaogulan* leaves in the urn and sealing it, I lay down on the bed and fell asleep.

"The man who chases two rabbits catches neither," the ruby begins.

Oh, no, not rabbits again.

"I once sacrificed myself as a rabbit," the emerald contributes.

"Rabbits are very clever creatures," the opal comments.

All well and good, but at the moment, rabbits, bunnies, hares, and leverets are not what I wish to discuss. My anger rises like a moth to a fire.

"Shen Lung!" I scream, "Show yourself, Shen Lung! I demand to speak with you!"

"Someone is sour," the red gem admonishes, "Remember the consequences of anger!"

"If you hold onto that bitter, burning coal of anger," the green jewel lectures, "you will most assuredly get burned."

"The sweetest fighter is never angry," the milky white stone bleats.

The sound of flapping wings grows louder behind me. I turn away from the wall and the stones. Shen Lung hovers in front of me.

"You called, my servant?" The great lids lower across his bejeweled eyes.

"You were right, my Lord! I do question your decision to assign me this undertaking. Tian Mei serves Lao Peng You. I have no standing to proceed with this particular task."

"First of all," he snorts a dusty wind from his nose. "You need to calm yourself before we can continue this interview. I am not accustomed to being summoned like a hunting dog."

He maintains correct reasoning. I am but a man, and he is a god. How imprudent of me to request an audience, but I feel profoundly troubled by this situation. Who else could I speak with?

"Yes. Who else could you speak with?" His head moves in a slight motion from side to side. "Have you encountered some difficulties?"

"The servant belongs to Lao Peng You."

He scowls. "No one belongs to anyone else, Hao Lan. Their relationship endures as one of employer and employee. Not your concern." Another snort.

"Even so, O Great One, Tian Mei is but a youth. I cannot in good conscience treat one so young like bartered bean curd."

The dragon's eyelids open to their fullest. "I understand your concerns, Little One, and how they might produce the conflicting emotions you currently experience. I shall ask you to proceed as directed, without further questioning my judgment. All will be revealed in time, and what you perceive by the light of day may unfold in a different way under the moon." He flaps his great wings.

As I feel the wind engulf me, I accept that I must swallow this pickle and obey my overlord.

"Yes, Shen Lung. I shall do as you have commanded."

He lifts his immense body and looks down. "You will be rewarded greatly for your obedience and filial piety." Up he ascends into the sky. "And… Hao Lan… stop complaining so much!"

"I have met the dragon," the ruby brags.

"The dragon is one of the myriad things," the emerald informs.

"I am the dragon," the opal offers. "You are the dragon, we are all the dragon."

An intense light pierced my eyelids. The bright moon swam in the celestial heavens directly outside my window, curtailing my dream state.

I peered into the courtyard. No one else seemed awake at this late hour. Unable to sleep, I considered a stroll in the garden to help relieve these apprehensions regarding my appointed task.

Along the path, statues of people and figurines of animals cast faint shadows in the moonlight. I marveled how the perceived shapes differed from the light of day. Shen Lung had mentioned things might tend to appear altered under the moon. I stopped at the fountain to meditate.

A touch on my shoulder startled me. When I turned about, there knelt Tian Mei, face lowered.

"You could not sleep either?"

The servant's head moved side to side, the silky raven hair swinging in rhythm.

I contemplated the challenges and complications if *I* could not talk. Attempting a conversation would prove difficult.

"Perhaps fate brought you here because I have been asked to speak to you."

The obsidian eyes I encountered previously looked up into mine. The lava flow in my chest began again.

I took a deep breath and sighed before continuing. "A force greater than you or me has requested that I explain something for your consideration." Why would I address this servant like an equal? Something did not feel quite right here.

I presumed the nod signaled me to go on.

"Do you know what immortality is?"

Another nod.

"Lao Peng You and I are two Immortals. We could live forever if we abide by a few simple rules."

Tian Mei continued to stare up into my eyes. I could not look away, even if I tried.

"I have been commanded to offer you this immortality that he and I share."

A smile.

"However, I also need to explain what this would mean for you."

A nod.

"Please listen very carefully to what I have to say."

Another nod.

"If you choose to accept this gift, you will never grow old, but you will never be able to have children either. In order to maintain your immortality, every so often you will have to…"

How does one explain the intricacies of adult intimate behavior to a young person in a tasteful and proper manner?

"…to ingest a man's seed, either here"–I pointed to my mouth–"or here," and I indicated the other end with a grimace, not knowing if I had to explain what *seed* meant. "There are one or two things unavailable to Immortals, as I myself am still learning. One significant disadvantage is that we cannot drink tea. Do you like tea?"

No response.

"If he has not yet done so, Shen Lung, the heavenly Blue Dragon, will appear to you in a dream. From time to time, he might give you… assignments to complete."

A few blinks.

"Well, in any case, if you do decide to accept the offer to become an Immortal, we shall have to spend some physically intimate time together. I do not expect you to comprehend what that might involve, but please understand that there may be some unpleasant or uncomfortable worldly business between us."

A nod.

"I shall leave you to contemplate these words. Please let me know what you decide. Any questions?"

Two round, large, moist, dark eyes beamed up at me. How silly. A mute person could not ask questions.

"Can I be assured that you understood all I told you?"

Nod.

"I shall return to my suite now. Please visit me at your leisure."

It took a great deal of determination and much self-control to turn away and return to my rooms. I had complied with Shen Lung's request and invited a mere youth into the ranks of the Immortals. Experience has shown that my little bird did not work with women. But Shen Lung informed me I would be able to perform when the need arose.

I had no desire to corrupt one so young, but I also had no desire to disobey the god who held my very life in his very sharp claws. If I did not comply with his instructions, I could find myself a decrepit *Jiangshi*, hopping my way back to Wu Chu like an undead bunny.

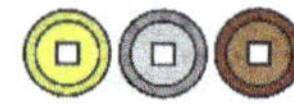

The rapping at my door made a faint noise, but I heard it. An hour or so had elapsed since my encounter with the young plum eater. The throbbing lava rushed up into my ears, and it felt as if my head might explode.

Tian Mei stood outside, hands clasped at the waist. I beckoned the servant in and closed the door behind.

"Have you made a decision?"

A nod.

"So quickly?"

More nodding.

I could only imagine Shen Lung appeared to the servant and presented the same information as he did with me. The dragon probably preferred someone who would not speak back.

"What have you decided?"

Tian Mei reached to untie a sash and open the servant robe. I knew I should look away and not gaze upon this youngster's virgin body. However, once the fabric parted, I realized that no youngster stood before me. Neither a woman nor girl!

The most beautiful–and largest–little brother I have ever witnessed poked out from his midsection. It resembled a gently curving cucumber.

Even though Tian Mei had a man's body, he presented himself to the world as a young woman. My brain sparked as I recognized how this might be a great advantage in the time ahead if I could find a way to acquire him from the Marquis. To the rest of the world, we would appear as a man and his lady, but in private, he could provide the seed of immortality I required. I would no longer need to seek the favor of male strangers. However, that would mean disobeying Shen Lung's order to make Tian Mei an Immortal.

His eyebrows raised in a question. Did he want to know if I liked what I saw? Might he want me to administer the gift of immortality? If only he could verbalize his inquiry. What would he ask?

He smiled and touched his bird in flight. It beckoned me, but I could not grasp why. I had not felt this fascination with little brothers before. My knees buckled.

Tian Mei caught me before I fell down and guided me to the bed. Once our flesh met, I knew what I wanted and how I wanted it. Even though I had recently taken my nourishment from Daniao, the kitchen worker, a craving for seed screamed and roared within my brain.

The young man removed my trousers in one motion, pulling the leg openings away with both hands. Pale silk fluttered across the room. My feet rose into the night as if under phantom control. Using his saliva, he prepared himself for pleasuring us both. I accepted his readiness to burst my chrysanthemum.

The sensation of his penetration induced more of the lava stream around my heart I had already experienced in his charming presence. I must have produced a loud groan because he put a shushing finger up to his painted little lips.

With each subsequent thrust my spirit rose further into the heavens, the moonlight through the window showering us with rabbit love. Over and over and over and over, he impaled me with such intensity and affection as I had never known.

Fire within me burned hot and fervid, and I could no longer contain myself. Without a touch, my own seed shot out in ribbons landing on my face, in my hair, and beyond. I did not know if I issued any noise, but from the excitement and pleasure I experienced, I should have produced a wild mating call that all the beasts for many *li* around could hear.

Seeing his tightly closed eyes, I could only imagine he felt something similar. The pounding ceased and he climbed on top of me, hugging me, kissing my neck and shoulders.

Never having been loved like this before, neither by man nor woman, this new sensation proved quite alluring. I kissed him back with great passion and enthusiasm. Before long, both of us appeared ready to repeat our sacred act.

I had no screaming desire for more seed as when another man touched me and could not understand why I wished to do this again so soon. But if it meant that Tian Mei would spend more moments with me, I wanted to encourage that.

This second time, he entered me from behind, lying front-to-back on the bed, reaching his hand around to pleasure me. The intensity did not feel as formidable, and the finale took longer to achieve, but the hot lava within my body flowed with more furor as I gave myself to this young man who masqueraded as a serv-ant girl.

We fell asleep together, him behind me, hugging me, holding me, loving me.

11. The Roll of the Dice

"It is more shameful to distrust our friends than to be deceived by them," the ruby instructs.

"When one is in love, one always begins by deceiving oneself," the emerald chimes in. "And one always ends by deceiving others."

"All warfare is based on deception," the opal quotes from Sun Tzu.

"Why are you all talking about deceit?" I ask.

"Is it not clear?"

"Are you feeling guilty about something?"

"Deception is outside the flow of things."

It seems the three of them want to gang up on me for some reason I cannot understand. I enjoy it more when they just mumble unintelligible epigrams.

"Shen Lung has requested specific action from you."

"You have not complied with his instructions."

"Pihua! It is all pihua!"

"How can you know what I have or have not done?" I inquire.

"The son's only gift is obedience," the red jewel intones. "Sour."

"Nothing is so obedient as a disciplined mind," the green gem suggests. "Bitter."

"When one follows the flow, he is in nature," the sparkly white stone imparts. "Sweet!"

Once again, they attempt to convey a message I cannot quite grasp in the moment.

Persistent knocking at my door woke me.

"*Huoban*, are you awake?" Lao Peng You called. "I can't find Tian Mei anywhere."

Before I could answer, I felt a small hand cover my mouth. Of course. The missing servant. When I looked at the person connected to the small hand, he put a finger up to his lips. I nodded and he pulled his hand away.

The Marquis cried out, "Hao Lan?"

Footsteps trailed off.

"Does he know you are a man?" I stared into the dark moons of Tian Mei's eyes.

He nodded.

"I see. This does complicate things, does it not?"

He nodded again.

"You need to leave while he is not out there. Perhaps you can go back to the garden. Tell him you fell asleep out there." Oh, wait. "You are not able to tell him anything."

He shook his head.

"Do you want him to know you were here with me?"

Again, head shaking to indicate *No*.

He picked up his robe, slipped into it, kissed me on the cheek, and left the suite. My heart paused. I needed to depend on the boy's own abilities for dealing with his master.

This new set of rooms has pleasant facilities for bathing oneself, and I prepared myself to face the day and Lao Peng You in a most leisurely fashion. This also gave me time to reflect on what happened last night and how I finally shared my bed with another person. My old self would have wished for a woman, but at this point in my immortal existence I needed someone who could supply me with long-life nourishment on an ongoing basis. How pleasant to have the same person for that fulfillment. It would mean a great deal to me with someone this lovely. Surely, this path would bring admonishment from Shen Lung.

When I arrived at the food table, my *huoban* sat motionless, not eating, shoulders slumped. "Is something concerning you, Marquis?"

He looked up with slightly reddened eyes. "My new servant, Tian Mei, has run away. I cannot find her anywhere. Have you seen her?"

Not a question I would choose to answer with total, outright truth. "Have you checked the garden? I saw her there last night, sitting on a bench under the moon."

"No, I have not." He jumped up and paraded toward the path. I followed.

A few steps around the first bend, Tian Mei lay curled up on one of the benches.

"Tian Mei!" my *huoban* proclaimed, "I was worried that you had run off. Did you sleep here all night?"

I imagined he would not like to answer that question. He bowed his head and smiled.

"She must have fallen asleep out here. Lazy girl! Come, eat breakfast!" Lao Peng You grabbed Tian Mei by the elbow and dragged him back to the food table. The young man looked back at me with a coy side glance as his master hustled him away. I nodded, attempting to provide a bit of reassurance.

Deception. The word stung my mind.

Back at the food table, the Marquis ate from his bowl while Tian Mei stood in the kitchen. I sat with my *huoban*, "Are you planning to play Mahjong today?"

He nodded. "Of course. And you should return to the table as a sign of respect to Lord Nanhai and General Sima. You left rather precipitously yesterday."

"But we all dined together last evening," I countered.

"Yes, but you have not yet surrendered any of your coins to them."

Apparently, my *huoban* had a special plan for me. "I am to lose to our esteemed visitors?"

"Yes." He continued to munch on a fish, which he washed down with rice wine.

"That does not seem fair. Why should I be the one to contribute my money? What about you?"

He raised a faint smile. "You do not need to let them keep it, *huoban.* Just allow them to hold on to it for a short while."

I see. Out of *respect* I should let them have some of my coins and then win them back. Respectful, perhaps, but rather discourteous overall. Oh well, I shall end up with more than I had started.

My stomach grumbled. I moved to the food display and assembled a few things in a bowl: cold rice, plum slices, and a bean cake. I still distrusted the *zongzi*, even though they appeared and smelled delicious.

As I sat, Lao Peng You looked over. "No *Jiaogulan* this morning? Are you already disgusted by its revolting taste?"

In my haste, I had forgotten to bring some leaves with me. "Marquis, it appears I have left my suite without it. I shall have some rice wine this morning instead." I reached for the bottle in front of him.

He blocked my arm and cried, "No!" This move surprised me as he usually espoused rice wine. "I will have Tian Mei get some leaves for you." He clapped three times and the servant appeared. "Tian Mei, go to the Baron's suite and bring a handful of the *Jiaogulan* leaves from that container you cleaned yesterday."

The servant bowed and ran off to my rooms.

"That is not necessary, Marquis. I am fine with –"

"No," he interrupted. "It is quite necessary. I must give the young one more commands to follow in order to instill obedience."

Tian Mei scurried toward me with a fistful of leaves.

"Now, take those leaves to the kitchen, crush them into a pot with hot water, and bring that–and a cup–back for the Baron."

The servant bowed yet again and ran off to the kitchen. I felt a twinge of jealousy as I watched my *huoban* dictate orders to my new lover, but the boy was his for the moment.

"Discipline," stated Lao Peng You. "Administer it early and often if you wish a deferential servant."

This reminded me all too much of my days in the cinnabar mines at Dong Ping. Each new supervisor would attempt to instill a sense of obedience into us by shouting unnecessary and contradictory orders over and over. They seemed to think that barking like a rabid wolf made us fear them. It only served to engender hatred and distrust. I could only imagine the same thing happening with Tian Mei.

Later that morning we joined Fa Sha, Lord Nanhai, and General Sima at the Mahjong table. Lao Peng You indicated I should play, and he stood off to the side, observing.

"I do hope you will be able to complete a game with us." Fa Sha squinted his remaining eye at me.

"As do I." I gazed to heaven and sat.

Lord Nanhai handed me the bone dice. "We shall let you roll for position first."

I dropped the pair of cubes in the bowl. Looking back up at me, the two dice displayed one pip each, which some people referred to as *Eyes of the Snake.*

"It does not appear you will be East," observed General Sima.

"It does not appear," I repeated and handed the dice to him.

Throughout the play, any time I rolled the cubes, they displayed only the side with one dot. After the third such repetition, I felt nervous.

"The odds of that happening again are infinitesimal," observed Lord Nanhai.

"One in 60,466,176, to be exact," the Marquis stated.

The three of us stared at him in disbelief, Fa Sha's eye fully open.

"Why do you all look so surprised? I have studied the mathematical arts at great length. I can tell you the chances of turning up a Red Dragon, a Flower, any tile you choose at any point in the game." Eyebrows raised even farther. "How do you think I got to be such a good player?" He grinned, seeming rather satisfied with himself.

At the end of play, I had rolled *Eyes of the Snake* five more times. I lost considerable sums to both the Lord and the General, only to win them back twofold. My personal fortunes amounted to more than it would cost to buy the entire valley of Dongting outright. Perhaps I should consider such a purchase, if only to justify my ill-gotten title.

That evening, Lord Nanhai and General Sima joined us for dinner again. I found it difficult to keep my attention on the table while Tian Mei stood off to the side during the entire meal. I tried as best as I could to not look at him, which proved quite challenging. Very pretty as a young woman, I believed every other man wished they could have some time with him alone. The urge to keep him all to myself swelled within, inflaming my breast. They say two tigers cannot share one jungle.

As I left the table, I observed Daniao looking at me from the kitchen. I had never known the tender touch of another man in my life. Suddenly, I had two people–at the same time–who seemed interested in being with me. My mind felt overwhelmed and confused. While I had never sought the affections of men before, it appeared they would become my primary source of intimacy.

Back in my suite, I contemplated the consequences of my disobedience. Shen Lung would surely be dissatisfied with my actions. I could only hope he would understand my reasons and grant me this one wish.

Knocking on my doorframe sounded faint, barely audible. Had Tian Mei come to pay me another visit? I rushed to the door only to find Daniao standing there.

"Baron, I hope I am not intruding." He seemed intent on entering my rooms.

"No, Daniao, of course not. What brings you here?" I observed a swelling in his pants.

He faced downward and shuffled before speaking. "I was hoping I might be able to… well… spend some time like we did before." The obvious bulge casting a shadow.

I felt fond of him and enjoyed our previous visit, but since I met Tian Mei, my focus shifted. "Daniao, I appreciate your request, but I am unable to fulfill it just now."

"So sorry to bother you, Baron," he turned away, head hanging low.

"Wait," I said for some reason I did not understand in the moment. He faced me again. When I noticed his teary eyes, the words came to me. "I want you to know that I very much enjoyed our encounter, but I do not know if I can repeat it. I hope you can accept that."

He bowed with reverence. "Yes, Baron." Off he went into the night.

I lay on my bed, heart churning, until I finally fell asleep.

"Hao Lan!" The voice of the Blue Dragon echoes through my skull. "Hao Lan!"

When I open my eyes, it appears I am standing on a great barren plain, something like I would expect the Gobi region to look like, desolate, unforgiving. Above me hovers a great blue beast with wildly whirling, iridescent eyes.

"Yes, my Lord."

"Have you completed your assignment?" he roars.

This question surprises me because he should know the answer.

"I have not yet accomplished the objective, but I have begun."

"I see." His fiery tone diminishes, but not much. "Have you explained the terms of immortality to our candidate?"

"Yes, my Lord, I have."

"And is the candidate willing to accept the gift we wish to give?"

"I do not know, Shen Lung."

"Do you mean you do not know, or you do not wish to know? Which is it, my little servant?" the anger returns.

It becomes difficult to answer his questions with the whole truth.

"The candidate is mute and cannot speak."

"Communication is still possible." He bellows and snorts. A huge plume of dust rises in a cyclone from the ground nearby.

"Of course, O Great One, but the candidate has not yet indicated a decision." I hope that answer mollifies him.

"Hmmmmm." The speed of the wings flapping slows a bit. *"And when do you think the candidate will give a response?"*

How can he expect me to predict such an event? I imagine he knows the answer and wants to see if I can figure this out.

"That is not for me to say, my Lord. I am but your humble servant."

"A humble servant who may have ulterior motives, I suspect," he snarls. The great wings flap hard enough to stir up dust from the ground.

I choke and cough. *"My Lord, I live to serve you."* I try to bow, but the dust is too thick.

"If you do indeed live to serve me..." He snorts. *"Complete your assignment without delay!"* The majestic dragon rises.

"I shall enquire again at my next opportunity, O Great One."

"See that you do, Hao Lan. See that you do." He disappears into the rising cloud of black dust.

Once again, the bright moon bathed my suite through the window, rousing me. In the garden, a shadowy form lingered along the path. I left the room and approached Tian Mei, who stood near one of the benches.

A smile spread all the way across his beautiful little face as I approached. Two orbs of polished coal beamed at me. I signaled for him to follow me back to my room.

Once inside, I checked to see that no one had observed us and closed the door.

The guarded manner in which he held himself seemed different. "Are you all right?" I had concerns about the way Lao Peng You treated him.

Tian Mei nodded, but I could see a scratch on his right cheek that powder could not cover.

"Did your master strike you?" I pointed to the wound.

He lowered his head.

"It pains me to see the way he handles you."

Tian Mei looked into my eyes once more.

"I worked in a cinnabar mine before... well... before I became immortal." I thought it best to save that story for another time. "I know how it feels to be downtrodden."

He nodded.

"Tian Mei, I have something very important to discuss with you. Please sit." I indicated the end of my bed.

He sat in the fashion of a hesitant dainty lady, arms folded, ankles crossed. How long had it taken him to acquire these behaviors?

"As I told you before, I have instructions from a force greater than you or me. At some point I have to bring you into the community of Immortals, but when I do that, it will mean that I can no longer obtain sustenance from you. Do you understand?"

He shook his head *No* in slight motions.

"I wish I knew how to explain it better." I trod a razor-thin line with this. "People like us require the seed of men who are not immortal, in order to maintain their longevity. If I give you the gift of immortality, I can no longer thrive from *your* seed. Is that clear?"

His head bobbed in slow nods.

"We have a decision to make."

Our gazes met.

"Yes. You and I, both. We need to make this choice together."

The grin on his face seemed to indicate appreciation. Perhaps no one had ever included him in a decision before. As a mute, he could not speak up for himself.

"Here are the options: I can refrain from giving you the gift of immortality, which means you would age normally and that I could continue to receive sustenance from you."

He smiled.

"In the alternative, I could make you immortal, but then I would have to look for sustenance elsewhere, as would you."

His head shook from side to side, and he frowned.

"According to my instructions, I am supposed to tell you about immortality and ask you whether you wish to receive the gift. I have accomplished that."

He nodded.

"Then I must ask you if you want to become immortal under those terms."

He turned his head to the side.

"When I ask you if you wish immortality, you are free to answer as you feel."

He faced me and nodded again.

I looked directly at the lovely young man, wanting to hug him, keep him safe.

"Are you ready to answer my question?"

He nodded.

"Well then, do you wish me to give you the gift of immortality?" I held my breath, hoping beyond hope that he would choose what I wanted him to choose.

He just stared at me, then smiled. After several moments, he moved his head slowly left then right, again and again. I grabbed him and hugged him and kissed him.

"Thank you," I whispered.

We lay down on the bed together, just holding each other. At some point I must have fallen asleep.

"If either wealth or poverty are come by honestly," the red stone begins, "there is no shame."

"It is best to be honest in all things," the green stone contributes, "not just when it suits us."

"Be honest with those who are also honest," the milky white stone adds, "and also be honest to those who are not."

I feel a light kiss on my right cheek. When I look to see who committed this act, a petite young woman stands next to me. She wears the traditional coarse-woven, dull-colored fabric of peasant clothes, similar to what I wore back in Wu Chu.

"Please do not tell my husband, the old farmer," she requests. "He is very jealous."

A massive man in dusty farmer's clothes appears. His head resembles a lumpy ginger root, and his face looks to have been bashed by a sharp rock several times. In his right hand, he holds a rusty, but sharp-looking, bident hayfork.

"Did you kiss my wife?" he growls with a voice reminiscent of the rice mill.

"I did not, sir." I turn to the young woman, and she nods.

"That is good," he acknowledges. "Because if you had, I would have to kill you." He shakes the hayfork as if intending to use it on me.

Fortunately for me, his threat is immaterial. He can attempt to kill me all he wants. I have survived Gu poison, and I believe assault with a hayfork would probably tickle.

The pretty woman shuffles back to her husband. He looks at her lips and then at me.

"Did my wife kiss you?" he snarls. "Because if she did, I shall have to kill her." He shakes the bident again while scowling at the woman.

So, here lies the heart of this conundrum. If I tell the truth, the farmer will kill the woman. If I lie, the woman is safe, but I have spoken an untruth.

"If you lie to me, and I discover the truth, I shall kill you twice!" He waggles the hayfork.

Kill me once, shame on you. Kill me twice, shame on me.

I must consider my options. While my life may not be in immediate danger, if I do not solve this particular riddle with correct reasoning, I know it will come back to haunt me again.

"My good sir," I begin, trusting the appropriate words would fill my head as I spoke. "Those are but two possibilities. However, there are two more that we must consider before passing judgment."

His face scrunches in confusion. "Pray, do not attempt to take advantage of my educational insufficiency. I do not fully understand what you say, but please proceed. I shall attempt to be patient." His grip on the fork seems tight enough to snap the pole.

"Consider the possibility that your wife did kiss me, and I do tell you about it."

He scowls.

"Please, sir, I am just enumerating possibilities, not declaring what transpired. In this case, anger toward your wife would be justified, but you should have no dispute with me because I spoke the truth to you."

The farmer's baffled appearance persists. Blood pounds in my ears. At least I have delayed the looming conclusion.

"The final possibility to consider..."–I take a breath to calm myself–"...is that your wife did not kiss me at all, and there is nothing to relate to you. You would then have no reason to harm either me or your wife."

He looks down at the dirt, up at the sky, at his wife, at me, at the fork.

"Only one of these scenarios preserves your wife. If you wish to keep her, the last proposition appears the most reasonable." I smile down at the woman, and she smiles up at her husband's tormented expression.

There. I had illuminated the situation with clever logic, did not admit guilt, and did not condemn the beautiful young woman. I hope that satisfies him.

"I do not like you!" he screams. "You fill the air with confusing babble!" He charges at me with the hayfork lowered in gouging position.

A light kiss on the right cheek woke me. I saw the back of Tian Mei's robe as it passed out the door, which brought joy to my heart. He had slept with me again and would be able to return to Lao Peng You's rooms before the Marquis discovered his absence.

So much subterfuge:

–The underhanded confederacy at Mahjong.

–My appropriated title of Baron.

–Wang Yue's attempt to determine my immortality.

–The Emperor's underground empire.

–My effort to mislead Shen Lung.

–The love between me and Tian Mei.

As in all good tales, the transgressor will receive punishment or comeuppance at some point, burnt by the very fire employed to deceive others. In this particular tale, however, it grew increasingly difficult to determine exactly whom the transgressor might be.

Once I readied myself for the new day, I headed to the food table, this time with a small handful of leaves. As expected, Lao Peng You sat before a bowl teeming with food, stuffing his mouth. Tian Mei stood off in a corner. Daniao peeked out from the kitchen. Before sitting, I approached Daniao to request hot water and a cup. He fulfilled my wish without a word. I thanked him, put the leaves in the pot, began counting my breaths, and returned to the table where my *huoban* sat eating.

"Good morning, Marquis. I hope you slept well." After setting the cup and steeping tea on the table, I took some rice and beancakes for my bowl. *Eleven... twelve...*

He looked up with bulging cheeks. A few chews and a swallow later, "Yes, very well thank you. I hope you are prepared for another exhilarating day at the Mahjong table."

After yesterday, I am not sure I want to spend another *exhilarating day* rolling *Eyes of the Snake* every time. Perhaps I could return to the distant part of the garden and continue my walking instead.

"*Huoban*, I am not sure that I shall be joining you this morning. My wished-for walk in the garden ended prematurely the other day, and I desire to go back and follow the other paths." *Thirty-and-seven... thirty-and-eight...*

"As you wish." He waved his hand. "I had hoped you would help me empty the coffers of Lord Nanhai and General Sima before they return to Moling tomorrow."

"Perhaps I can join you later in the day for the dramatic finish you so much enjoy. Do you anticipate fireworks?"

He paused in thought. "Yes, that would please me very much if you could be there for the spectacular conclusion." He issued a complacent smile.

I glimpsed Tian Mei abiding in the corner, a furtive gaze at me every so often. The lava flow within my chest began again. My future happiness would be agreeably augmented if I could get the youth away from the Marquis.

Exactly seventy breaths had passed, no more and no less. I poured the tea into the cup.

"*Huoban*, how have you been getting on with your new servant?" I asked with a fleeting look before taking my first sip.

His eyebrows lifted and his head tilted a bit. "She has much to learn. I do not know what that bloated ball of blubber ever saw in her."

I believed I knew just what Wang Yue saw and felt fairly certain the Marquis saw it as well.

Lao Peng You pointed a finger in Tian Mei's direction. "She is disrespectful, unhelpful, and arrogant."

Which I interpreted to mean the servant did not obey the master's every wish with unqualified obedience.

"However, I intend to break her of these bad habits. For if she wishes to continue in my employ, this situation must improve."

"Oh, my," I blurted without intention. "Oh, my," I repeated to suggest I was sympathetic to Lao Peng You's difficulties, not those of Tian Mei. "Perhaps you might desire a change of servant, *huoban*."

"Oh, no," the Marquis declared. "This one has been sent to serve me, and we shall work together to forge a bond of mutual respect."

Which I interpreted to mean Lao Peng You would continue to erode and wear down Tian Mei until the servant submitted to the master without question or objection. Poor Tian Mei. Browbeaten and mute. I certainly would not wish to live at the end of my *huoban*'s puppet strings.

"Please keep in mind you cannot force a plant to grow by tugging at it." I could not think of anything else to say without giving away my true feelings for his servant.

He aimed a half-lidded eye in my direction. "More of your Confucian wisdom?"

"My concerns linger with *you*, Marquis. You sound frustrated with the current circumstances. Perhaps you can soon reach a satisfactory state." I took a few more bites of the meager meal I had assembled followed by some *Jiaogulan* tea.

"Thank you, my friend. How are you getting on with Daniao?"

I had been staring at Tian Mei, and the question startled me. "Daniao?"

"The kitchen fellow. I have seen him go to your suite a few times, and his adoring regard for you is unmistakable. Perhaps you have found a suitable ongoing companion for yourself."

"Yes, the fellow is quite pleasant, indeed. I have enjoyed our time together. I shall consider your suggestion very thoughtfully."

Of course, my preference would have been to whisk Tian Mei away from the Marquis and have just the two of us travel around until we had enjoyed everything there is to see in this astonishing world. From the way my *huoban* talked about Tian Mei, it sounded like he would never entertain the idea of releasing the servant from his indentures. At least not just yet.

Lao Peng You looked at me with a quirky smile. "I just want you to be happy, Hao Lan."

I wondered if he really knew what would really make me really happy. "Thank you, *huoban*." I stood after finishing my breakfast. "I believe I shall now begin my journey into the outer garden. I wish you well at Mahjong."

"Thank you, Baron. I look forward to you joining us later in the day."

I started down the path through the garden to the crossroads.

Three claps rang out followed by the sharp cry, "Tian Mei!"

My body convulsed.

As I meandered along the garden path by the creek with the mossless stones again, I considered how to procure the servant from Lao Peng You without damaging our association. It already taxed my mind without end to maintain a tenuous equilibrium in my interactions with Shen Lung. The blue dragon could terminate my insignificant existence at any moment, should I displease him. I desired to wrestle the servant away from the Marquis, but any method for this goal eluded me in the moment.

I reached the intersection and stood before the granite bench beneath an old gingko. Three paths diverged ahead of me. All of a sudden, I felt rather drowsy. I decided to take a brief rest before I pressed on.

Sitting on the stone bench, I survey the first path, the one with red dirt. In the center of the lane, a teapot and cup sit on the ground, as if someone had placed them there for me. I stand up, walk to them, and crouch down. The aroma smells much like Jiaogulan steeped for exactly seventy breaths, no more, no less. I pour from the pot into the cup and taste. It is, indeed, Jiaogulan, but it has a slightly sour taste.

I stand up and bring the teacup with me as I take my first steps along the barren path. This narrow route proceeds along the steep side of a mountain. On my right, a jagged cliffside up. On the left, a sheer drop of a li or so. The challenge appears remaining in the center of the lane as I follow along.

After a few twists and bends, I see a figure ahead in the road. As I approach, I recognize Daniao, who smiles at me. I finish the tea and hand him the empty cup. He tosses it over the side of the mountain and places a hand on the back of my neck.

The touch of his skin ignites passion within me. I bend down and pull at his drawers, freeing his little brother. When I begin sucking on it, Daniao moans with pleasure. The rapturous sounds reverberate off the mountainside throughout the valley. At his climax, he grunts so loudly, the path starts to crumble beneath us.

To keep from falling into the deep valley, I run back toward the bench and gingko. I look behind to see Daniao tumbling down the steep cliff, but there is nothing I can do to help him. I sit again to catch my breath.

How horrible! My friend's pleasure led to his demise. The scene replays itself before my eyes.

When my heartbeat slows, I look at the beginning of the second path, the one leading into the green woods, I spot a plum on the ground, as if someone had left it there for me. I walk to the fruit, pick it up, and take a bite. Very juicy, but a bit bitter.

This trail leads up and through one of the stands of trees atop Changshou Shan. I continue to nibble on the stumbled-upon plum. After a while, the path levels out, and I see the misty valley below. A bit farther the trees become dense. Sunlight no longer shines through them.

From behind one of the maples steps Tian Mei. He smiles at me. I finish the flesh of the fruit and hand him the stone. He tosses it into the trees, reaches out, and takes my hands. As soon as our flesh touches, fiery passion ignites again. I must have him inside me!

The young man uses gentle force to push me down toward the forest floor so that I am resting on my hands and knees, like a dog. He pulls down my trousers and plucks my willing chrysanthemum. The intense pleasure causes me to gasp and moan. In and out he goes, again and again. While he does not utter any sounds, I sense his impending explosion. When he empties his seed, the sensation of warm fullness reminds me of the hot water colon therapy my physician used to administer.

As I look back to my lover, trees around us begin to tumble. Tian Mei stands up, and a large mulberry tree falls on him. My heart turns cold when I realize I cannot save him. I run back through the jumble of toppling trees to the gingko again and sit on the bench.

This is horrible! The two men with whom I have most recently shared intimacy have just been killed following pleasure. I pray to the gods for no more deaths.

On the third path, the one leading into the white stones, I spy on the ground a blank Mahjong tile, which represents the White Dragon. I pick up the sweet-smelling bamboo piece and follow the winding trail down into a narrow valley full of pale, rugged rocks.

A high-pitched voice reverberates, "Two men fell into a raging river. One attempted to fight the current, hoping to take control of his situation. As he struggled in vain, the rapids dashed him into a sharp rock, killing him."

I do not like this story.

"The other fellow," the voice continues, "merely relaxed, letting the current gently carry him safely to shore."

I look at the undecorated tile and toss it away. The earth trembles. White boulders fall all around me. As I run back to the gingko, the voice sings out again, "Which man will you be, Hao Lan? Which man?"

The largest stone I have ever seen heads directly toward my face.

I sat up with a start. It appeared that, once again, I fell asleep on the bench. The deaths had only been part of a dream, my thanks to the gods.

The position of the sun indicated mid-afternoon. I felt it would be best to return to the game area and assist Lao Peng You with his masterstroke.

These various paths would have to wait for yet another time.

12. Topsy-Turvy

Back at the Mahjong table, Lao Peng You sat with Lord Nanhai, General Sima, and one person I did not recognize. It did not matter because just as I approached, my *huoban* issued the familiar, "I shall settle with you later in private. You must now leave the table as you have no more money. Next!"

The Marquis saw me approach and beckoned with an open hand as the unknown unfortunate walked away. "Baron, I hope you are coming to join us."

I nodded and sat in the vacated position.

Lao Peng You clapped his hands three times. "Tian Mei! Retrieve the Baron's coin purse from his room."

My fists balled in reaction to the harsh command.

The servant bowed and sped away without looking in my direction. I so wanted to gaze into his eyes again but knew that must wait until later.

"Lord Nanhai, General Sima, how nice to see you again." I nodded to each of the visitors. "I hear you are leaving us tomorrow."

"Yes, very early in the morning," Lord Nanhai responded. "Our carriage arrives before dawn. We must return to Moling as soon as possible."

"Have you considered taking a boat down the Yangtze River?" I suggested. "The Marquis and I had a rather enjoyable voyage recently."

Lord Nanhai glanced at General Sima with a snicker. "Some people do not travel as well upon the waters as others."

The General lowered his head and blushed.

Tian Mei returned with my purse. I made sure not to touch him because I knew it would ignite my passions. When he dropped the bag into my hands, I took a calming breath before saying, "Thank you, Tian Mei."

"Do not encourage the help!" scolded Lao Peng You. "I do not want my servant to believe we appreciate the work any more than I've already paid for!"

Tian Mei backed into a corner, bowing and groveling.

My word! I worried that if I could not develop some sort of scheme to get him away from the Marquis, this sort of maltreatment could result in permanent injury.

After a few hands, our totals remained about the same as when we began. My mind kept drifting off to Tian Mei, the garden path, and the terrifying dream. From time to time my *huoban* had to prompt me to play.

On one hand, I attained Mahjong with a worthless Chow, a few Pungs, and a pair of White Dragons, not a very high paying hand at all.

Lord Nanhai took notice of the tiles, and his face twisted into a pallid, frightened expression.

"What is troubling you?" I questioned. "Has a black crow perched on your gravestone?"

"Did you not notice, Baron?" He pointed a knobby finger at the tiles.

"Notice what, my lord?"

"You can invert all of them without change." His face continued to pale.

I looked again and observed the curiosity. Without intention, my hand consisted of tiles that appeared the same when turned upside-down: the White Dragon, the One, Two, Four, Five and Eight Dots, the Two, Four, Five, Six, Eight, and Nine Bamboo.

With widest eyes, he pronounced in a rather serious tone, "It is the *Topsy-Turvy* hand. Everything will now be different for you."

Lao Peng You laughed in scorn. "Such nonsense. Superstitious piffle."

Lord Nanhai turned to the Marquis. "Mark these words, my friend. Many things are about to change."

My *huoban* chortled and snorted. "Tian Mei! Bring us a new flask of rice wine!"

Change approached in a single stride. After a few hands, Lord Nanhai and General Sima accumulated most of the table's wealth. The Marquis and I had lost nearly all our coins. His principal plan comprised possessing our visitors' wealth, not the other way round. Lao Peng You glanced at me sidelong with a fearful look I had not yet witnessed.

The session ended when Lord Nanhai produced a hand known as *The Wriggling Serpent*: single Bamboo tiles One through Nine, a Pung of Green Dragons, and a pair of East Winds to match his position. A limit hand, and neither the Marquis nor I had sufficient coins left to settle our debts.

"Gentlemen," the Lord began, "it has been a pleasure playing Mahjong with you both again. I see that you do not have sufficient coins to cover the score, but let us not quibble among friends over such a trifling amount." He and the General stood, shoveling all the coins into their purses. "Perhaps the next time you are in Moling, we can give it another go. However, we must turn in early and cannot dine with you. A good evening to you both." They toddled off to their rooms.

"Of all the white-eyed things…" Lao Peng You trailed off. I could only imagine the anger after he had anticipated his *dramatic finish, fireworks optional.* Again, he appeared ready to launch himself skyward without the thrust of fire medicine.

"*Huoban?*" I prompted.

"They must have figured out our system and used it against us!" he proclaimed. "And then, to dispatch us with *The Wriggling Serpent*! What gambling rogues they are." He hung his head and shook it.

Use of *The Wriggling Serpent* seemed to have a hidden meaning attached to it.

Words popped into my mind. "It is more shameful to distrust our friends than to be deceived by them."

"Piffle," Lao Peng You dismissed.

"Perhaps some food will help you feel better and take your mind off of this pecuniary insult," I proposed as I stood.

"Perhaps you are correct, *huoban.*" He rose. "Perhaps you are correct."

We walked to the food table and shared a rather quiet dinner.

That night I waited by my window, looking into the garden, hoping for Tian Mei to return. My eyes kept closing despite wanting to remain awake, and I finally dragged myself to bed.

"They must often change, who would be constant in happiness or wisdom," the red gem begins.

"When words are both true and kind they can change our world," the green jewel continues.

"If you do not change direction, you may end up where you are heading," the sparkly white stone concludes.

It would appear tonight's lesson involves change. My life has certainly seen a great deal of it in the last moon. I became immortal, possessed wealth beyond belief, traveled upon river and sea, discovered a lost treasure, visited the Emperor at his underground palace, and flew on dragons. None of which could have ever happened had I remained a poor, wretched cinnabar mine worker from Hunan.

Behind me I hear an unusual noise, like dried seeds rattling in a bottle, or rain on dry land. I turn about and observe a long-haired man with a short beard wearing a bamboo peasant hat sitting on a woven mat. He throws down a collection of sticks from a cup, then divides them into groups, over and over again, counting them out, placing some between his fingers as he does so.

I observe the proceedings and walk toward him. Every so often he makes a mark on the ground alongside the mat.

"May I inquire as to what it is you are doing?" I ask.

He looks up without an expression of surprise, as if he knew I had been standing there all the time. "This is Yi Jing."

My raised eyebrows must have communicated lack of knowledge.

"From The Classic of Changes," *he informs me.*

Now, I see where the subject of change fits in. I had not heard of that particular book before.

"By counting the yarrow sticks, I generate a pattern of six lines, some broken, some unbroken." The design he had scratched reveals one broken line, three solid lines, one more broken line, and, at the bottom, a solid line. "This signifies Skinning"–he points at the set of lines–"which indicates inevitable change."

"What does that mean?" I ask.

The man tilts his head and closes one eye. A few moments later he says, "I am not sure. What do you think it means?"

How am I supposed to know the interpretation of something I have never seen before? Perhaps this is part of the lesson.

"I have heard that if you never change direction, you may inadvertently get to the destination you were originally heading toward in the first place." I figure that a good response as any.

He wrinkles his face. "That makes no sense at all."

"I agree. I don't understand it either, but I did hear it recently. Or maybe something very close to that."

The fellow wipes the dirt, erasing the set of lines. He picks up the cup and puts the sticks back into it. "Perhaps you would like to give this a try." He hands them to me.

"And what am I supposed to do?" I cannot count the exact number of sticks, but it has to be at least thirty.

"Choose one of the sticks and place it here on the ground." He points to a spot where he had scratched the lines.

I kneel on the mat, pick one of the twigs, and place it accordingly.

"Now, dump the rest into one pile."

I do so.

"Divide them into two sections, left and right."

This seems arbitrary. "Must I count them so that they are even?"

"Oh, no!" *the man responds.* "Uncertainty is part of the experience."

Uncertainty has certainly been part of my experience. I split the pile without counting.

"Do I really need to know this?"

"It has become necessary for you to learn the Yi Jing. If not today, then tomorrow."

My loud exhale of exasperation causes him to turn a wary eyeball toward me.

The old man explains the complicated system, and I make every attempt to follow his directions for counting and placing the yarrow twigs. We count over and over again, resulting in three groups.

"Nine," *he declares.* "A large number. Gather the unused stalks and repeat this process two more times."

Not only do I find this complicated, it feels repetitive and a bit boring.

Following his instruction, I have three piles.

"Large, large, and small. That is an unchanging broken line." *He draws two short marks in the dirt.* "Now, perform the whole thing again." *He returns the sticks to the cup and hands it to me.*

With all the confusion from this painstaking procedure, I take a calming breath before proceeding.

I repeat the exercise until he draws a sixth line, another broken one. The pattern looks like this:

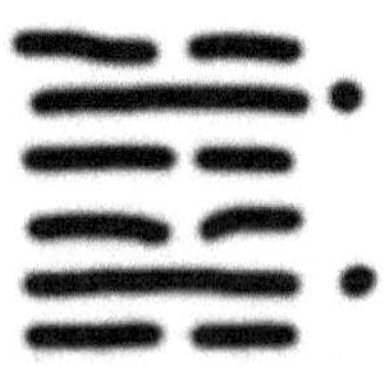

"What does that mean?" I ask.

"It represents The Gorge."

I wonder if it refers to the deepest part of the river under the bridge from our boat voyage, the only gorge I can think of.

"It indicates great calamity, the depth of sorrow, a crisis," he explains.

Not the gorge I had in my mind. "Does this represent the past, present, or future?"

"Yes, it does," he responds. A rather confusing answer that reminds me of the opal.

Should it refer to the past, it certainly describes my life before meeting Lao Peng You. In the present, it might mean meeting Tian Mei. As for the future, that does not portend well.

My curiosity begs: "Does this belong to me, you, or someone I know?"

"Only you would know that."

It could also describe my huoban's horrible loss at the Mahjong table earlier in the day.

"What are those two dots off to the side?" I point to the extra marks.

"Those indicate changing lines. They become their opposite."

Changing lines? Further change to the changes? This system appears much more complicated than expected. "What do they signify?"

"If I remember correctly..." He looks up at me, studying my face. "They say you can do nothing to stop the crisis, but neither will it get worse."

That sounds marginally better than an unstoppable, worsening crisis.

"And once you apply the changes, you get this." He wipes the dirt and draws six broken lines, like so:

"What does that one mean?"

He gazes at the new design as if in meditation. "Did you observe that both of the patterns you generated can be viewed equally from top or bottom?"

"Now that you mention it…" Another repetition. *"Would that be Topsy-Turvy?"*

"I am not familiar with that concept."

As I contemplate this whole ritual with sticks, I realize there might be a simpler way to accomplish a similar result.

"Pardon me, but this stalk tossing and counting is rather complicated. Would it not be easier just to throw dice or a few coins to obtain the different lines?"

The man shifts his head from side to side. "I imagine it would make things move along faster, and it would allow each of the lines to appear in equal probability."

"Yes, I believe that would also be a benefit."

"No," he responded. *"The yarrow stick method is derived to give you more time to consider your question as you create the patterns. Also, certain lines appear less frequently than others. All part of the design."*

"I see." Probably best not to rock this boat. *"And what is the new arrangement?"*

"This"–he points to the lines in the dirt–*"is called* The Field.*"*

Perhaps I shall become a farmer in my old age. "Is there an interpretation for this?"

"Yes, it signifies following instructions, following them precisely, and without deception."

In a swirl of blue dust, the long-haired man transforms into Shen Lung. It should have been obvious. I stand and bow.

"Hao Lan," the dragon begins, "You have once again forsaken my directions!" *Wind churns as he flaps his wings.*

"My Lord." *I bow again.* "I am not sure I understand what you mean."

"Little servant"–*his eyes whirling*–"did you ask the candidate about immortality?"

"Yes, my Lord, I did."

"Did you not prompt the candidate to answer in a fashion that would benefit you?" *he bellowed.*

"Shen Lung, I presented the information to the candidate and requested a response. I do not believe I attempted to influence the answer."

"You do not?" *he roared.* "Is that your belief?"

"Yes, my Lord."

"Hmmmmmmm," *the dragon droned.* "And what are your feelings toward this candidate, Hao Lan?"

I cannot misrepresent my mindset here. The Blue Dragon will know if I dissemble. "Shen Lung…" *I pause in hopes of having the correct words fall into my head without effort.* "I have, indeed, developed a fondness for the young servant, Tian Mei. I wish to continue receiving seed from him."

"I see," *he purred.* "You do realize that without immortality in time he will age and die, as mortals predictably do."

I had overlooked that inevitable outcome. "Quite true, O Great Dragon."

"However, if the candidate accepts the gift of immortality, you can no longer receive nourishment from him."

"Yes, my Lord."

"What a conundrum, Hao Lan. To live a few years in relative comfort with someone you enjoy now or to have an eternal escort who cannot supply you with the nourishment you require." He scowls and flaps his wings a bit faster.

"A difficult choice, O Great One."

"Then please explain to me why you wish to bond with this particular person." Dust rises about, making it more difficult to breathe and speak.

"The young servant presents himself to the world as a woman. This affords me the security of having a companion who appears female. In private I can obtain nourishment without having to approach other men surreptitiously."

The dragon honks, the ground shakes. "Are you saying you find intimate relations with other men shameful?"

"No, O Great One." I had better phrase my feelings correctly. "It is that my upbringing taught me to seek a woman for companionship. I am now unable to fulfill that duty, but I still have a drive for female intimacy."

"Yes, I see that." He blinks. "However, from now on you will only be intimate with other men. If you cannot accept this, perhaps I should consider terminating your immortality." The dragon looks off into the distance. "Did I not mention that one of your group will be departing soon?"

"My Lord," I gasp. "Please give me the chance to acclimate myself to this distinctive lifestyle. I have only had but one moon cycle as of yet. I believe I need more time."

"True. You reason well, Little One." He seems to be calming. "I have known of your affection for the candidate. It is heartwarming and pleasant." I think he smiles, but I cannot be sure. "However, what must be done, must be done. I shall give you two weeks more to complete your assignment. If you do not give the candidate the gift of immortality by then, I shall deal with your disobedience in a rather unpleasant fashion. Do you understand me?"

"Yes, my Lord. I must bring Tian Mei into the circle of Immortals within two weeks." I do not wish to find out what *rather unpleasant consequences he has in mind.*

"Very well, Hao Lan. Use your time wisely." He flaps his powerful wings, lifting himself off the ground. "And please–please!–stop complaining so much!" Shen Lung flies off behind me.

"You should live as you advise others. Do not advise others as you live," the ruby states.

"Eat to live, but do not live to eat," the emerald relates.

"When eating grapes, do not spit out the skin. When not eating grapes, spit out the skin," the opal instructs.

With that, I feel hungry.

I woke to the smell of fresh bean cakes and a quiet knocking at my door. When I looked outside, there stood Daniao with a bowlful of cakes.

He presented the food and bowed. "Good morning, Baron. I noticed you did not appear for your morning meal. I took the liberty of preparing something for you to eat in case you were not feeling well."

I took the welcome offering with a smile. "Thank you, Daniao. I appreciate your kindness. Would you like to come in?"

He shook his head. "No, Baron, I must return to the kitchen. Perhaps we can visit another time."

"Another time, yes."

Daniao walked off. As I watched his departure, I realized he could be my customary source of seed once I have given immortality to Tian Mei. The kitchen worker seemed willing, and he appeared to enjoy my company. Shen Lung granted me two weeks to comply with his request.

I closed the door and sat at my table considering a few options. After a couple nibbles of fresh bean cakes, I heard a faint rapping.

This time, Tian Mei appeared, and my heart somersaulted. I bade him enter. His eyes jumped to the bowl of cakes.

"Are you hungry?"

He shook his head.

"Does the Marquis feed you?"

He shook his head again.

"It would please me to share my meal with you." I took a bean cake from the bowl and handed it to him. "I shall not tell the Marquis." I put a finger up to my lips to indicate the confidence.

Tian Mei shoved the whole cake into his mouth and swallowed in one gulp. He must have been very hungry. I gave him another, and it disappeared just the same.

"It seems the Marquis does not take very good care of his servant."

Unblinking eyes stared at me.

"If you were my servant, I would want to give you the best life possible."

He smiled.

"Then again, I would not wish to have anyone in my servitude unwillingly."

Tian Mei approached, arms wide, as if to hug me, but if our flesh connected, I would have had an overwhelming desire for his seed. I did not wish to be intimate at that moment because I needed to confront him about my assignment from the blue dragon. I held my hand out to stop him.

"Please, be careful. Once we touch, I get an insatiable urge to have you inside me."

He smiled a big, grand smile.

"Yes, I enjoy that as well, but right now I need to discuss something very important with you. Please, sit." I indicated my chair.

He shook his head and remained upright. Perhaps servants could not sit while others stood.

I calmed myself and continued. "Shen Lung explained to me that I must give you the gift of immortality soon. I believe you understand that once I have done this, your seed will no longer nourish me."

He nodded.

"I want to find a way to get the Marquis to release you from your bondage. If we do not, you will end up serving him the rest of your life, which, as an Immortal, could be quite lengthy."

Tian Mei shuddered.

"Yes, that is quite a daunting thought. While Lao Peng You has treated *me* quite well since we first met, I have observed him mistreating *you*, and that upsets me very much."

He lowered his face.

"I want to give you the gift of immortality within the next day or so."

The servant opened his robe, exposing an extremely desirable body.

"No, not now. It is not the right time." In this moment, I must steer my boat where the winds direct. "Perhaps tonight, after the Marquis has retired for the evening." It would gratify me to have him once more before the gift makes his seed ineffective.

He did up the robe and nodded.

"Until this evening, Tian Mei." His name tasted like warm, sweet bean curd in my mouth. I opened the door and observed his willowy, girlish form as he shuffled away.

One bean cake remained. Delicious.

I grabbed some *Jiaogulan* leaves and went to the kitchen. "Daniao, may I have a pot and cup?"

He brought me the requested items and set them in front of me.

"Daniao," I whispered so that others would not hear, "I require your services this evening."

His eyes popped.

"Yes. Can you be at my suite just past moonrise?"

He nodded with a small grin.

"Until this evening then."

I walked to the food table expecting to see my *huoban*. But no. I sat and drank my tea. I waited for quite a while, but my friend and Mahjong partner did not appear. Perhaps the embarrassment of yesterday proved too much for him.

After I emptied the cup, I tapped it to read the leaves. The image of a dragon looked up at me. The voice of all-knowing, all-seeing Shen Lung echoed in my head, "Stop complaining so much!"

Following my tea, I strolled along the garden path as far as the gingko and bench. Fearing another terrible dream, I did not sit down. I looked along the other three paths as far as I could see without stepping onto them. No dreams, no messages, no voices.

When I walked back to the courtyard, I stopped at the bench where I saw Tian Mei that first night. I sat down, felt the cool, firm stone under my hands, and thought about the wonderful, intimate experiences we have shared since.

I did not see Lao Peng You all that day, and he did not come to the food table for dinner. Something must be terribly wrong.

After the evening meal, I returned to my suite to await the visit of Tian Mei. I had instructed him to come back after my *huoban* had fallen asleep. If the Marquis remained inconsolable, he may not be able to sleep.

The library in my suite possessed a copy of *The Classic of Changes*, and I read some material regarding the strange game with yarrow sticks. It told of the *Yin* and *Yang* lines, the possible changes, the combinations of Trigrams, and the sixty-and-four Hexagrams. So much to learn.

About an hour after dark, I heard the sound of wagon wheels on the path outside. Through the window, I observed Lao Peng You get out of a cart. Tian Mei followed, lugging a large bag. His head turned in my direction for an all too brief moment. I beamed.

The two of them went to my *huoban*'s suite. I could only hope that Lao Peng You had exhausted himself and would fall asleep soon.

As I read the *Yi Jing* book, designs floated in front of my eyes, making patterns of solid and broken lines. I must have been staring at the pages much too long.

At last, I heard the anticipated knock at the door. I placed the bamboo slats on the table and ran to let Tian Mei in.

Before I could get the door all the way open, he reached through and attempted to hug me. I hoped my *huoban* had not maltreated him.

"Tian Mei, did the Marquis hurt you today?"

When he looked up, I noticed his cheeks had some new scratches, and the face powder had been scraped away in a few places.

"Oh, no." I held him tight. The poor fellow. I must get him away from Lao Peng You somehow. The sooner the better.

"Did Shen Lung, the Blue Dragon, appear to you in a dream?"

He nodded.

"Did he provide you a new name?"

He nodded again. It seemed pointless to ask because he could not speak. I took some paper from the table, inked the brush, and handed it to him. He wrote two characters.

"Zhong Shi?"

He nodded.

"Zhong Shi, it is." I returned the paper and brush to the table. Tian Mei, soon to be Zhong Shi, came up from behind and put his arms around me. Once our skin touched, my hunger took over. This time, I wanted to taste him, to know what that joy would have been like had I been able to partake of it on a regular basis.

All I had to do was part his robe, and his large little brother reached up to meet me. I worried it would not fit in my mouth because I had never encountered one as great before. It took some maneuvering and clever adjusting, but I did manage to get half of him down my throat. His flesh smelled sweet, salty, musky, delicious.

Even though I lacked practice in the art of pleasuring another man, my amateurish attentions caused him to writhe and shiver. I could barely breathe with him crashing his hips into my face. At the point I felt as though I might suffocate, he blasted the most tasty fluid into my mouth. It had flavors of soy and bok choy. Once he withdrew, I licked my lips, enjoying the anticipated delight.

Tian Mei fell backward onto the floor. I helped him up and guided him to the bed. He lay back, and I raised his legs. The welcome sight of his blossoming chrysanthemum made me grin, and my little bird responded, eager for its first flight.

Shen Lung had informed me I would be able to perform my duty when the time came. Thankfully, his reasoning stood firm.

"Are you ready, Tian Mei?"

He nodded with quickening tempo and spreading grin. My chest filled with the warmth I had come to know in the presence of this wonderful person. As long as we could preserve our green mountain, we would never want for firewood.

When I penetrated the lad for the first time, it felt like being inside a warm, moist bean cake. Unbelievable pleasure amplified as I slid myself out and in, deeper each time. I must have been erupting thunderous moans because he put a finger to his lips. It would prove difficult to remain quiet during the most blissful experience I ever enjoyed in my whole life.

When the pressure within me had built to its highest point, I warned Tian Mei, "You will be blinded by a bright, white light. All will be well after a few moments. I shall be here with you, and I shall not leave you. Do you understand?"

He nodded.

I began my final thrusts just as another thought occurred to me. "Soon after, you will feel very hungry. I have arranged a meal for you."

He nodded again. When he winked at me, I could no longer control myself. Burst after burst fired from the depths within me to the depths within him. Even *I* experienced the bright, white light and almost passed out. Fortunately, my grip on his ankles helped me steady myself.

There. Once again, I completed an assignment for the Blue Dragon. The person from whom I had hoped to receive my eternal nourishment transformed into another Immortal. We would no longer be able to satisfy each other's nutritional needs.

When I gazed down, I saw my companion quivering. He trembled and pointed to his mouth. I remembered this ravenous sensation from *my* initiation.

A knock at the door startled us both. I hugged the boy and attempted to disentangle and go to the door, but he clung tightly. "Your meal has arrived. Please, let me get it for you."

He let go with what seemed great reluctance. I grabbed my robe and opened the door for Daniao.

"Thank you for being here, my friend. I have a favor to ask of you." I indicated Zhong Shi on my bed.

"Is that not the servant of the Marquis Pichan?" he asked with raised brows.

"Yes," I answered. "Please. You will receive what you have come for."

He walked to the bed. Zhong Shi reached out and pulled down Daniao's trousers, freeing the cook's engorged organ. The young servant suckled, making gurgling sounds like he might choke.

Given my recent pangs of jealousy when observing the young man with others, it seemed odd that I felt no such turmoil observing the activity before me. A business transaction. Nothing with problematic emotional layers to kindle my fears of losing him. Something I must prepare myself for as we learned to make our long-lived way in the mortal world together.

Several moments and grunts later, Daniao finished. Zhong Shi swallowed his first meal as an Immortal. He sat back on the bed with a wide grin.

The kitchen worker looked at me with an expression of curiosity.

"Thank you, Daniao," I said. "I do not require your further services this evening."

He frowned.

"But you and I shall speak in the near future. I have something of an arrangement to discuss with you."

He pulled up his trousers.

I opened the door for him. "Good night, my friend."

Daniao bowed and left.

From his idyllic expression, the newest Immortal seemed in heaven. He ran to me and kissed my face all over.

"You are welcome, Zhong Shi. Shall we sleep now?" I pointed to the bed.

All this activity exhausted me, and I hoped the young man as well.

As far as I could remember, we fell asleep in each other's arms, me thinking of wonderful and marvelous things.

13. One Character

"If you choose to do what you love," the ruby recites, "you will never have to work a day in your life."

"Know well what leads you forward and what holds you back," the emerald states. "Then choose the path that leads to wisdom."

"There are two alternatives," the opal shares. "Be clever and deceive others or avoid cleverness and be virtuous."

And here I am again, in the presence of the three wise gems. As before, their statements seem contradictory and confusing. Shen Lung instructed me to heed their teachings, weighing and considering each statement for its own truth. I expect someday they will make more sense to me.

Behind me I hear faint footsteps. I turn and behold an aged, slightly stooped gentleman with a short, grey beard. He appears wizened and sage, wearing the distinctive square, black hat of a great scholar. He holds a collection of bamboo slats with writing.

"You see before you an old man, a teacher, some people would say," he tells me. "Some identify me as master." He blinks and looks behind me at the wall with the three gems. "And some call me an old fool."

His gaze returns to me, as if I am supposed to do something or say something.

"You need not do or say anything at all." Apparently, he reads minds as well. I wonder if he is Shen Lung in disguise, once again, testing me. "You are quite young for an Immortal, Hao Lan, but you have great potential."

This gentleman knows my name. And he seems to have more faith in my abilities than I do.

He extends his arms with the bundle of bamboo pages, urging me to take them. "Here is all the wisdom you will ever require. Read these and learn the keys to all great mysteries."

As I collect the slats I ask, "What is this?"

He smiles and blinks, "This is The Classic of The Way. *I have spent my life collecting and sifting through moments of pain, sorrow, happiness, humility, forgiveness, and acceptance. This is the result of my analyses and knowledge, the summation of my teachings." He winks at me. "A sweet gift for you, my sweet child."*

I look down at the pages of staggering and overwhelming writing. First, The Classic of Changes, *and now this. It might take years to get through it all. Fortunately, I have many, many years ahead of me.*

"When you are thoroughly familiar with the contents and concepts therein, you may wish to share these ideas with the rest of the civilized world. Some may listen, but most will not. A few will rise in anger at what you have to say, others might accept these words as irrefutable truths."

It feels like quite a daunting task for just one person. An obvious question occurs to me. "Did you try to instruct others?"

His face assumes a wry, wise, and amused little grin, "How do you think I got the sobriquet Master *or* Old Teacher?"

"Yes, of course." How silly of me. "May I know your proper name so that I can acknowledge and tribute you personally, Master?"

"I have a name–or rather–I had a name." He looks up to the heavens as if it were written in the clouds. *"Long forgotten, hardly ever used."* His eyes return to me. *"Names are unimportant. Ideas are everything."*

It feels like he has given me the very keys to the Universe. His experience, his knowledge, his wisdom, his truths.

"The Universe, yes. It was once mine." The fellow steps forward and pats me on the shoulder as he passes. *"It is now yours. Use it very, very mindfully. Farewell."*

With those words he steps through the wall of solid gold and silver with the three large gems as if it were a gentle waterfall.

"Well, what do you think of that?" I ask myself.

"Follow the rules," the red jewel states, *"even though they can be sour."*

"Follow your path," the green gem advises, *"even though it may be bitter."*

"Follow that man," the white stone instructs, *"for he is most certainly sweet."*

I shake my head in disbelief. "A wise old man hands me a pile of bamboo pages to study, disappears through your wall, and that is all you can say? You are supposed to be my guides, my mentors, my advisors. I perceive no insight here. Where is your counsel? Where is your wisdom?" I glare at them with many questions.

"By three methods we may learn wisdom: first, by reflection, which is noblest; second, by imitation, which is the easiest; and third, by experience, which is the sourest."

"If a man can control his mind, he can find the way to Enlightenment. All wisdom and virtue will naturally come to him, even if it is bitter."

"Knowing others is intelligence; knowing yourself is true wisdom. It is sweet."

"All this discussion of wisdom." I stamp my foot and shout, "What has it gotten the three of you? As long as I have known you, all I receive is words, words, and more words."

No response.

"What is wrong? Where are your words, now?" I stare at each of the gems in turn. "Normally, you have a comment for everything." Their lights diminish to darkness. The wall melts before my eyes, disappearing, vanishing into a golden vapor. Behind it lies a beautiful landscape: a lake with birds, a grassy meadow, tall, narrow, snow-capped peaks in the distance, clouds perched on the mountain tops.

I step over the line where the wall once stood.

Ferocious knocking at my door woke me.

"Baron! Baron! I cannot find Tian Mei anywhere!"

He would not know that Tian Mei no longer existed and could not be found anywhere. However, I did not want my new partner, who slept in the bed next to me, to get into any trouble with my old partner.

"*Huoban*, please calm down. Your servant is here with me."

Yes, in fact, the young man had spent the entire night. I pointed to *The Classic of Changes* on the table. He donned his robe and went to the book.

I donned my tunic and opened the door.

Lao Peng You peered into my suite, squinting around, searching for the wayward servant.

"Tian Mei! You have duties to perform! Return to my suite immediately and prepare my clothes for the day." He pointed in the general direction of his rooms.

"Marquis," I said in my calmest voice possible. "I could not sleep past dawn this morning. Upon rising, I saw your servant standing in the garden. I asked for assistance with deciphering the *Yi Jing*. It is most confusing, and the girl seems to have a working knowledge of this particularly complicated system."

Lao Peng You gazed at Zhong Shi with an arched eyebrow. "Indeed. How... convenient." He turned his disbelieving look at me. "I told you *this*"–he pointed at the book–"is piffle."

"I find it rather fascinating, *huoban.*" My face flashed a polite smile. "I intend to study it in hopes of attaining some perspective on our existence and, perhaps, some guidance along the way."

"Yes, well, some guidance and perspective can be helpful from time-to-time, when one requires such nonsense. However, now I must prepare for the day." He turned to the servant. "Back to my suite with you," and then to me, "*You* I shall see at the tables later." Without another word, they departed my rooms.

My eyes followed Zhong Shi.

After they left, I contemplated the scene we had just played. Once again, I had prevaricated to hide my true actions and feelings. Words from the three departed gems regarding love and deception stung in my head.

After my own breakfast, I joined Lao Peng You at the Mahjong table. His servant stood in the corner, as usual, waiting for the master to bark orders.

An hour later I grew tired and rose.

"Sit, my friend," the Marquis entreated. "One more hand." He raised his eyebrows, imploring me to remain.

One more hand proved a disaster for him and the other players. I sat East, and when I declared Mahjong, I had acquired all the One tiles from the three suits (Characters, Dots, and Bamboo), a Pung of East, and a pair of White Dragons. This entitled me to all the coins on the table.

"Marquis," I stood and addressed him as I collected my winnings. "Thank you for suggesting another game. It has proven most profitable." When I nodded and smiled, he produced a sour frown.

I returned to my suite. Zhong Shi followed my movements as best as possible with Lao Peng You observing everything within his sight.

That afternoon, I strolled to the bench under the old gingko. For some reason I did not understand at the time, I sat and relaxed, even though I did not feel tired. Several breaths later, I fell asleep.

"Hao Lan," the voice of Shen Lung calls.

"I am here, Master." Darkness envelops me when I open my eyes.

"Please, keep your eyes closed, Little One. The darkness will blind you."

Always one to follow the dragon's rules, I close my eyes.

"Once again, you have completed the task I set before you."

"You are my Lord, O Great One."

"Ha, ha, ha, ha, ha," he bellows.

I am grateful that I can still amuse him.

"Yes. And you have completed my command well within the time allotted."

It sounds as though another task will follow.

"I have a request for you."

A request? Usually, he has commands or assignments. What could he possibly want to ask me to do that did not involve a direct order?

"Yes, it is a request, not a command or assignment. In your last dream you received The Classic of The Way.*"*

"Yes, my Lord. The old man handed me a bundle of bamboo."

"The old man," he repeats, mocking my use of the phrase. "That old man, *as you put it, was the most sage scholar in all of history. Never again will someone with his intellect walk our soil and engage our people."*

"He seemed quite learned."

"Indeed. He was quite learned. A good student."

"Your student?" I hope that does not sound too incredulous. "Was he also an Immortal?"

"Oh, no." The dragon blinked. "That one was too wise for immortality. One lifetime was all he required."

Too wise for immortality? What does that make me?

"Can you comprehend the writing of The Classic, *Hao Lan?"*

"Yes, my Lord. It is standard Seal Script. My parents made sure I could understand it."

"Good. I would like you to read the book and absorb its teachings."

"Shen Lung, I do not have the book. It is only in my dreams."

"Yes, I am well aware of that, Little One. Each day you will return to this spot and learn while dreaming. Is that clear?"

"Yes. That is your request. I shall read and learn from the book."

"Very good. Open your eyes and begin."

I part my eyelids. Long sheets of orange-yellow silk with writing hang from bamboo frames about an arm's-length taller than a man. They appear to contain the same teach-ings as slats from The Classic of The Way.

The fabric undulates, even without a breeze. Dozens of these banners stand all about me in a broad, flat meadow with a rippling stream nearby. The first page begins: "The Way that can be discoursed is not the eternal Way."

For the next few weeks, I spent my time divided between the Mahjong table, the bench under the gingko, and Zhong Shi. Occasionally, he and I would engage Daniao after the Marquis fell asleep for the night. The three of us paved the road to a supportive, mutual friendship, each receiving what he needed from the others.

My earnings from Mahjong increased, and my knowledge of *The Way* blossomed as well. Some of the lessons from the Old Master, such as, "The sage is guided by what he feels, rather than what he sees," applied to the game of tiles likewise.

I asked Zhong Shi if he received nighttime visits from Shen Lung. He nodded. Part of being an Immortal, I suppose. We all have our individual relationship with the Blue Dragon, and we all have our separate assignments. I could only hope that the young fellow has been able to satisfy our Lord's demands.

On the Fifteenth day of the Eighth Month, we observed the Mid-Autumn Moon Festival at Changshou Shan. Origins of the celebration–clouded from antiquity–arose from a tale about Chang'e, beloved wife of our great hero Hou Yi. The gods rewarded him with an elixir of immortality, which he gave to his wife for safe-keeping. While her husband was away, an evil man attempted to take the potion by force. Chang'e swallowed the elixir to keep it from him. Her body floated up into heaven, and she became a celestial being, the Moon.

Well, that is how some of our pointless traditional festivals have inaugurated, and we kept perpetuating the old myths. At least this festival included good food. For instance, the Moon Cake, a flaky, round, palm-sized pie filled with savory meat, a flavorsome treat.

Lao Peng You had Zhong Shi work with Daniao to help prepare this special meal. The two servants walked around with trays full of these delicious-looking pastries. When Zhong Shi stopped near me to serve another guest, I reached for one of the cakes. He shook his head and moved the tray out of my grasp. I found it curious that he did not want me to partake of them for some mysterious reason.

Across the way, I saw my *huoban* stuffing his face with cake after cake. I still cannot understand how he could eat so much yet remain the same size. Perhaps another of the many benefits of being an Immortal.

Zhong Shi pointed to a container of pumpkin and taro. I scooped some of the mixture into a small bowl and tasted it. The pale, clay-like color of the fruit mix smelled like moldy leaves, but the flavor more than made up for it. The mélange tasted like a blend of sweet spices with a hint of osmanthus blossom.

Following the meal came music and dancing. While I did not desire to participate, I enjoyed watching the others who moved in rhythm and displayed their acrobatic abilities. From time-to-time, I looked for Zhong Shi. He could not get far from Lao Peng You, who kept ordering him to retrieve bowl after bowl of food.

The following day, Lao Peng You appeared at my suite looking peaked, pale, parched, and a bit paunchy.

"Come in, *huoban*, come in. You appear unwell."

He entered with slow steps, not his usual burst of energy.

"Baron, I fear something is not right with me. I feel out of balance." He winced and sat with shaky movements denoting pain, as a man in his advanced years might.

"What can it be?"

He shook his head. "I am quite uncertain, but I do believe it is best that I journey to Chongqing to pay a visit to the great physician and soothsayer, Hua Tuo."

"Yes, that seems appropriate. When will you depart?"

His listless eyes turned to me. "That is why I am here. I wish you to accompany me. Traveling by myself would be unwise."

"But you have your servant to keep you company." I would miss Zhong Shi. The young man had sown a blossom in my heart, more so than I could have ever intended. We treated each other with kindness and respect, more than either of us received from Lao Peng You.

The Marquis waved a dismissive hand, using what energy he had left. "That useless *wangba* does nothing for me. I need *you, huoban*. Please." His reddened eyes moistened with tears of discomfort. "Please."

It pained me to hear him speak that way. I have never been able to understand his disdain for the servant. Perhaps it had something to do with his desire for revenge upon Wang Yue, Zhong Shi's former master.

"Will Zh... Tian Mei"–I almost forgot to use his original name–"be remaining here at Changshou Shan while you journey?"

"She will–unfortunately–come with us." He scowled. "I cannot trust to leave the girl here alone. She might run away."

And who would blame such a browbeaten youth.

Until I can devise a way to acquire the servant from him, I must respect my *huoban*'s behavior, whether I condoned it or not. Also, if I accompanied him to Chongqing, I would not be separated from the beloved Zhong Shi.

However, Shen Lung requested I spend some time each day reading from *The Classic of The Way*, and I have so much more to learn. Nevertheless, it would have been uncharitable for me to refuse a request from the one who saved me from my own early death.

"Of course, *huoban*. I can be ready tomorrow morning."

"Good." He rose at a slow and discomfited pace. "I shall see you at dawn."

The next morning, the three of us set out for Chongqing, Lao Peng You, Zhong Shi, and me. Without dragons or boats, it would be a two-day journey by oxcart. Our provisions included food and drink for a week. And a Mahjong set.

At this time of the year, some of the leaves had begun to lose their green color, turning to a ruddy tone. The air smelled of honey, and the birds kept us company along our way.

The first night we stopped by a stream and slept under the burnished sky. At one point, I looked at Zhong Shi then heavenward just in time to witness a trail of fire across the field of stars. An omen, of course, but who could say whether good or bad. We smiled at each other.

Lao Peng You's condition worsened the next day. He seemed older, paler, fatter. After a few hours, he could no longer steer the wagon. Fortunately, I had observed him enough times and could take over the reins. Zhong Shi sat next to me while my *huoban* rested in the back of the cart.

By nightfall we had reached the tenuous Wushan Bridge across the Yangtze, a spidery ribbon high above the churning waters. I first saw it in a dream, where Shen Lung sailed us down the river and indicated I would encounter the structure again. Soon after, when Lao Peng You and I sailed with the unrivaled Xin Yue, I observed it from below.

Beholding the span from this perspective, the slender thread terrified me, and I wanted to put off the inevitable as long as possible. I suggested, "Let us camp here, behind that hill and make our river crossing at first light."

Neither of my companions objected. Zhong Shi prepared dinner using the provisions we had brought with us from Changshou Shan. After the meal, we talked for a while, discussing our previous journeys, adventures at the Mahjong table, and Lao Peng You's favorite food delicacies. Near midnight, we all fell asleep in the cart.

I stand halfway up the side of a snow-capped peak. Black stone, like onyx, beneath my feet forms a narrow path. Only a few brave little pine trees have dared to sprout from the almost vertical wall. A slight wind wafts the clouds around. Perhaps, I am ascending up into Heaven itself.

"Do not be silly, Little One," the voice of Shen Lung rings out. "You are not going to Heaven. At least not today."

I feel relieved. One can never be sure with the Blue Dragon.

"*Shen Lung,*" *I call.* "*I have concern for Lao Peng You. He does not appear well.*"

"*Yes, I know.*" *He flies into my view and hovers near the mountain.*

"*What is wrong with him?*"

The dragon's eyes whirl as if he needs time to consider a response. "*He has displeased us and will receive appropriate punishment.*"

Appropriate punishment does not sound like a leisurely boat trip down the Yangtze River. I glance at Shen Lung. "*Was I the cause of his disobedience, O Great One?*"

"*Ha, ha, ha! You continue to amuse me, my little servant.*" *The blue beast smiled.* "*Your behavior is not in question… at the moment. However, I shall advise you to refrain from uttering untruths. It is not becoming for someone of your station.*"

Untruths? What had I said? Oh yes. I have told a few small lies regarding the conduct of Tian Mei, who has become Zhong Shi.

"*Once you begin with falsehoods, it might be difficult to return to the path of correctness. But because you are not using these untruths to better yourself or damage others, it is of little consequence for the moment.*"

I find that very reassuring. It helps me to realize my affection for the boy has altered my usual obedient behavior.

"*How are your studies with* The Classic of The Way *going?*"

I understand that by accompanying my huoban *I have not complied with Shen Lung's request to read from it every day.* "*The book is thoughtful and immense. I am not even halfway through it yet.*"

"And, still, you are taking time off to accompany your associate on a journey."

"Yes, my Lord. Lao Peng You requested I travel with him. He gave me my new life, and I did not want to disappoint him. I hope this does not displease you."

He grins. "A few days in the life of an Immortal are of little importance compared to the dedication of your friendship. Of course, it also keeps you with your precious Zhong Shi, does it not?"

I avoid answering the insinuating question. "Can you tell me what will happen to Lao Peng You?"

The Blue Dragon glowered at me. "It is not your concern, my little servant."

"But he is my friend, my Lord. Without him I would be nothing. I would be a sickly miner in Hunan or, more likely, dead." I bow in obeisance, nearly falling off the side of the mountain.

"While it is true that he did bring you into the circle of Immortals, since that time he has not obeyed subsequent commands and orders from his overlords. He has been dis-obedient in ways that concern us greatly."

"Of course, my Lord." I bow again, but not as far. "You are my Master. I shall obey in all things."

"That is good to hear."

"O Great One. It is you who hold my life in your… well, you who hold my life. My obedience to you is paramount."

"Indeed. For example, if I tell you to leap off the side of a mountain, you would leap."

"Yes, Master."

"Go ahead, then. Leap."

"What!?" He wants me to jump from the side of this cliff? It must be at least a li to the bottom from here.

"Yes. Leap. Demonstrate your obedience to me now. Follow my command. Leap!"

"Have I offended you in some way that you are unhappy with me, O Great One?" I attempt a dainty bow, just to make sure. "I shall make every endeavor to return to your good graces, if only you would allow me the opportunity, my Lord."

"Not at all, Hao Lan. You have never been out of my good graces, *as you call it*. However, your scrupling has become rather annoying. Either jump now, or I shall push you off."

Before giving it another thought, I take a big breath and leap into the air, not knowing where I might land.

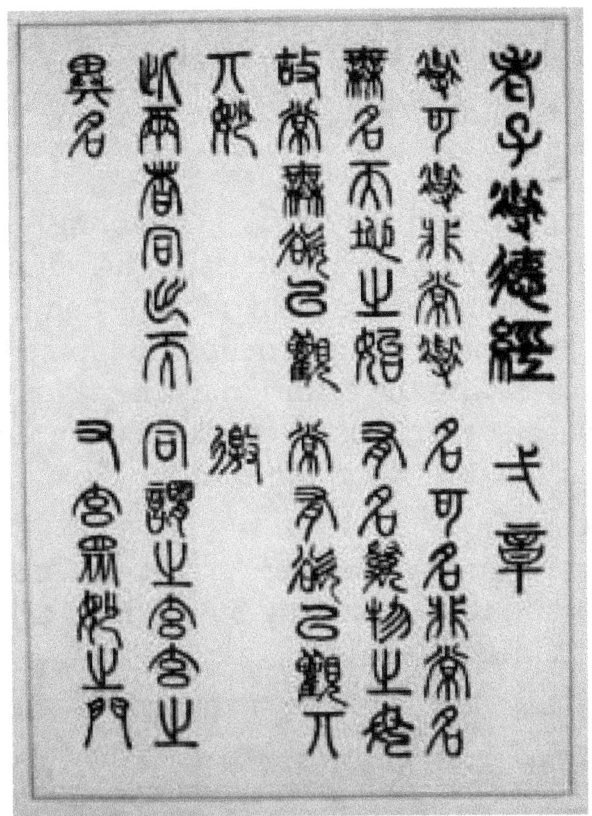

Page one **from** *The Classic of the Way*

14. The Gates of Heaven

I awoke around daybreak, trembling from the dream. Footsteps caught my ear. The sounds grew louder. Without moving the rest of my body, I opened my eyes just enough to discover who loomed nearby. Two men wearing the traditional white cloth of merchants had discovered our makeshift camp. Most likely hungry, they probably smelled or saw our food supplies.

"Good morning, gentlemen," I said as I arose. Sensing no reason to be anything but polite, I asked, "Did you want something to eat?"

Before they could answer, Lao Peng You bolted up. "We are not in the business of providing aid to strangers," he spat. At least his lovable old self still persisted somewhere within that bloated and inflating carcass.

One of the men bowed. "We beg your pardon, my lords. My friend and I are not here to take handouts from you. It is not gifts we seek."

The Marquis studied and appraised them. "Then what *do* you seek? I warn you, my friends and I are quite capable of defending ourselves if you attempt any sort of highwaymanship."

If it had been their goal to rob us, they had already squandered their advantage of surprise. Lao Peng You tended to see the worst in everyone. I, however–through the teachings of *The Way*–have learned to be less hasty in judging others.

The unfamiliar man smiled. "I believe you misunderstand our intentions. We seek you for the honor of playing the sacred tile game of Mahjong. This cart bears the emblem of Changshou Shan, which–I believe–is a mountain resort a few days from here."

"Yes, you are correct in that," I responded. "How is it that you know of Changshou Shan?"

He looked back at his comrade, then at me. "It is well-known in these parts as a place one can go for rest and recuperation. Unfortunately, it is quite expensive and beyond the means of common peddlers, such as ourselves."

"The cost of staying there can be quite prohibitive," I replied while keeping an eye on Lao Peng You. My concern for his health persisted, especially in light of these unknown visitors.

"It is said," the intruder continued, "the grounds are like that of Heaven itself."

The lush and beautiful gardens satisfied *my* desire for serenity, but I did not know if I would liken the rest of the setting to Heaven. "There is some beauty to be found there, certainly." I looked back at the Marquis, whose distrustful focus remained on the interlopers. "Is there some way we may be of assistance to you?"

"It has been years since we had the pleasure of playing with the medicinal tiles and wish to enjoy a few games, if it is not an imposition."

My main concern remained delivering Lao Peng You to the doctor before he got any worse. "Gentlemen, I appreciate your curiosity, but–as much as we would like to accommodate your wishes–we did not bring a Mahjong set with us."

Yes, I knew we had one in the cart, and, yes, I knew I told untruths again, but I felt compelled to get my *huoban* to safety as quickly as possible.

The fellow's laughter reminded me of a donkey. "I hope your Mahjong play is better than your attempt at deception." He pointed to the back of the cart, where the tiles could be seen.

"Well, what I meant to say is that my friend here"–I pointed to the Marquis–"is quite ill, and I am accompanying him to Chongqing to see the famous physician, Hua Tuo. I did not want to embarrass him by disclosing his current, life-threatening condition."

The hee-hawing stopped and the merchant bowed with reverence. "I am most sorry, my lord. I did not realize your associate lies within the jaws of the tiger. We shall leave you to your errand of mercy." They turned and walked away.

"Wait!" Lao Peng You's voice called out, faint but still audible. "There is always time for a game. How many coins have you brought with you?"

The men returned to the cart and showed a few gold coins, a handful of silver ones, and a bag of copper.

My *huoban* looked at me with sad eyes. "Surely we can grant these fine gentlemen at least one round, Baron." His speech diminished with each wheezing breath. "We would not want to disappoint our new friends."

I threw my hands skyward in exasperation. "If that is your wish, *huoban,* so be it." Even in the throes of his own demise, avarice reigned.

The two fellows joined us as we sat in the back of the oxcart. We did not even bother to ask their names because they would only be with us a short while. As

Zhong Shi did not play Mahjong, he stood off to the side observing us.

After the second round, Lao Peng You showed signs of further tiring and puffiness.

"Marquis, perhaps we should start for Chongqing now," I suggested. Even though the thought of crossing that terrifying bridge turned my blood cold as blind charity, I wanted my *huoban* to receive the attention he needed.

"One more hand, Baron. Just one more hand," he gasped.

I could only hope this *one more hand* worked out better for him than the last time he requested such an additional game. His previous insistence upon playing *one more hand* ended up with me acquiring vast wealth.

We rolled the dice. Tiles clicked and flew. Winds, Dragons, Flowers. All arranged and disarranged in front of us until, finally, the familiar call.

"Mahjong!" The Marquis had a fully concealed hand. I could not guess what he held. As he displayed his tiles one-by-one, my eyes opened wider than a plate of Moon Cakes. He had assembled a Pung of One Dots, one each of the Two through Eight Dots and a Pung of Nine Dots, a special limit hand known as *The Gates of Heaven*. This allowed him to claim all the coins in play. Coughs intermingled with greedy glee as he collected his winnings.

"Thank you, gentlemen," I said. "I believe the time has come for us to take the Marquis to Chongqing."

The others backed off the cart and walked down the path. I heard their grumbling as they trotted away.

"Tales about that guy ring true. Such a cheater. It felt like shooting shadows at sand."

"True, but at least we know for certain."

"He looked so much older than I expected."

"More pungent than ancient ginger."

"*Huoban*," Lao Peng You coughed. "I do not feel very well at all. Please, let us proceed."

Zhong Shi and I prepared the cart. I could not take my mind off the precarious-looking Wushan Bridge we needed to cross to get to Chongqing. So long as my companions accompanied me, I hoped I would be able to draw up the courage for the journey ahead to wade through boiling water and scorching flame.

With me and Zhong Shi in the front, and Lao Peng You in the rear, I started the oxcart back toward the mooring of that frightening bridge.

I stopped the cart at the precipice. Before us loomed a walkway of slender rope and brittle bamboo, at least one full *li* above the raging Yangtze River. The wooden slats strung together resembled *The Classic of The Way* given to me in a recent dream. I have heard people say, "Third time lucky," and I have seen this crossing twice before.

"Let us go!" commanded Lao Peng You from the back of the cart.

A Moon Festival drum pounded within my chest. I looked at Zhong Shi, and he stared back at me. Neither of us seemed very confident about what we must do to help our companion.

The space between posts holding the ropes appeared too narrow for our vehicle to pass between them. "*Huoban*," I began, then halted. My gaze shifted back and forth. "I do not believe this bridge is wide enough for the oxcart."

"Of course, it is not wide enough for an oxcart." He produced several raspy coughs. "You stupid egg."

My breath ceased. He had never insulted me in all the time we knew each other. I had done everything possible to get my *huoban* to this point, including disobeying the Blue Dragon. If he persisted in such discourteous behavior, I might consider dumping him out and heading back to Changshou Shan with Zhong Shi.

"You leave the cart here, and we *walk* across the span." He struggled to lift his distended body so he could descend to the ground. Unfortunately, he had expanded to the size of an overfed camel and could no longer accomplish this maneuver unaided. His silk tunic ripped at the buttons, exposing swelling and ashen flesh. "Tian Mei! You must assist me."

The young man looked in my direction with widened eyes, as if to ask for guidance. I had none and shrugged.

"Get over here now!" the Marquis yelled as he fastened a bulging coin purse to his waist sash. "Do not make me beat you yet again!"

Zhong Shi stepped to the back of the cart and attempted to help Lao Peng You to the ground. The sight of the willowy youth making awkward efforts at bearing the weight of this bloated Immortal made for a comical scene. My hand rose to cover an unsolicited smirk.

I stood observing the efforts, gawking at the spectacle. Wind blew up the gorge, and a gentle breeze graced us with its slightly salty river scent. This soothing aroma distracted me for a moment, diminishing the anxiety.

Once he reached the ground, my *huoban* set off toward the bridge by himself like a clumsy bird, determined to get to the other side no matter what. Due to his increased size, he gave the impression of a one-man parade. His tattered, fluttering tunic resembled garish banners foretelling imminent doom.

I waited near the cart, immobilized with dread, Zhong Shi at my side. He slid his hand to mine and gave it a squeeze.

The Marquis glanced back at us. "Come on, you two scared bunnies! Do not be silly little turtles."

We both looked at the treacherous bridge. I had considerable trepidation and sweaty palms. Whatever Zhong Shi might have been feeling, he could not have expressed with words, but his hand trembled around mine. I concluded not to cross that rickety path of possible death, even if a hungry bear and several venomous snakes appeared behind us. Immortals should be allowed to have legitimate concerns for their own safety and wellbeing, unfounded as those fears might sound.

"Look!" Lao Peng You shouted. "I shall demonstrate to you there is nothing to fear. This bridge is as sturdy as..."–he pointed to the beast who pulled us to this location–"well... as an ox!" He attempted to establish the strength of the anchor post by hitting it with his hand, but the halting and jerky movement of his arm came across as absurd. "Watch!" came the command as he stepped out onto the splintered bamboo slats suspended by fraying ropes.

Cun by *cun*, he advanced toward the opposite bank. The bridge swayed as he progressed but showed no sign of imminent collapse.

"See, I told you it was safe." He smiled back at us as much as his pudgy face would allow.

The breeze intensified. I crossed my arms and watched the span oscillate up, down, and side to side. Nothing could be said or done to make me comfortable enough to follow. I remained resolute and would have preferred sitting on a distant mountain watching tigers fight among themselves.

"Ass fairies! Ass fairies! You two are useless, old turtle eggs." He turned away and resumed his slow and deliberate crossing.

As we watched in amazement, Lao Peng You increased in size before our eyes. His arms and legs swelled, his head puffed out, his belly expanded.

A distinct *pop! pop! SNAP!* drew our attention to the rope holding the walkway. My rapidly degenerating *huoban* turned to look at the source of the startling noise. "Uh oh..."

Perhaps the unremitting, overindulgent eating caused his body to balloon to a humongous size. It appeared as though his advanced age had caught up with him all at once. What hair remained turned white and fell out. What I could see of his eyes–almost hidden behind mushroomed cheeks–registered surprise like I had never seen before.

"How… is… ?" he managed to squeak out before the bridge shattered with a loud *CRACK!*

Bamboo slats flew in every direction as the ropes gave way. Zhong Shi and I gasped in unison, holding hands for mutual support.

Lao Peng You clutched a swinging strand with what strength he had left. His overblown bulk whipped around with the flaying ropes. Up, down, up, down. All over. Finally, as if propelled by a blast of fire medicine, his heft flew high into the air, exploding overhead into ten thousand little pieces. Coins dispersed in a shower of gold, silver, and copper. They shimmered in the early morning sunbeams, imitating the fireworks he had fancied so much. The Marquis did relish a *dramatic finish*.

I shed a tear in memory of the person who delivered me into this life. All my good fortunes stemmed from associating with Lao Peng You. His passing marked a distinct crossroads for me. While I may continue to drink from a privileged well, I shall never forget who dug it for me.

"Thank goodness *that* is over," came from a distinctive, deep male tone.

I turned to the person standing next to me, the only one within sight. My mouth opened as far as possible. "Did… you… say something, Zhong Shi?"

"Yes," responded the mellifluous voice. "I said, *Thank goodness* that *is over*." He shot a playful smile back at me.

"You mean you could speak this entire time?"

He nodded.

"Why did you tell the Marquis you were mute?"

His head turned side to side. "I never told him any-thing of the sort."

I found his golden manner of speech mesmerizing.

"Because I never spoke, he merely assumed my muteness." Zhong Shi winked.

"Now that I hear your voice, I don't ever want to stop hearing it. The sound is honey to my ear."

"Thank you, Master Hao." He blushed and glanced down. "However, I shall only be verbalizing in your presence alone."

"Why is that? You speak so beautifully."

Zhong Shi closed the flowery silk robes with his soft, small hands. "Because most pretty little ladies do not have big men's voices."

Of course. I nodded. In perpetuating the masquerade of being a young woman, he had to remain silent. Another lovely surprise demonstrating astute wisdom from one so young. This revelation endeared him to me even more.

Having relatively good health and meeting the unex-pected love of my life seemed like miracles to a poor miner from Hunan province. As long as we served Shen Lung and did not upset the blue dragon, we could live many years in comfort.

From my wins at Mahjong, I possessed more money than the two of us could ever spend in multiple life-times, which we both had ahead of us. Any location would serve our needs, and we could live wherever we liked.

"Shall we return to the mountain?" I asked.

He bowed in curt agreement.

On the return drive, I felt compelled to inquire regarding the climactic scene we had just witnessed. "Zhong Shi, do you have any idea what might have happened to Lao Peng You that would produce such an extraordinary display?"

"Yes." He nodded. "Once you bestowed the gift of immortality upon me, I no longer provided the nourishment he needed to maintain his longevity. In addition, I made sure I was the only man from whom he received seed. The Marquis had no idea that I became an Immortal."

I marveled at how my new companion managed the delicate situation and looked at him with renewed appreciation. "You mean to say you intentionally caused the end of his life?"

"It was not *my* idea alone." His eyes focused on the road ahead. "Shen Lung suggested this strategy. He expressed how Master Lao affected and upset him."

"It pained me to see my *huoban* abuse and frequently harm you. Every moment I wanted to do something to help, but it was not my place to intervene."

"Well-reasoned, Master Hao." He glanced in my direction.

"Please, call me Hao Lan. I am not your master. You are a free man… or woman, as you choose."

"Thank you, my eternal friend. I could no longer stand his treatment of me either. As Tian Mei, the servant girl, I was obliged to submit to his self-centered will and overly authoritarian discipline. However, as Zhong Shi the Immortal, I felt unable to endure that intolerable path."

"No, of course not," I agreed. "And you will not be *my* servant either. As far as I am concerned, we are equals in every way."

"If that is your preference, but I would gladly serve you through the rest of eternity, Hao Lan."

His speaking my name sent shivers throughout my body. "I believe the Blue Dragon will surely instruct us on how to conduct ourselves."

"Certainly." He grinned. "But we shall continue the pretense of me being a young woman, yes?"

My inclination would have been for a proper female companion, but this might have been as close as I could ever get. "Perhaps it is time for the young woman to become a lady. I believe that has advantages for both of us, yes?"

His smile lit up the rest of his adorable face. I felt quite blessed.

"Yes, if that is what you would like. However, we would not want to disobey Shen Lung," he cautioned.

"No, indeed not," I responded. "Look what happened to Lao Peng You."

"I believe he got what he deserved. Even the *Yi Jing* suggested this outcome."

My eyebrows raised in amazement. "And do you think that is what would happen to us should we stop taking the seed of immortality?"

"I would imagine so," he replied.

"But it was so dramatic!" I exclaimed. "I would prefer to go out in the quiet murmur of shadows."

He grinned at me. "It might have very well happened that way, but to ensure the success of this plan, I put crushed black tea leaves into the Moon Cakes, just to make sure."

We looked at each other and broke into unbridled laughter.

That night, we stopped near the roadside and concealed ourselves, pulling the cart into a circle of trees for shelter. We talked and cuddled, enjoying the pleasure of spending an entire night together without fear of Marquis Pichan discovering us. If I had to live through the next few hundred years, at least I had found someone with whom I wished to spend that time. Zhong Shi came as close to a perfect mate as I would ever expect to find. Falling asleep in his doll-like arms felt nearer to Heaven than I ever hoped to get while still alive.

I stand on the black mountain again. Closer to the top, farther from the abyss below.

"*Very well done, my little servant.*" *The Blue Dragon floats into view.* "*You have completed my assigned tasks, for now.*"

"*Yes, my Lord, as you have instructed me.*" *I bow.* "*I take it Zhong Shi replaced Lao Peng You in the circle of Immortals.*"

"*You are correct, Little One. Lao received his consequence for disobedience. You received your reward for right action.*"

"*My reward, O Great One?*"

"*Zhong Shi is your reward, Hao Lan. I knew what you wanted and provided it for you.*"

"*Thank you, my Lord. Zhong Shi is a wonderful companion. I look forward to spending many years together.*"

"*And many years you will have. However, one suggestion, if I may...*" *He breathes a gentle snort.*

"*What is that, Shen Lung?*"

"*Do not allow him to learn Mahjong!*"

We both chuckle.

"*Little One,*" *he says,* "*look around you. Tell me what you see.*"

I press against the side of the mountain for balance. Perhaps I have an aversion to heights, especially after the recent bridge events. "*I see clouds, trees, a mountain.*"

"*Look down,*" *he commands.*

"*I would prefer not to, my Lord.*"

"*It is safe. I would not have you harmed in any way.*" *His words sound somewhat comforting.*

Far below, I see a river and a meadow. Bamboo frames held familiar saffron silk banners.

"*Hao Lan, that is where you began your journey. Now, you are near the top of the climb. Keep in mind that you may never reach the apex of the mountain, but you have also traveled quite far from where you started."*

The dragon reasons well. If I did not have such a fear of looking down, I would have been able to compare the distances much better.

"You have performed splendidly, and your assistance has been most valuable. You will return to Changshou Shan and learn the rest of The Classic of The Way.*"*

"Yes, my master. Do you wish to have Zhong Shi learn it as well?"

"That is a good question, Little One." He grins. "However, his expertise is with the Yi Jing. *The two of you can provide guidance to those who request it. Your wisdom and his insight will be most helpful to people who seek illumination and enlightenment. Just remember that not everyone will be prepared to receive the message at the time you wish to share it."*

"Of course, my Lord."

"And now, I shall bid you farewell."

"Farewell? Am I never to see you again?" That would be a great loss for me, as Shen Lung has provided much in the way of support and instruction.

"Do not worry, my servant. I shall appear to you from time to time as I require your assistance. For now, enjoy your lives, share your learning, and be exceedingly generous to those around you."

"Indeed, I shall, O Great One. Thank you."

He turns, flutters his wings and begins to fly away.

"Oh..." He cranes his head back toward me. "Hao Lan!"

"Yes, master?"

"Do not complain so much!"

I stand and watch with a few tiny tears as he flies off into the clouds.

Back at Changshou Shan, Zhong Shi moved his few belongings into the suite with me. I hardly played Mahjong after that. Only when old Fa Sha requested my presence would I return to the table. Oddly enough, he kept his one remaining eye on the game and never asked what happened to Lao Peng You.

I continued my study of *The Classic of The Way* and Zhong Shi studied the *Yi Jing*. Occasionally we would take the sedan I purchased out into the country for a day or two. Usually, Daniao accompanied us and prepared our meals, as well as provided us with his seed.

Those around us continued to age, and, eventually, we needed to move from Changshou Shan. I felt sad to leave that oasis on the mountain where I had obtained immortality and met my beloved. After Daniao's death, Zhong Shi and I traveled, searching for another spot to settle down, but no such place called to us.

Once enough time had passed, we returned to the resort. No one knew who we were by then. Fortunately, no one occupied my old suite, and we lived there until, once again, we had outlived our new set of acquaintances.

15. Fenghuang

Zhong Shi and I traveled throughout our great land over the next hundred years or so. Due to our immortality, our appearance changed little with time. We enjoyed each other's company and relished learning about the history of places we explored together.

When requested, I instructed others on the *Tao Te Ching*–lessons from *The Classic of the Way* silk banners in my dream–and he demonstrated the *Yi Jing*. It gave me a sense of pride to relate the philosophies and beliefs I learned over the many years.

I had acquired great wealth from the gambling, and we lived like princes. However, my fortunes could not last forever. Whenever our coffer neared depletion, I sat in on local Mahjong games to replenish our coins. Never did I use Lao Peng You's method of employing a confederate. Neither did I teach Zhong Shi the ways of the game with the medicinal tiles, as Shen Lung had suggested. Besides, he had no interest in Mahjong after observing his former masters' conduct.

But no matter how beautiful the setting, how exotic the food, how peaceful the harmony of the land, no other place ever said *Home* to us.

During the fourth time we returned to Changshou Shan, my immortal dream life resumed.

"Hao Lan!" a familiar but distant voice cries out. The Blue Dragon returns to my life after an absence of two thousand moons. My chest swells at hearing his call.

I keep my eyes closed, just in case. In previous dreams he directed me to do so for my own safety.

"You may open your eyes, Little One."

My body recoils at the phrase. If you have lived a few hundred years, it feels most uncomfortable when someone refers to you as Little One. However, compared to Shen Lung, I am just a mere child.

I stand in the courtyard of a great palace, not the one I visited years ago in Xian. This one appears newer and grander.

"Do you recognize this place, Hao Lan?" the dragon inquires.

"I do not, O Great One. It is most magnificent."

"It is the Endless Palace in Chang'an. I shall send you there a few days hence. You will meet with Liu Xin, the Emperor Ai."

I recall a previous assignment from many, many years ago. "Do you have a message I must present to the Emperor?"

"I do not." Shen Lung hovers in front of me and blinks. "This time, you are the message."

Such astounding information causes me to shudder. "I am the message?" This makes no sense, but when does the Blue Dragon have to make perfect sense?

"Yes, my servant. I am sending you on a very special mission, one that will shape this world for the next ten thousand generations to come."

The thought of such great responsibility prompts me to swallow, but my throat tightens so that I cannot. "I... I... I... hope I can live up to your expectations, my Lord." I bow.

"I have no doubt you will." He blinks again. "That is why I have chosen to send you and Zhong Shi."

At least I will have my faithful companion for support. "As you wish, O Great One." I bow again for formality sake.

"You will speak with the Emperor and his grandmother, the Consort Fu."

I can only hope she will be more pleasant than Lady Xing, the last dowager I faced at a palace. "I live to serve you, my Lord."

He smiles. "And soon you will serve another, Hao Lan."

My eyes widen in surprise. "Shall I no longer provide you with assistance?"

"Ha, ha, ha, ha. That time will come, but not for quite a while." He hovers around, tail lashing the air, before continuing. "You will meet a new teacher, one whose life has been foretold by many, including Confucius and Buddha. You will learn from him, and he will learn from you."

"I fear I have nothing to impart to such a great teacher, my Lord." I bow again.

"You have much to share, Little One." I cringe once more at that phrase. "You and Zhong Shi will instruct and influence the new teacher, and he will share these principles with his people."

"And this one person will cause great changes?" I ask because I have doubts and am not sure I fully understand my mission.

"The right person with the right message in the right place at the right time can, indeed, encourage new ways of thinking."

"It seems unlikely that one person can bring about such change."

"Consider some of the names you know: Confucius, Buddha, Lao Tzu, Sun Tzu, Emperor Qin. These were men who not only changed the course of human events, but their names endure the centuries. In the future, other individuals will initiate further changes, and people in the years beyond will know of them. The teacher you encounter will be one of these people. Your guidance leads to a set of progressive revolutions that spread throughout the world."

"As you wish, my Lord." The weight of such a great deal of responsibility causes my shoulder to slump.

"Tomorrow night, look up at the Western sky. You will see a great star in the heavens. Keep your eye on that star, Hao Lan. Let it be your guide."

A star for a guide. This sounds like an old myth I heard as a child. However, it seems our principal journey does not begin until we reach Chang'an, many li *from here.*

"And how, may I ask"–with trepidation on my part–*"shall we be getting to the palace?"*

"I believe you know the answer, Hao Lan. Otherwise, you would not have to ask the question."

Dragons! *I hate traveling by dragon, and he knows it.*

"Someday you will thank me for this expedition. Perhaps not today or tomorrow, but someday, certainly." He turns and begins to fly away.

"Shen Lung!" I call out. He turns back. *"Thank you. Thank you for everything."*

He smiles. *"Don't thank me just yet, Little One. Wait until you have seen this through, and then reconsider bestowing your gratitude upon me."* He turns and flies off.

The next night I looked up into the Western sky, as Shen Lung had instructed. Zhong Shi stood next to me.

"What are you looking at, Hao Lan?" No one else was around, and he must have felt comfortable speaking.

I pointed up at the bright light in the heavens.

"Oh, my," he replied. "What is that?"

"A great star, so I have been told."

Zhong Shi looked at me with his cute nose pointed upward. "Shen Lung?"

I nodded.

"Ah," he responded.

"I shall explain all later."

We stood in silence, gazing up at the miraculous object hovering high above. *How can something so far away affect our lives here?* I wondered. After half an hour or so, we retreated to our suite.

Three days later, two yellow dragons landed in the courtyard at Changshou Shan. Zhong Shi and I had prepared ourselves for a long journey. We hoisted our bags and mounted the magnificent beasts. I attempted to be stalwart for my friend, as he had not yet flown upon a dragon's back. It had been a few hundred years for me, but, as with many things, you never seem to forget how to ride. I attempted to imitate the posture used by Lao Peng You, sitting tall and unbending, as if posing for a portrait.

Our flight took us over high mountains, tall trees, and wide rivers. As we flew, we took turns pointing out interesting scenery to each other. Even after ten generations, Zhong Shi and I still shared a loving and blossoming relationship.

About an hour later we circled down into the courtyard of the great palace Shen Lung had shown me in my dream. Guards stood in attendance as we landed. We slid to the ground, took up our bags and followed several soldiers.

The guest accommodations here did not differ much from those at Emperor Qin's palace. Rooms fit for two princes: flowing fabrics, many pieces of art, cushions.

A messenger led us to the throne room, a great, airy hall. Bright, celebratory, regal. Above ground. Even after so many years, I felt the excitement of rushing waters within my breast and attempted to maintain a placid visage.

For my previous court attendance, I had been blind-folded, ushered through a maze of halls to a gloomy, subterranean throne room, and forced to keep my forehead on the floor so that I could not see whoever spoke.

On a raised platform in front of us sat the Emperor Ai. He appeared young and robust. His face seemed too long for his head and the lips bore red paint, as a noblewoman might apply.

Seated to his left, an aged woman, whom I assumed to be his grandmother. She kept her hair in the traditional bun of youth, but many, many wrinkles suggested many, many years.

On his right stood an attractive young fellow, simply dressed, stiffly poised and neck stretched, as if *he* ruled the realm. His arms bustled with shiny, bejeweled bracelets.

"Hao Lan, Zhong Shi." The Emperor stood. "How nice of you to grace my throne room with your presence."

We bowed so low our noses almost touched the polished metal floor. "Emperor, the pleasure is ours."

The woman's mouth pursed, as if she had just chewed on a piece of the sour and bitter Buddha's Hand fruit.

The Emperor turned his head toward Zhong Shi then back to me. "Does your companion wish to give proper respect as well?"

"We apologize, your Highness, but my companion does not speak." I bowed.

Emperor Ai scrutinized Zhong Shi. "Does not speak… or cannot speak?"

The well-appointed young man leaned to the Emperor's ear and whispered.

"I see. Well. That explains the circumstance." He sat.

Consort Fu spoke with a smoky, raspy voice. "Get to it, Xin! Send them on their way before it is too late!" She raised her trembling arms like a haunting specter.

"Yes, grandmother." He asked us, "Did the dragon explain the purpose of this audience?"

I bowed. "Shen Lung instructed me that you would be sending us on an expedition to meet a great teacher."

"Correct." He nodded to the young fellow and glanced back at us. "Did he mention the prophecies regarding this great teacher?"

Zhong Shi and I looked at each other with blank expressions. I turned back to the Emperor. "A few, your Highness, but my companion and I would enjoy discovering any exceptional information you wish to share with us."

Fu pointed a bony finger at us. "Tell them, Xin! Tell them!"

"Yes, grandmother." Fluttering eyelids hinted at his frustration with the older woman. "The wise scholar Confucius once told of a great teacher who would arrive in the West. Zoroaster also predicted such a prophet. Even the great Buddha spoke of a Holy One who would rescue us and save the world. I am not sure, however, that we require rescuing and that our world needs saving." He chuckled at the attempted wit. When he saw no one else join in, he stopped. Then the rest of us laughed in an effort to placate him.

What a responsibility for one man! To have his life foretold by several great ancestors and have such expectations put upon him. I could only imagine how difficult his seasons would be.

"Buddha also requested," the Emperor continued, "that we seek out this Holy One and do a *good deed*." He looked at me and Zhong Shi in turn. "That will be your contribution." His finger aimed at us. "I am sending you with a delegation from Yindu, the empire to the West, where Buddha began as Prince Siddhartha Gautama. From there, you will proceed to the land under the great star in the sky." He pointed upward. "It is many thousands of *li*, past Ar-Hsi, beyond Li-Kan, and I believe the land is now part of an expansive empire ruled by light-skinned warriors."

I looked at Zhong Shi, and he looked back at me. My mind flooded with questions, but we could not address the Emperor unless requested. We were about to embark on the most wonderful adventure of our lifetimes, but the lack of more detailed instructions concerned me. Tension in my throat would not abate.

"You, Hao Lan, are the greatest scholar of the *Tao Te Ching*–so I am told–and you, Zhong Shi, are the most learned with the *Yi Jing*."

We looked at each other then back at the Emperor. I had no idea such celebrity shadowed us.

"I have chosen to send the two of you to this great teacher as a *good deed* so that you may impart your wisdom in hopes of assisting him with his consequent struggle to save this world."

The young man next to the Emperor whispered in his ear once again.

"Oh, yes. Thank you." He turned back to us. "I am sending Dong Xian, my personal advisor"–he pointed at the fellow next to him–"with you to assist in diplomatic activities." The Emperor winced and put his clasped hands to the side of his abdomen. "That is all." He rose in a slow fashion, one palm pressed on his flank, turned, and walked away from the throne as we bowed in obeisance.

Consort Fu looked down at us. "What are you waiting for? Go! Hurry!"

A messenger escorted us back to our quarters.

Around midnight, the door to our room opened, even though I had locked it from the inside.

"Who is there?" I called out.

"Sssssshhhh," came the reply.

I recognized the silhouette of that young man who stood next to the Emperor earlier in the day. He looked behind himself as he crept in and shut the door without making a sound.

"Hao Lan, Zhong Shi," he whispered. "I need to discuss a few things with you before we embark on this journey. May I come in?"

A useless question as he had already entered our room and closed the door. His curious behavior aroused my suspicions, and I focused on his movements.

I heard rumors of him being more than just an *advisor* to the Emperor. Even though both men were married, people gossiped about them being lovers as well.

He lit a lantern.

"A curious time for an official visit. How may we be of assistance, Dong Xian?"

The intruder studied both our faces before proceeding. "You two have secrets."

One could make that statement about any pair of people. Also, it came from someone who had secrets of his own to conceal and protect.

"Do you care to be more specific?" I replied. "We have so many secrets. To which do you refer?" I glanced at Zhong Shi, and he smiled.

The uninvited visitor faced me. "You are an Immortal, and you"–he turned to Zhong Shi–"are not a woman."

I could have feigned shock, but at this age, it did not feel worth the effort. My companion maintained his composed expression. However, such information could be used by an unscrupulous fellow to blackmail us. It seemed he believed this knowledge brought him some power over us.

"Your point, Master Dong?"

"My point, Baron Dongting…"

Nobody had called me that in years. I had forgotten about my erstwhile title.

"…is that I can expose the both of you as frauds."

Zhong Shi and I looked at each other with an unspoken question.

"To what end, Master Dong? Neither of us really cares what you do. You are not the only person who has that particular information."

He scowled. "I can make life difficult for you, Dongting."

After my time with Lao Peng You, I found this fellow's amateurish and awkward approach amusing. "I see. So, this is an effort at extortion. You attempt to strong-arm us for some unknown purpose."

"Call it what you will." He sneered. "I just want you to know who is in command of this team."

I could not help but smile. "Master Dong, there is no need to lord your position over us. We have no desire to control our mutual venture."

His eyes narrowed.

"We follow orders from someone much more powerful than you, yourself or–in fact–the Emperor, himself," I continued. "And, besides, I believe it is *we*"–I indicated my companion and myself–"who hold dangerous and potentially damaging information about *you*."

Dong Xian's eyes opened wide. "And just what is it you think you know about *me*, Baron?"

I blew him a kiss. "You and the Emperor, sir. Cut sleeves?"

His mouth rounded into a circle of disbelief. "How dare you! Other, lesser men have died for speaking that way to me. I could have you killed for such a statement!"

I could not refrain from laughing aloud. "Ha, ha, Dong. You accused me of being an Immortal. How do you plan to slaughter one?" Zhong Shi and I giggled together.

His face reddened. "I warn you. Do not make light of me. You will discover I am not one you can easily outwit."

The man's raw arrogance would surely be his ultimate undoing.

"Your attempt at intimidation carries no weight with us," I advised.

Sweat formed on his forehead. "If I cannot dispatch *you*, then I shall claim the life of your companion!"

I took a deep breath before responding. "Zhong Shi also happens to be an Immortal. I doubt your efforts would harm him."

Dong Xian's smoldering expression reminded me of the times when a frustrated and angry Lao Peng You appeared ready to propel himself upward without the assistance of fire medicine. "Then I have no choice but to expose your secrets! Everyone will know you are charlatans!"

I shook my head in disbelief. "Neither of us cares if you share your knowledge with others. Therefore, you have no leverage over us, sir. Can you not see that?"

Dong Xian sighed. "You are a shrewd *wangba*. I shall grant you that, Baron."

"Perhaps, Dong. And how do you propose to keep *your* secret safe?"

His face blanked. "As we shall be traveling together for a while, I hope I can trust you not to expose us." The tremulous tone sounded weak and falsely brave. His rigid posture suggested defensiveness.

This advantage allowed us some leverage. "Of course not, Dong Xian. However, you do have something Zhong Shi and I require. Should you comply with our wishes, your secret is safe with us."

"Comply?" His voice shot up an octave. "What is it you need from me?"

I nodded to Zhong Shi. He moved across the room to yank down our guest's pants. Dong Xian gasped then smiled. My companion proceeded to satisfy his and the advisor's necessities. My turn followed.

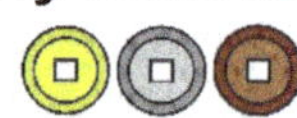

The next morning, another messenger summoned us. He instructed Zhong Shi to bring the yarrow sticks with him. We followed through hallways and passages, arriving in a small, dimly lit salon. At one end sat Consort Fu flanked by attendants. The elderly dowager glowered and scrutinized us as if we conveyed unfavorable tidings.

"Did you sleep well?" she asked in a bland manner that suggested she did not care one way or the other.

"Yes, Consort Fu," I answered. "The guest room is quite luxurious. Better accommodations than we are used to at even the finest places we have visited.

"Glad to hear that," she droned.

I believed she would have responded the same way no matter what my answer.

The dowager looked at a servant. "Tea? Would you like some tea?"

We both shuddered at the thought. "No, thank you, my Lady. It is most generous of you." I felt no need to explain our aversion to the popular beverage.

"Hao Lan," she barked. "My grandson, the Emperor Ai, mentioned that your companion is an expert at the art of *Yi Jing*. Is this correct?" Her burning eyes pierced mine.

I quivered and looked over to Zhong Shi. He nodded.

Lady Fu asked, "Did you bring your yarrow sticks with you?" He held out his hand with the fifty stalks. "Good! I need you to assist me."

"We are at your service." I made a slight bow.

The old woman stepped down from her ornate lacquered chair with assistance from an attendant and approached Zhong Shi. "There is a matter for which I must find counsel. Demonstrate how to do this."

Because Zhong Shi did not speak in public, we developed a way to communicate, especially when giving *Yi Jing* readings. Years ago, he found a thin, flat piece of slate in a river. With a brush and water, he wrote characters that appeared for a few moments before evaporating. In this way, I could read what he wished to say.

My companion demonstrated the frustratingly slow method of dividing and counting, over and over. The clacking of sticks chopped through the musty air. After a while, he drew a set of lines.

"What does that mean?" she croaked. "I have seen the trigrams before, but I am unaware of their specific interpretation."

The first set of words he wrote forewarned me unpleasant information would follow. After that disappeared, he gave me the initial interpretation.

"Ah, Lady Fu. My companion says this arrangement indicates great potential, especially if you can avoid temptation and stay within the flow of all things."

"Thank you. Most helpful." A tiny smile appeared. "You may leave now." She began to walk away.

Zhong Shi shook his head.

"Please, wait, Lady Fu," I requested.

She paused.

"These changing lines will produce yet another interpretation."

Her head rotated slow as a turtle to face us. "Changes? I do not like changes. What are these changes?"

My companion had long ago explained how the lines with dots indicated they switched from broken to unbroken, or the other way round, adding an additional dimension to the trigram reading.

Zhong Shi drew another set of lines, which I revealed to the Emperor's grandmother.

My companion wrote a message.

"My Lady, the changing lines suggest a growing evil and the necessity to deal with inferior persons. Misfortune follows most definitely."

Her eyes hardened, her lips puckered.

"I feared this outcome. Not what I wished to hear. What else do those little sticks say?"

Another set of characters appeared on the writing tile.

"Oh, dear." My throat swallowed without request. "I am not certain how to express this."

"Say it! Just say it! I may look like an old woman to you, but I am stronger and heartier that most men your age."

I attempted to suppress a giggle because I had seen almost two hundred summers more than her. Most men my age had died.

"The final reading points to a total collapse, a lofty goal beyond your reach, unrealized unfounded expectations."

With eyes ablaze, Consort Fu fell to the floor in a heap. "Death!" she shrieked. "Death and destruction! Not again!" The distraught woman sat up and swung her arms as if fighting a multi-armed adversary. "Not again..." The flailing ceased when she covered her face.

Guards jumped forward and escorted us back to our quarters.

Once they had left us, I asked Zhong Shi, "Did you concoct that interpretation?"

"No. *She* selected those trigrams. Why would I devise something so horrid? I have no reason to wish harm upon such a nasty old grandmother from the other side." He examined my face for some clue.

"Sorry to ask, Zhong Shi, but the reading devastated her so. It appears to have dashed any hopes for riding her grandson's reign to higher power." I gazed up at the intricate ceiling. "Perhaps she knows about Dong Xian and the Emperor. Xin–as she calls her grandson–has yet to produce an heir. She has no way to maintain her precarious position." I glanced at my partner. "I had thought you might have been endeavoring to shock the old woman into an early death."

He chuckled. "I am not so calculating as she, Hao Lan."

The next morning, a guard instructed us to pack for our journey. After the day's first meal, we proceeded to a staging area, where a team of elephants awaited us. Servants strapped our belongings to one of the beasts.

Zhong Shi, Dong Xian, and I rode atop another in a small sedan.

"What did you tell the old lady?" the Emperor's advisor asked once we had seated ourselves.

As the elephant walked, our bench swayed left to right, up and down. This method of travel felt bumpier and bouncier than a dragon, yet still less upsetting than a ship on the open ocean.

"Consort Fu asked us to assist her with a situation. Zhong Shi showed her how to cast the yarrow bundle. Is she not well?"

One eyebrow on his well composed face rose. "She is at the point of saturnine death. I do not know whether I should castigate you or congratulate you."

His response confused me. "My Lord?"

"The old woman attempts to control Xin for her own whims, but she unquestionably managed to teach him how to be Emperor. He does not listen to other people very much. It is probably just as well if she dies."

His tiny smile seemed unguarded.

"Xian… may I call you Xian?"

He nodded.

"I know the relationship between the Emperor and his grandmother remains quite complicated. Are you not his main advisor?"

"In name only. He appointed Fu Grand Empress Dowager recently, and it is her conviction that she rules the country through her grandson."

Which meant her death would leave Dong Xian as the sole voice in the Emperor's ear.

"By the way, Baron, at our first opportunity, I would enjoy a repeat of the entertainment from the other evening."

The three of us grinned and glanced sidelong at each other.

Our travels took us south and west, past the large mountain range separating us from the country of Yindu, our first destination. The elephants proved most worthy as transportation, even though they ate mounds of food several times a day.

Every night the Western Star burned bright, calling all those who gazed upon it. *Follow me, follow me*, it beckoned.

At one point we crossed the large river Padma. Our huge beasts waded through, ignoring the raging current. The water almost came up to our sedan.

Eventually, our caravan arrived in a walled city named Taxila, and we proceeded to a grand palace made of white, polished stone. The lavish statues and decorations illustrated what I imagined the inhabitants of this dominion worshipped as gods. People with many sets of arms, men with elephant heads, women with oddly shaped bodies. What kind of superstitious beliefs did these foreign and backward folks have?

The servants of King Gondophares Gaspar treated us like visiting dignitaries. Once arrangements had been made, we prepared to journey toward our western destination with Gaspar and his entourage.

It is at this point I chose to end the first installment. My life continued on for hundreds of years more, but the following chapters presented even more challenges than this first set.

Perhaps when I feel ready to share more of the tale, I shall pick up the ink brush again and relate my experiences to the rest of the world.

Until then, I urge you to emulate water. It fills out the shape of its container, it tastes best when not stagnant, and it sustains all our lives.

Longevity has its benefits, but also some detriments, as I have learned and shared. Fortunately, Zhong Shi and I shall always have each other, discovering new things every day, sharing what we have with those less fortunate, and tending to our private garden born from the seed of immortality.

Glossary

Listed below are some of the unfamiliar words and phrases used in this book.

Mahjong Terms:

Chow – A sequence of three tiles in the same suit, *e.g.*, Two, Three and Four of Dots

Kong – Four tiles exactly the same, *e.g.*, four North Wind, or four Five Character

Limit – The predetermined maximum amount of money that can be paid to a player on any single hand

Mahjong – A winning hand, usually comprising of four sets (chows, pungs, or kongs) and a pair

Prevailing Wind – Each round (4 games) one of the winds is given double value

Pung – Three tiles exactly the same, *e.g.*, three Red Dragon, or three Seven Bamboo

Tai Feng – A sequence of tile exchanges executed before playing the first tile of a game (Modern players refer to it as the Charleston)

Wall – A formation of tiles 18 side-by-side and two high set in front of each player from which the game tiles are drawn

Wash the Tiles – Moving the face-down tiles on the table in a random fashion, similar to shuffling cards

Cultural References:

Ar-Hsi – Ancient Chinese name for what we call Persia

Celestial Mother – Xi Wangmu, also referred to as Queen Mother of the West, wife of the Jade Emperor, ruler of heaven

Chang'an – Capital city of China, and eastern terminus of the Silk Road

Chongqing – A large city on the Yangtze River

Chungnan – An imperial city along the Wei River shaped like the Big Dipper constellation (called The Plough, in China)

Classic – An authoritative text, *e.g.*, 'The Classic of Tea'

Confucius – Kong Qiu (551–479 BCE in our dating system), nobleman who published his beliefs on morality, correctness, justice, and sincerity

Consort Fu – Imperial consort, dowager grandmother of Emperor Ai

Ding Cheng Zhuan – "The brick to balance the fort"

Dongting – A region in northeastern Hunan Province

Dong Xian – Advisor to Emperor Ai, with who he maintained a surreptitious relationship

Fenghuang – Chinese equivalent of the phoenix

Fulu – A town in northwestern China, near Jiayu

Gu Poison – The venom from the survivor of a battle among several caged poisonous animals, usually scorpions, centipedes, and snakes

Guizhou – Southern province up the Pearl River from Hong Kong

Hexagram – An arrangement of six Yin/Yang lines, comprising two Trigrams

Hong Kong – Translates to "Fragrant Harbor"

Hua Tuo – Physician who first used anesthesia (a blend of wine and cannabis powder) in surgery

Hunan – A province in the south-central part of China

Huoban – A term that could be used to mean 'good friend,' 'mate,' or 'business partner'

Jiangshi – A hopping undead being, similar to a zombie but everlasting like a vampire

Jiayu – A village in northwestern China, near Fulu

Kan Pei – Traditional toast meaning "Empty Cup"

Koan – A teaching story with contradictory elements

Kunlun Shan – The mythological mountain where the gods live

Leveret – A young hare less than one year of age

Li-Kan – Ancient Chinese name for what we call Syria

Liu Xin, Emperor Ai – Han Dynasty emperor, who had a surreptitious relationship with his advisor Dong Xian

Moling – A city near the mouth of the Yangtze River, now known as Nanjing

Monkey King – A mythical primate born from a stone with supernatural powers

Moon Rabbit – The image Westerners call "The Man in the Moon"

Moxibustion – Traditional Chinese medical treatment using burning mugwort to stimulate energy flow

Osmanthus – A fruit-bearing shrub used for its apricot or peach scent

Passion of the Cut Sleeve – Homosexuality, referencing Emperor Ai, whose male lover once fell asleep on his arm and he had to cut the sleeve to sneak away

Pearl River – Empties out into what is now Hong Kong harbor

Pichan – A region within Xiyu

Qin Shi Huang – United warring provinces and became the first Emperor of China

Shennong – An ancient ruler of China (approx. 5,000 years ago) who modernized farming practices

Sun Tzu – A general and military strategist, author of *The Art of War*

Taijiquan – A system of ritual martial art exercise that Westerners call Tai Chi

Tao Te Ching – The text by Lao Tzu comprising 81 chapters that is the basis for the Taoist philosophy, which encourages its followers to live in harmony with the life force around them

Tasseomancy – Using tea leaves to predict the future

Trigram – An arrangement of three Yin/Yang lines

Wuchang – A city along the Yangtze River now known as Wushan

Wushan Bridge – The bridge across the Yangtze River near Chongqing that connected the cites of Wuchang, Hanyang, and Hankou

Xian – The capital city of the first Emperor, Qin

Xiancao – An herb used in Traditional Chinese Medicine

Xianyang – Isolated city where Emperor Qin's palace stood

Xiansheng – Polite form of address to a man: Sir

Xiongnu – The Mongolians

Xiyu – An isolated region in the far northwest of China

Yangtze River – The longest river in Asia, spanning almost 4,000 miles from the glaciers of Tibet to Shanghai in the east.

Yi Jing – Divnation system that Westerners refer to as I Ching

Yin and Yang – Opposing energies, generally classified as female and male

Yindu – What the Chinese called India

Zhao Gao –Emperor Qin's advisor, a eunuch, who tested for loyalty by showing candidates for office a deer and telling them it was a horse, determining whether the candidate would deny the obvious truth in deference to him

Insults:

Banana People – Chinese people who live abroad and have lost their sense of culture and history
Bunny – Male homosexual, usually the passive partner
Chrysanthemum – Anus
Egg – Testicle or offspring
Little Bird – Penis
Little Brother – Penis
Longyang – Homosexual, referring to the lord who was the lover of King Wei
Pihua – Feces, 'shit'
Piyan – Asshole
Rice Bucket – Useless person
Silver-haired Chicken – An older woman's genitalia
Steamed Buns – Breasts
Turtle – Penis
Wangba – Whore
Wangbadan – Son of a whore, bastard
Yinhu – Female genitalia

WAYNE GOODMAN has lived in the San Francisco Bay Area most of his life (with too many cats). When not writing, he enjoys playing Gilded Age parlor music on the piano, with an emphasis on women, gay, and Black composers.